REALLY,
a WORST-CASE SCENARIO

REALLY,

a WORST-CASE SCENARIO

B. P. NOLAND

iUniverse, Inc.
Bloomington

REALLY, A WORST-CASE SCENARIO

iUniverse books may be ordered through booksellers or by contacting:

iUniverse
1663 Liberty Drive
Bloomington, IN 47403
www.iuniverse.com
1-800-Authors (1-800-288-4677)

ISBN: 978-1-4759-0111-5 (sc)
ISBN: 978-1-4759-0112-2 (hc)
ISBN: 978-1-4759-0113-9 (ebk)

Library of Congress Control Number: 2012904730

Printed in the United States of America

iUniverse rev. date: 03/30/2012

ACKNOWLEDGMENTS

THE AUTHORS WISH TO ACKNOWLEDGE the able assistance of and advice from Cindy and Greg Scheibel, especially in providing invaluable constructive comments and their editing service. Without the expert advice from our iUniverse editor, Sarah Disbrow, this book could not have been developed into publishable material. A fellow iUniverse author, Sharon Wilson, generously answered procedural questions, and helped edit. Lucy DuPertis edited our first draft, and most of her comments are included in the book. Richard Lanham gave us a gun lecture. Thanks to all.

CHAPTER 1

V AL NEVER KNEW WHY RON wanted to buy an antique grandfather clock—especially a Hentschel Steinway grandfather clock with starburst mahogany, cable-wound triple-chime movement, and a six-piece beveled glass. It was in the far corner of the living room, stood ninety-three inches high, and played Beethoven's Ninth Symphony, *Ave Maria*, or Westminster Chimes on the hour, every hour. It was manufactured around 1900. The sale price was $14,439. Holy smokes.

What Val liked most about the clock was that it had a secret compartment indistinguishable to the human eye. Val just happened to visit an antique dealer south of town who pointed it out to her. This was where she kept her Glock. The Steinway belched out Beethoven's Ninth Symphony.

Damn, it was midnight and Ron still had not called. Where could he be and what could he be doing? His work often kept him out late, but usually he called. Val felt that she was missing important information when Ron didn't call and update her, especially with the election scheduled in a month.

The problem with politics is that temptations are around every corner. Val wasn't so concerned about Ron, but it seemed that some women around politicians become like rock groupies and will do anything for attention.

Only today, in the committee workroom, Val had witnessed this sexy, petite blonde walking up to and handing Ron her thong panties. Val lost her temper and flew into a rage. She slapped the woman across the face and verbally assaulted her. The woman silently slithered out the door, and Val ran after her, screaming up a blue streak.

As the woman disappeared around the corner of the building, Val stopped chasing her, recovered some of her composure, and reentered the room.

Embarrassed, she apologized to the election workers for her outburst. Many of the women were very supportive. One of the volunteers told Val she was probably headed to Will Brown's office. He was one of Ron's opponents. The woman would find out quickly she couldn't do any good over there. According to rumors, Will had lived with a male partner for years.

This all seemed contrived to Val, and she vowed to figure out who the young blonde woman was and who else might be involved.

Ron was upset at Val for running after the woman and told her she had cost him a vote. Val told him they would make up for it because she had some friends she could get to vote twice. But Ron, who was not known for having a sense of humor, did not find that amusing.

Val followed her tirade with her favorite soapbox sermon that the greatest hazards politicians face are the ongoing sexual temptations. Many fail miserably on this score, probably because they start believing all the crap sycophants feed them. Maybe everyone is horny. Maybe it is ego. All politicians have strong egos. The more success they experience, the larger the ego.

Ron looked at Val and thought he had heard this song before.

CHAPTER 2

Valarie and Ron Steadman have been married for seventeen years. They met at a social gathering at Georgetown University while working on their college degrees. Val received her degree in biochemistry, and Ron had a Doctor of Jurisprudence degree. Yes, Ron is a lawyer.

When the Steadmans moved to Centerville, New Mexico, Val began working in the Chemistry Department of the university and has worked her way up to and is currently the head of the Biochemistry Department, specializing in molecular and structural biochemistry.

Val is about five feet six inches, with auburn hair curling around a slightly full face, pert nose, greenish-brown eyes, and a firm, shapely body. She keeps her body firm and toned by working out with Julian Michaels four times a week, weight lifting and riding her stationary bike. She has a body to die for and a personality to match. She always lights up the room when she walks in or makes an entrance.

Ron presently is mayor of Centerville, a city of about nine hundred thousand, and is running for reelection. When they first moved to Centerville, Ron was a special agent in the criminal investigation division of the FBI. Ron broke two cases wide open, one involving a money-laundering operation and, the other, a state transportation department bribery that resulted in two road commissioners going to jail for embezzlement. The cases received wide publicity and helped Ron become a hot political prospect. A successful mayoral election followed a few years later.

Up to about thirty years ago, Centerville was a sleepy little town of about eighty thousand, a hub of a large farming area where the major crops are still wheat, hay, and other grains. Enough oil wells are scattered around to make a few people wealthy.

Centerville is located in the high southwest desert of New Mexico, where the Rio Grande River meanders south. The climate dominates, with huge blue skies, great vistas of mountains, and plenty of sunshine but little rain. Centerville receives only about eight inches of rain annually, most of it during the late summer during a so-called monsoon season. Heavy, hard thunderstorms hit, usually in the afternoons. When the river is in its low-flow period, water is pumped from a large underground lake for urban and farming use. Irrigation canals run parallel to the river southward through the state, and then along the Mexican border.

A bonanza struck about thirty years ago, when the city was chosen as the new site for a Japanese auto manufacturer. Related industries started appearing, and now the city has a thriving, growing economy with all the associated sprawl problems. Large shopping malls became the vogue. Downtown started to decline and people became concerned. City government officials responded with a downtown capital improvement program. A new city hall, county courthouse, judicial complex, and two new hotels appeared on the skyline. The vibrant downtown led an area-wide economic revival.

Ron is tall, about six feet one, not too thin and not too heavy. With blue eyes and plenty of blond hair, he is personable and handsome. He exudes confidence when talking and gives everyone the feeling he's addressing them personally.

Ron has been a successful mayor. He accomplished most of his previous campaign promises, including stable government operations, employee raises, paved streets, and increased police patrols; and he encouraged successful city development.

This strengthened the business community. He supported open-space acquisitions and expanded city parks and recreation programs without raising taxes. Even so, it's a close race. The last poll showed Ron leading by 2 percent—46 percent to 44 percent, with a third candidate having the remaining 10 percent.

However, satisfying everyone has proven impossible, and environmentalists are never satisfied. Their attitude has always been "what have you done for us lately?" Val's reply is, "Do you mean this morning?" In fact, one environmental group has their own candidate, Will Brown, the rumored homosexual.

Ron met with Will Brown to discuss different scenarios in the current election. Will said he thought he could support Ron's campaign. Ron thanked him. When Brown announced his candidacy the next day, Ron remembered a quote from Harry Truman when the same thing had happened to him.

"The son of bitch lied—he's running against me."

And sure enough Truman's opponent announced the next day.

Anyway, Ron was in a meeting with his campaign manager and his public relations people, finalizing campaign expenditures. Money was important, but the meeting should not have lasted this long.

Val had a busy day scheduled for tomorrow, trying to evaluate a stem-cell experiment that appeared to be going down the drain, literally. Val cleared her mind, went to bed, closed her eyes, and let the world and its problems disappear.

CHAPTER 3

THE ALARM SOUNDED. IT WAS 5:00 a.m. Val jumped out of bed, turned it off, and headed for the shower.

Ron was home and was sound asleep. He had climbed into bed without waking her. Val decided it wasn't worth the hassle to wake him. She was feeling really good this morning and really didn't want to bitch at him.

Val loved her research job directing the stem-cell farm laboratory at the medical school.

Remembering that Steve was to be in the laboratory today, she dressed with a little more care. Down deep she knew somehow her feelings bordered on wrong, but all things considered, she really didn't care.

Steve Janson is one of the medical students who works with her in the laboratory. Like Ron, he's tall, about six feet one, has dark-brown hair, and long eyelashes with soft brown eyes that seem to twinkle with amusement. His carefree attitude was obvious, and his mouth, slightly wide for his face, already showed smile lines.

Steve was one of the many students she had supervised, but he was different. He was a few years older than the average first-year medical-school student, having spent several years in the military. His maturity exceeded previous students' by far.

Thinking about him, she really had no idea just how old he was, but smiling, she admitted to herself that whatever his age, it had to be several years younger than her thirty-nine years. That aside, she found him extremely attractive, sexy, and with a wonderful sense of humor, one far beyond his years. He took her work very seriously and was very proud of all she had accomplished. She looked forward to the days when he was present in the lab. Based on different and frequent comments he had made, sexual tension was in the air, but nothing overt.

He was enamored with her, for sure, but she hadn't decided how far her feelings for him would go. His admiration has been good for her. Playing second fiddle to Ron and his career sometimes left Val with emptiness.

Val walked into the garage, got into the car, and was backing down the driveway when Ron came bouncing out of the house, shouting, "Stop! Wait, come back! This is important!"

As Val drove the car back into the garage and got out, she started complaining that she was already running late. However, the look on Ron's face startled her enough to make her forget her anger, and she asked him, "What is it?"

Ron grimaced and asked, "Do you remember Amy?"

Puzzled, Val shrugged, thinking he looked kind of cute in his red, white, and blue flag pajamas.

Exasperated, Ron yelled, "Did you hear on the news what happened last night?"

"No," Val replied, "TV wasn't on this morning."

Ron said, "Remember the panty girl, Amy Johnson? They found her body last night in the alley behind our campaign headquarters. She was murdered."

"Murdered?" Val said stupidly. "Murdered?"

Ron said, "Yes, behind our office. They found her about ten o'clock last night. We were still meeting inside at that time. The police believe the body was moved to the site but are checking it as the scene of the murder." Ron whispered, "She was left naked."

Val said, "God, that's awful. How do they know she was murdered, Ron?"

Ron replied, "She was shot at close range."

Val asked, "Did any of you hear anything or notice any strange activity out of the ordinary? Did you see anybody who didn't belong?"

Ron said, "The police questions were redundant. Remember, Val, there is a door to a little storage area back there, before the door to the alley. It would mask some sounds. Besides, a strong person could carry her easily and lay her down quietly. She was small, you know, probably only weighed 110 to 115 pounds."

"I felt the whole incident was staged. It was so obvious," Ron reflected. "Even though you made short order of the panty incident, some people will blow it out of proportion with the sex records of other politicians."

The whole scene played over in Val's mind. People were going to formulate their own opinions once it hit the papers. Her verbal blasts yesterday played into this, and she repeated that thought to Ron.

He looked at her with that funny expression he got when his mind started computing some data and then started working around how the data would affect the election. He seemed to have little concern about Val's feelings. How many votes he might lose was his focus.

Val pulled out her cell phone and rang the lab.

Her boss, James Lorensten, dean of the medical school, was already at work; and she quickly told him something had happened and she would be in later. The dean wanted to know if he could help, obviously curious, so she told him he would receive a full report later.

Ron and Val headed back into the kitchen as she suggested they have coffee and discuss all the ramifications of the situation. She brewed the coffee while Ron went into the bedroom to dress for the day.

CHAPTER 4

RON WENT TO THE REFRIGERATOR, took out the orange juice, and asked Val, "You want some?"

Val shook her head as he tipped the carton and downed a big gulp.

Ron looked at Val and said, "We need to—" He was interrupted by the doorbell.

Ron groaned, "What now?" He sat down at the kitchen table, continuing to drink the orange juice while Val went to answer the door.

Val opened the door and exclaimed, "Oh!" She faced a man wearing a pair of blue jeans and pulling a tan Windbreaker into place as he smiled at her.

He said, "Mrs. Steadman, I'm Joe Maxwell, homicide detective." Joe flashed his ID, but Val hardly glanced at it.

Joe said, "As you probably know, there was a murder last night. Do you mind if I come in? I have a few questions for you."

Val swallowed. "Okay." She opened the door and led Joe down the hallway and into the kitchen.

As they entered the kitchen, Ron stood up.

Joe said, "Hello, Mayor." Ron extended his hand, and with eyes locked, he and Joe firmly shook hands.

"Lieutenant, you're still in blue jeans," Ron said.

"Yes, just haven't had time to change yet."

Val said, "Would you like some coffee, Lieutenant Maxwell?"

Joe nodded.

Ron asked, "Has anything changed about the murder since I left last night?"

"Well, we understand Mrs. Steadman had a run-in with Johnson yesterday afternoon. That's why I'm here. I would like to ask a few questions."

Val brought the coffee and sat down next to Ron.

Joe took a sip of coffee and then said, "Mrs. Steadman, where were you last night between five and eight o'clock?"

Val responded, "I was here in my home. I got here at five twenty-five."

"Was anyone here with you?"

"No, I was home alone."

"Did you call anybody? Did you get any phone calls?"

"No, no one called."

"Do you own a gun?"

Ron jumped to his feet and said, "That's enough. We would like our attorney present for any more questions."

Joe said, "Okay, have your attorney call me as soon as possible. You well know, Mayor, time is of the essence early in a murder case. Who is your attorney?"

"Don't have one yet. We'll let you know."

Joe handed his card to Ron and left. "We'll be talking to you soon." He walked through the hallway with Val following behind and went out the door. Val closed the door and returned to the kitchen.

Ron said, "Damn, that stupid gun. Why did I ever give that to you?" Ron raised an eyebrow. "Val, where is the Glock?"

Val said, "It was for my birthday, remember? You thought I should have it for all the nights I spend alone in this house. I've never had a need for it anyway. I've stashed it away in the big clock."

"Oh, the old Glock-in-the-clock trick." Ron smiled and then changed expression. "Damn gun. I wish I hadn't bought it. It is only a matter of time before the police discover we own a pistol."

Ron sighed and continued, "I'll talk with Chief Pirwarsky when I get to city hall. We will arrange a meeting with our attorney and Lieutenant Maxwell. This must be handled professionally from our end. The staff and I were together for hours last night working on the campaign. We all can vouch for each other."

Val said, "I am a little concerned. I can't prove I was home. I arrived home about half past five, give or take a few minutes. A couple of people did see me leave the medical building. I didn't see anyone in the neighborhood when I drove home, but I still can't prove where I was. On the other hand, they will never place me anywhere else."

Ron moved to Val. He placed his hands on her shoulders, paused, and then looked deeply into her eyes. He kissed her softly on her lips. Nuzzling her neck, he uttered, "You will be okay, Val."

Val shifted into Ron, feeling his body next to hers. She put her arms around him and placed her head on his shoulder. She inhaled and then softly sighed.

Ron gently pushed Val away and spoke. "We can expect the police to delve into your confrontation with Amy Johnson. I never met the girl until yesterday. The whole evening was a bad dream. What was the significance of Amy handing me her underwear? I never met her before. Was it supposed to embarrass me? Was it to embarrass you, or was it to light your fuse? I just don't know. Just a pair of underwear by themselves isn't very meaningful."

Val joked, "Unless they were yours. Was she returning your panties, Ron?"

Ron laughed, "Don't joke around, Val. The girl is dead."

"You're right, Ron. Nothing funny about it. They were way too small for you anyway."

She had to smile a little but continued, "However, it must have been more than an impulse, especially with me standing there. Maybe she didn't even know me. Hey, wasn't that reporter from the newspaper, Andy Stricker, there?"

Ron said, "Oh my goodness, you're right. Andy must have received a tip. Andy hardly ever just shows up at the campaign office. His being there adds creditability to the story. I need to talk to Andy and see why he was there."

Ron joked, "Val, when the police question you about your threats, just tell them you threaten to emasculate me at least once a month, and I'm still here."

"You're all heart, dear," Val responded with a smile on her face but with a feeling of despair. They embraced and kissed.

What a way to start the day.

CHAPTER 5

THE STEADMANS STARTED PREPARING FOR the media frenzy that was sure to be coming their way. It was urgent to have a meeting at their house as soon as possible.

Their house, a Western-style ranch design, located in an upper-middle-class neighborhood, could be called sprawling if the square footage were larger. Only 2,800 square feet, it was just the right size for entertaining. The Centerville Art Museum furnished historical pictures and photographs for most of the walls on a loan basis. The Steadmans held social parties frequently, and the house is perfect for this function.

One room, adjoining the master bedroom, had been set up as an office. This room was sparsely decorated, but in it were their computers, two desks, and a conference table with chairs. Two televisions, primarily for watching the local and national news, sat on one wall. There were three bathrooms, one for the master bedroom and two located off the hallway.

A circular driveway led to a large custom-made double door made of South American oak.

The house occupied about one-half of the one-acre property. The other half acre came in handy for parking guest vehicles when necessary.

They built the house and moved into it shortly after Ron became mayor, and it served them well most of the time, but right now, easy accessibility was a problem. The street and vacant lot next door were crammed with news media vehicles. A sensitive person would feel like a hostage, especially when the doorbell rang constantly. One reporter yelled, "We know you're in there. Can't you come out and give us a few minutes?"

Ron placed a call to Charles McKay, his campaign manager, and Mike Bronson, his public relations advisor. "We're under siege here! Reporters are everywhere!"

Charles mentioned he would be over immediately and hoped they could quickly work up a finished product for minimizing adverse publicity from the events of the previous evening.

Mike said he was on his way.

Ron planned a press release and wanted their input. Ron told them, "At this point our goal is to fully cooperate with the investigation and let them know we have nothing to hide. The police interviewed everyone at the campaign headquarters and took their statements last night."

Val called Jay Barnes, who was on retainer by the campaign committee. Although Jay was not a criminal attorney, he had been their personal lawyer for years. He was known as an expert cross-examiner in a courtroom. He would help prepare Val in responding to anticipated questions about her supposed involvement.

The most frustrating part of politics was the backstabbing, character assassination, and mudslinging, which sometimes tended to stick. Being in the limelight, especially running for mayor in a city the size of Centerville, changed some people. Many opponents pulled out all stops and certainly didn't consider the ethical or moral implications of their actions. After all, to the victor go the spoils. Losers may give up and disappear or live to fight another day.

It is unconscionable to think that someone in this political arena was involved in a murder and death of a young girl. Val privately couldn't fathom the possibility. But she swore on her mother's grave that she would find the killer. After all, she's the person who was going to be up the proverbial creek without a paddle. She had no choice but to work on a worst-case scenario.

With all the noise and interruption of the doorbell and telephones, the team could hardly hear themselves think. In consideration of his neighbors, Ron entered a bathroom—it was quieter—and called the chief of police, George Pirwarsky. Ron requested an officer or two be sent to control the noise and traffic outside.

After he hung up, Ron went back into the kitchen and reported, "The police are on their way. Chief Pirwarsky has advised his detectives, headed by Joe Maxwell, head of homicide, to interview all of us, some as follow-up, to find out what we know about the murder. He didn't seem to know that Maxwell had already tried."

Ron continued, "Chief Pirwarsky also stated he would inform the media that since this was a murder investigation, no information could be released at this time. He suggested that Val and I not comment on the ongoing investigation. I agreed with Chief Pirwarsky. This meeting should be aimed toward responding to ancillary questions only."

Ron headed out to massage the media while Charles and Mike questioned Val about the panty incident and what she knew about the murder.

This did not take very long since she knew nothing, but she informed them she had been home alone, had no alibi for the time of the murder, and that was the reason Jay Barnes was there. The balancing act was how to protect her legal rights while minimizing the effect on the campaign.

One issue centered on how to anticipate the political attacks they might expect from one or more of the opponents—again, a worst-case scenario.

Val explained to them Ron's idea about a possible conspiracy that went wrong. Charles jumped up from his seat and spouted, "That's it, and it has to be." The others agreed and decided the basic response would be that the incident was an attempt to embarrass Ron, probably by an opponent.

Charles McKay was about thirty-one years old but had been in political campaigns since his first year in college. He worked on Ron's first mayoral campaign as a volunteer and then went on the payroll of Senator Michal's last election staff.

He then worked for the National Democratic Committee as a field agent, before signing on with Ron's reelection. Being ambitious, he saw this job as the last step before going big time in running election campaigns. Intelligent, energetic, and persuasive, Charles performed well.

If Charles had a weakness, it was that he hit on every desirable woman. He considered women a bonus of his work. Charles stands almost six feet tall, with a body most women find attractive. Broad shouldered and slim, with dark, swarthy looks and a great smile. Many women working on the campaign were enamored with him.

Mike Bronson presented an entirely different physical appearance. He was redheaded, with freckles, and bubbled with optimistic enthusiasm. He was five foot eight and built heavy. About twenty-nine years of age, he frequently showed up in plaid pants.

He had been in public relations with a marketing firm before joining the campaign. Mike probably wanted to stay on as Ron's PR director after the election.

Mike looked at Ron and asked, "Do you have a busy day at city hall, or will you be able to devote part of the day to the campaign?"

Mike went on to explain, "I am concerned about priming the telephone workers on filtering various phone calls, questions about Amy Johnson, or who should field those questions."

Ron noted, "I will be available for people who want assurances from me personally and will come by the war room for direct contact with the volunteers on the matter. The telephone workers should be instructed on how to respond, but if a voter is not satisfied, I should be notified so I can respond personally."

Charles, in agreement, considered this a good approach. "The mayor can return calls where needed. Perhaps this might be a situation where Ron can also record a telephone message to be sent out to all the voters."

Jay Barnes thought that he and Val should have a private conversation concerning her legal rights and how she might respond to personal attacks. Then she could rejoin the others in the overall approach to the matter.

Val said, "I welcome any input regarding my problem. I have no alibi and I am a suspect in a murder. Let's get all our ducks in a row. The police have talked with you four, and you have backed up each other. That's a dead end for them. That leaves me."

Jay Barnes's age was middle forties. He married his college sweetheart when they both graduated from college. Shortly after joining a local law firm, he attained national attention by winning a lucrative personal injury lawsuit and then was off and running. He started his own firm and now has three or four associates.

Jay asked, "Val, please, tell me about your activities during the hours of the murder, between 5:00 and 7:00 p.m."

After her short review, Jay assured her she definitely would be cleared but advised her to retain Bob Reynolds, a well-known criminal attorney with a record of enough wins in court to be admired and envied by other attorneys. Jay downplayed her concerns about being alone but recommended caution by hiring the best attorney in going forward. He stated that most attorneys would recommend legal assistance from someone like Reynolds as early as possible in her situation. He offered to call Reynolds; Val accepted the offer.

Jay was sure Reynolds would want to sit in on her police interview and would counsel her to keep her statement short and to the point. Something along the line of, "Yes, I threatened her. She was way over the line, with her panties, and it was a spontaneous reaction on my part. She left and I never saw her again."

Jay said, "Call me if I can be of further help." He left to go to his office with his assurance she would hear from him or Reynolds in short order. Val, feeling neglected, hurried into the office room and switched on the TV. As Jay left the house, he was engulfed by the news media people and cameras. He fought through them, made it to his car, and left.

The team finished wrapping up the package. All agreed that Ron should express his condolences to Amy Johnson's friends and family. He should take Chief Pirwarsky's advice and not comment on the circumstances surrounding Amy Johnson's untimely death, other than to point out he had only met the girl the day before. A recorded phone message from Ron along these lines would go out. Ron would be provided a list of all people desiring a direct comment from him for return calls.

Ron would state that his campaign was on course and will stay on course, but he would be in frequent contact with the police to assure this case has the priority it deserves. There would be no public comment from his wife. She would do all she could do to cooperate with the police and help bring the investigation to fruition, when all guilty parties were arrested. Ron headed out again to brace the media and make his statement.

The team watched the TV as Ron made the statement, declined to answer questions, and came back inside the house.

Ron suggested to Charles and Mike, "Why don't you go to the war room and bring the staff up-to-date? I will be over later. This too will pass, and we will proceed toward election victory. The panty incident and subsequent murder, although dramatic and terrible, should not deter our efforts for victory."

Ron walked over to Val and said, "I need to go to city hall. My mayoral schedule is heavy today with budget and constituent matters."

Val responded, "I also have experiments running and am needed at the lab. If the police need to schedule my interview this afternoon, they should call."

Then thinking about the horde of locusts outside, Val shouted, "Who will run interference for me so I can back my car out of the garage?"

Charles called the policeman on duty to help him with crowd control. They would handle the crowd.

A couple of news media cars followed Val all the way to the medical school. They left her alone as she entered safely into the building and her lab—her other home, where Steve Janson and two lab assistants immediately started peppering her with questions. Telling them everything would be made clear later, she took Steve into her small office, closed the door, and briefed him on the flare-up with Amy Johnson, the murder, the meeting, and the campaign strategy.

Val, on the verge of tears, confessed to Steve, "I felt like I wasn't even at the meeting. It was like they were ignoring me.

All they cared about was the campaign. No one, other than Jay Barnes, offered any suggestions or any kind of support for me."

Steve immediately engulfed Val in his arms, looked down at her through his thick eyelashes with his big brown eyes, and whispered in her ear, "Val, I am here for you."

Val began to melt and her stomach tightened. *No. No*, she thought, *this isn't right*. She came to attention and swallowed as she gently pushed Steve away.

Lightly touching his arm, Val softly pleaded, "Steve, I need your support. Will you go with me to the police interrogation?"

Steve slowly ran his forefinger down Val's nose and touched her lips, winked, and said, "I will be happy to. Just tell me when you are ready to go."

CHAPTER 6

THE MEDICAL BUILDING WAS ABOUT twenty years old but had been meticulously maintained. Landscaping was particularly effective through the use of xeriscaping, using cactus, sage, and other southwestern desert plants. A large concrete area surrounded the buildings. It included benches and modern sculptures, but the outlandish ones made many laugh, like the complete 1957 Chevrolet sedan on a twelve-foot pedestal. Oh well, to each his own.

The laboratory building housed five large labs and the necessary warm and cold rooms. All were located on the second floor of the two-story building.

Val's lab, originally set up as a cell farm whose purpose is to grow new cells of different kinds, has been expanded into a stem-cell research lab to study the effects of new stem cells on existing tissue. With the governmental ban on stem-cell research now abolished, Val and associates were off and running in competition with the best labs around the country. The lab's location, just an hour and a half from a well-known national research laboratory, gave a good edge through collaboration to move along quite fast. She loved the direction the research was taking since it appeared so promising. Steve and Val had finished preliminary experiments and were in the process of adding to the number of animals tested. This strengthened their statistics.

This research work, always a tedious part of any experiment but a very necessary one, required successful repetition to validate findings.

Steve and Val recently submitted a grant proposal to the National Institute of Health for $7.5 million—$1.5 million per year for five years. This was the unwritten time limit for this kind of grant. All indications indicated approval. If grant progress was made to NIH's satisfaction, the grant could be renewed and the work continued.

The grant submission proposed that the university laboratories and cell farm facilities be upgraded in order to become a certified stem-cell research lab. Their proposal was based on their development of a new and vastly improved method for certifying the stem cells' viability and purity.

This method had not yet been published in a national journal, because university attorneys were in the process of patent approval for the procedure. Val expected approval because several other laboratories had successfully repeated her procedure, could testify the procedure as 100 percent accurate, and results were completed in twenty-four hours. This was a substantial improvement over procedures then used in labs around the world, where the results took days. Studies using pigs had shown that stem cells sometimes grow into tumors and morph into unwanted kinds of tissue, possibly forming bits of foreign tissue, such as bits of bone forming in the heart when they were supposed to be repairing heart tissue.

Many lines of stem cells did not seem to morph, but it was critical to weed out those that might. Lab procedures had been developed for solving these problems, but they were tedious and time-consuming. Val's new lab procedure improved the time problems.

Steve and Val had grown quite fond of pluripotent cells, which are cells that are able to develop into virtually every kind of human cell. They had recently attended a three-day symposium on how to grow these cells and how to keep them content and healthy.

Even though the government now allowed this research to be funded with government money, this work was still highly controversial and had become a hot political issue nationally. Some people saw the work as an attack on their religious beliefs.

Ron had always supported her in her profession. Indeed, he was proud of her. Nevertheless, in public they downplayed the subject of Val's work because of its controversial nature. Why beg for conflict? Experience has been that elections thrive on conflicts, and there are enough going around without this one. They were prepared to go on the offensive for their research if it became necessary. Extremists against any issue can make a lot of noise even though they may be a small minority. Also, everyone must be aware that although this research has the potential to be of great benefit to mankind, scientists working in this field know that unscrupulous people could cause damage to the programs by starting human treatment before research has been completed. As noted, this could result in unforeseen harmful side effects on the body. One of Val's aims in science was to stop this kind of scientific action.

CHAPTER 7

R ON RODE THE CITY HALL elevator up to his office on the fourteenth floor. As usual, several other city employees heading to their offices were also on the elevator.

Ron recognized one employee who was a paralegal in the city legal department, and who was known to be a loudmouth. He said, "Good morning, Mayor. Man, you and your wife blew the town open on the news today. The newspaper was pretty descriptive."

"BJ, since you work here and I assume you wish to continue to do so, I suggest you keep your mouth closed, or better yet, help us out by spreading the word on the incident being a set up by my opponents."

They reached the fourteenth floor without further comment.

A city organized like Centerville, under the mayor/council form of government, employed two types of people—the professional employee hired for his job expertise and the political employee, who was hired primarily to support the mayor.

Sometimes the political employee came with professional qualifications. A professional, like a hired mercenary, worked under the newly elected mayor's policy. Sort of like "The King is dead. Long live the King" philosophy. The professional planned on being in the job for a career, whereas the political employee usually only lasted as long as the elected official.

The mayor's office was the hub of city operations. A day in the mayor's office may offer unanticipated challenges, which made the job exciting. The clerk's office followed a set routine most every day unless an election was imminent.

Elections bring their own excitement to the city clerk, whose responsibility includes overseeing the election process.

Being mayor became a great balancing act between employees' motivations and varying loyalties.

There are always reporters snooping around looking for items of interest. Every once in a while they turn up something controversial. These were the news items that sell newspapers. Ever reporter's dream was to have his or her story on the six o'clock news.

One difference between private and political business is in decision making. The public sector has the ability to make crucial plans behind closed doors, whereas in politics, there is nothing close to a closed door. One way or another, reporters obtained information.

Ron opened the doors leading into the reception area, and there stood Andy Stricker, the *City Hall Times* reporter, and three TV crews.

Ron asked, "Didn't I see you outside my house this morning? How did you beat me here?"

Andy replied, "It's just my job, Mayor. How can I write the story without some statement from you?"

Andy Sticker, a city hall veteran, could have gone on to become an editor on another paper, but he loved reporting the mix-and-match work of city hall. He was bald except for some gray hair around the fringes of his head. His stomach led him around as he walked. Short of six feet by a few inches, he still weighed over two hundred pounds. His shirt always looked as if it were slipping out of his pants, and his red nose upheld the reputation of a good reporter, known to down a few beers when available.

Ron showed his put-upon look and said, "Andy, I would like to help you out, but you have my comments I made at the house this morning. My mouth has been literally zipped by Chief Pirwarsky. Look, it's time for me to take care of city business. Go talk with Chief Pirwarsky. There is one thing though—I saw you at the campaign headquarters yesterday. What made you show up yesterday at that particular moment?"

"My editor received an anonymous phone call that suggested we be at headquarters for a news flash. Good thing I was there. That was a good show. I vowed right then that I would never take on your wife. She has the fire of a dragon."

"Don't you see, Andy, information is being fed to you by my opponents who tried to set me up. You might want to remember that as we go forward. I'll give you first shot if any information becomes available."

Ron glanced around the work area, a large open area with a reception counter, dubbed as the war zone. Desks were strategically placed around the room for the office staff. There were several private offices at the back of the large work area.

The mayor worked out of a large corner office with an attached conference room. Next to the conference room was the private office of the chief administrative officer, Art Gallendez, more commonly called the CAO, followed by an office for the assistant CAO and two small offices for administrative assistants.

One wall in the conference room held pictures of previous mayors, called "the wall of fame" or "the wall of infamy," depending on the attitude of the person observing the pictures.

As Ron walked by his administrative assistant, Lupe Lopez, he smiled and greeted her in his usual morning way, "Buenos dias, Lupe." She smiled, and said, "Bueno dias, Mayor." She handed him a stack of telephone call slips. She told him that he had a stack of papers needing his signature on his desk, and if any additional information was necessary, she would bring him up-to-date.

Lupe's jet-black hair framed her expressive face and flashing black eyes. She dressed in bright colors and always lit up the room. Seeing the pleasant Lupe every workday morning helped start his day right, usually with a smile.

Lupe was an office gossip. Each morning, after their usual greeting, she would update Ron on office rumors. But today, Ron was inpatient. He asked Lupe if the panty incident and murder had made the rumor rounds.

She smiled. "Si, it's covered city hall."

Ron and Lupe often used office politics as a tactic for distributing information. Ron told Lupe it would be good to put the word out that the incident had been a setup, probably by one of his opponents. He knew Lupe represented a large family, and soon everyone would be talking about the setup.

Ron checked his first appointment of the day. The executive director of the Tourism and Convention Center and the finance and development director would be discussing budget problems. Ron had reserved fifteen minutes for them. The tourism director desired a budget increase because more conventions were being booked than anticipated when the budget was prepared, resulting in more office expenses. The finance director wanted deferral until he had a chance to review the request. He thought other options might exist.

But instead, waiting for him with Art Gallendez, was the shop's superintendent. Both had worried looks on their faces

"What's up, fellows?" Ron asked.

Art reported that a shop foreman and parts supply manager had been arrested for stealing and selling automotive parts from the city parts store. They had been under the surveillance of an undercover policeman, who had received a tip from a commercial parts competitor. The news media had the story.

"A new one, and on top of the panty murder, this hurts the campaign."

Art said, "Well, Mayor, we can't stop breaking news. Why don't you talk with Mike Bronson? Maybe he can put a positive spin on the story, like how the city will always weed out bad apples while you are mayor."

"Good thinking, Art. Give Mike a call and ask him to get on it. Ask Mike to try and set up the panty matter in tandem with the stealing story."

Then Ron ordered, "Art, you handle my first appointment concerning the tourism budget matter. Lupe, please cancel my other appointments this morning. Call Chief Pirwarsky and ask him to come over as soon as possible."

Essentially, Art Gallendez, CAO, acted as the mayor's chief of staff. Art handled the day-to-day working of city activities and tracked programs important to the mayor.

Large city government is big business in a political setting. Centerville had an annual operating budget of close to one billion dollars, with about twelve thousand employees. Based on budget allocations, the largest operations were water utilities, roads and streets, and police and fire departments.

There were twenty-one other smaller departments, all reporting directly to the chief administrator.

The government could be likened to a large private business operating as a holding company.

Art Gallendez, a Centerville local born into a large political family, decided government was for him and obtained a master's degree in public administration from New Mexico State University. His experience included responsible jobs in both state and local government. He and his family supported Ron's candidacy. When news media raised an issue of political payback upon Ron's announcing Art's appointment, Ron's comment had been, "He has the qualifications, and then some."

Art said, "Before you go, Mayor, based on what I heard this morning, everyone supports Val."

"Thank you. The media will take the routine task of drawing the stories out so they can fill the papers and airways as long as possible unless something more exciting explodes. I'll have a frank session with Chief Pirwarsky, and he will stay on top the investigation, I'm sure. We'll wait to see which assistant district attorney gets assigned."

While waiting for Chief Pirwarsky, Art briefed Ron on city operations, including a major zoning issue, utility line extensions, and counseling of a police sergeant on sexual harassment charges.

Art continued, "Councilor Cisco had been pressuring me to hire one of his nephews. The kid, eighteen years old, has no particular qualifications. Cisco has come by to see me about hiring his nephew three or four times. His wife, Rosa, has even called me at home. He came by this morning again and begged me to hire the young man. I still hesitated. Visibly showing discomfort, Cisco told me this was critical. Rosa had told him she wouldn't let him have any until Pedro was hired."

Art grinned from ear to ear and said, "As you know, Mayor, Rosa is one of the sexiest, most beautiful women in town, so I consented and told Cisco he should have told me how critical this was before. I told him to tell Rosa you got the job for Pedro. I'll start the process today."

Ron laughed and said, "We take care of the problems, don't we, Art? He now owes us big time. Ask Lupe to set up a meeting for me with Cisco. His family can assure I carry his district. Maybe he will knock on some doors with me."

After Art left, Lupe buzzed Ron. "Chief Pirwarsky will be over in a few minutes, but he wants to have a word with you immediately. He's on line one."

Ron picked up the phone, punched line one, and said, "Yes, Chief."

"I just received information that a patrolman was sent out with his partner on a marital dispute that got out of hand. The husband was shot in the ensuing conflict. The husband had a shotgun, would not obey an order to put the gun down, and pointed it at the patrolman. The patrolman shot him in self-defense. Jose Ortiz is the man's name, and he is in the hospital in critical condition. His wife and relatives are upset and making statements that the cops overreacted, Ortiz wasn't going to shoot anyone, and they would sue."

"Hell, Chief, the way this day has started, I think I'll go home and go back to bed. No matter what I would say, it would be misconstrued. Its best you issue a statement saying the incident is under investigation and the officer involved is on paid leave, pending the outcome. I'll see you in a few minutes."

Ron hung up the phone, leaned back in his chair, and swung his feet onto his desk. He closed his eyes and rubbed his forehead and eyebrows with his fingers. Things have to get better.

Ron also was worried about Val. He had to know if she was okay. He pictured her in his mind. He got excited just thinking about her and imagining the two of them together. When he closed his eyes, he could almost smell her presence. Ron picked up the phone and dialed her number.

After two rings, Val answered. Ron told her about his day and that he would be meeting with Chief Pirwarsky in a few minutes.

Ron whispered, "Val, can you get away for an . . . umm, lunch date at home? There we could at least talk in private."

Val whispered back, "I will be there a little after eleven, waiting for you."

A few minutes later, Chief Pirwarsky arrived in the mayor's office via the underground corridor that connected city hall with the justice complex, composed of the courthouse, jail, and the police department. Lieutenant Maxwell entered with him.

Lupe brought coffee for all, black and strong.

Chief Pirwarsky could play the part of a big city police chief in a movie. He pushed six feet five, had a military haircut with brown and gray hair stubs, a ramrod posture, and a deep voice. He chose police uniforms for dress and wore all the gold braids his position warranted.

The chief said he asked Lieutenant Maxwell to sit in because he was the lead investigator on the Amy Johnson case.

Ron said, "I am glad Maxwell is heading the investigation. By the way, Val and Bob Reynolds, our lawyer, will be available this afternoon if you want to arrange a meeting with your people."

Sitting at attention, if that is possible, Maxwell appeared ready to pounce but just said, "That's good. I will call her."

Although Ron had never met Maxwell formally, he had heard of his reputation as a smart, straight-talking detective who obtained results. Sitting ramrod straight with shoulders back, sharply angled facial features, and piercing brown eyes, Maxwell presented himself as a hard-nosed ex-marine who aggressively pursued his assignments with professionalism.

Ron initiated the conversation. "Chief, I am well aware that we have a sensitive matter facing both of us with Val and the murder. I am not about to ask you or any of your people to do anything other than perform your normal, complete investigation and go where the evidence takes you."

Ron explained his concern that one or more hotshot detectives, not Maxwell, might see this as a golden opportunity for personal glory.

The chief chuckled. "No, Mayor, I don't see that happening. Such extreme action isn't likely. Max will run this investigation and he is solid. He won't play politics. You know I support you and enjoy working with you. You have supported my efforts and department, and we are going in the right direction for law enforcement. Frankly, I don't think all the rumors concerning you can be stopped. We have 1,920 policemen in law enforcement, most with strong character. We can't control everyone."

Chief Pirwarsky added that even though his best investigators would work on this case, two other murder cases also were being investigated. All three had to be given top priority. He assured Ron that he'd keep it close to the vest and that his detectives were above reproach.

"You must separate the mayor's office from your wife's involvement. We can't have you involved or influencing a murder investigation. I can't control the district attorney, and I don't know anyone who can. That would not benefit either. Again, Max is the best detective we have. He is as competent and professional as they come. Also, Max will keep me informed. That will minimize any bullshit."

Maxwell joined the discussion. "Your wife and Amy Johnson had a public confrontation yesterday. The murder occurred late afternoon. We are busy compiling information. Frankly all we have right now on background relates to the confrontation Val had with Amy Johnson. We want the interview with your wife, and we will be thorough and impartial."

At first, Ron appeared surprised at Max's comments but then recovered and said, "Well, we are basically on the same page, and that is all I can expect."

Ron went on to mention he knew that Sergeant Ed Jones was retiring from the force next week and informed Chief Pirwarsky he would try to stop by to wish him well.

He related a conversation Jones and he had about two years ago. Jones stopped by one morning asking to see him. Lupe sent him in.

"He walked in wearing a uniform that looked as if it had been poured on—it fit so well. I complimented his appearance. Ed thanked me and then stated the uniform was why he wanted to see me. He asked if I noticed anything unusual about it. I replied, 'No, I don't.' He then pointed out his pistol was in the crossdraw position, but regulations required a straight-draw position. It was his opinion that the crossdraw offered a faster draw than the straight position. He had compared draws in both positions and cross was faster. I asked Jones if the matter had been discussed with his superiors. It had, but they would not change the regulations. I then asked Jones how many times he had drawn his gun in a crime situation, and he replied, 'None.' I told him it made him look like a gunslinger, and it wouldn't make for good PR to have photos of an officer not conforming to the dress code splattered across the front page of the paper."

Ron said that he concluded the discussion by suggesting Jones continue to pursue the matter if he felt strongly about it, but he, Ron, would not interfere in any way. He pointed out to Jones that any chief would be upset if a mayor interfered in internal regulations.

"I tell you that because this time, I believe I have to participate in the investigation. After Max interrogates Valarie, and clears her, I want you to swear me in as a policeman, and I intend to work some with Max and his team. Normally, a hands-on approach would not be necessary for me, but I don't want this investigation to screw up my election. Besides, I enjoy investigative work and miss it. With my field experience as an FBI agent, I offer the investigation a qualified, experienced person who can assume certain duties that otherwise would crowd your agenda."

The chief sputtered his objection to the idea and added, "How will the public respond to this? They'll think you believe you can't trust the police department to solve the crime, and what about the chain of command? I essentially will be out of the loop."

"Chief Pirwarsky, I'll make sure you know everything before anyone else. You'll be in the loop. After all, I can't work exclusively on this, and my election activities still will take more time than anything."

"Well, Mayor, you know my feelings, but I remain a team player. Max, do you have a comment?"

"Yes, I have a question. Mayor, do we have any ground rules on this or do we play it by ear? Chief Pirwarsky is my boss also, and I don't want to get in the middle of communication lapses where you and I discuss and act on a matter or the chief and I act on a matter and one of you isn't informed of the activity."

"Max, we'll play it by ear right now and work on communication issues as we go along. Thanks for your efforts so far. After I'm sworn in by the chief, we, all three, will get together."

After the chief left, Ron called Charles, his campaign manager, and told him about his conversation with the chief and then added, "Even though the chief assured me of a professional investigation, Charles, we should prepare a contingency plan for countering someone going after Val as the only suspect. After she is cleared, I'll be involved in the case." He informed Charles he would be at the war room after a late lunch, at approximately one thirty.

Charles agreed all contingencies must be considered and then suggested that Val record any interview and consider calling a press conference to review and comment on the police interview. Ron said that he liked the idea of recording the police interview but wasn't sure about a press conference. We must see the police response first.

Ron wondered if anyone had ever taken this approach before. If they played a recording of the police interview, the assistant district attorney assigned would go ballistic. He noted he would mention this to Val at lunch to get her reaction.

The rest of the short morning was routine. He met and congratulated a Girl Scout group for a citizenship award they had won, returned some phone calls, and referred people to the right department for solving their particular problems. Two personal friends had called about the previous day's incident and murder. One other call returned was for fun.

Several nights back, a neighbor had called Ron at home at 2:00 a.m. to complain about barking dogs. Two nights ago, Ron didn't arrive home until 1:30 a.m. He called the neighbor to inform him he had reported the barking dogs to animal control and hoped they could do something. He was sure the neighbor would complain about being awakened at one thirty. He had a call slip from the neighbor and returned the call. They agreed future complaint calls would be made during the day, both had a good laugh, and Ron picked up another two votes.

CHAPTER 8

A S RON LEFT THE OFFICE for lunch, he told Lupe he would be late getting back and could be reached at the campaign office after one thirty.

Driving home, he reflected on the crazy turns a campaign could take and decided that supporting Val and clearing her name was important to the election.

Then he visualized walking into their bedroom, unable to find Val. She would be hiding in the closet and would jump out naked. He felt excitement building up.

Ron arrived home, noted Val's car was there, and quickly went into the house. He headed for the bedroom, taking off his coat and tie.

The bed had been turned down, but where was Val? She wasn't in the bathroom either. When he stepped back into the bedroom, he heard Val bumping around in the closet. She stepped out of the closet fresh out of the shower, her body still moist, clad only in a black Oakland Raiders jersey with the number 24 on it. This was not at all what he had fantasized.

Ron's eyes slowly wandered over her body. How beautiful she was. He moved toward her, smiling wickedly. Val held up her palm out and stated rather gruffly, "I need to get lunch started."

She marched angrily past him and padded barefoot down the hallway. Ron followed, slowing just past the bedroom door so he could admire the movement of her hips and the way the shirt lifted just enough for him to glimpse her ass. Her legs were tan and shapely.

Val entered the kitchen and started preparing lunch. Ron said, "I understand you might be a little upset, Val."

She was trying unsuccessfully to gouge soup out of a frozen container into a pan. She slammed the spoon on the counter and turned to face him. "Cut the crap, Ron, I got no damn help at all this morning, not from you and not from anyone else."

"I'm sure you feel that way, Val, but—"

Val interrupted, "It is what it is, Ron. No help is no help."

Ron looked at Val. "Val, Val, please I am sorry for everything that happened this morning. I feel terrible, I really do. If there was any way I could go back and change it, I would."

"I don't believe you, Ron."

Ron gave her a fiery little smile. "I hope I can change that. You know you are the most important thing in my life. I love you. You want some help with that?"

He walked up behind her, put his arms around her, and held the pan to keep it from falling on the floor. He dumped the soup in the pan, set it on the stove, and turned the burner on low. He moved his hands to her back and began to massage it. All of the anger and tension began to leave Val's body. He slipped his hands around and cupped her breasts, kneaded her nipples, and moved closer to her. Val's body went limp. As she melted into Ron's body, she began to tingle inside. Val wondered how, after seventeen years, this man could still make her feel so helpless.

She turned to him, clasped her hands behind his head, and immediately became lost in his eyes. She whimpered, "I'm sorry I was so angry." They began to kiss, first softly and then more urgently.

Ron carried her to their bedroom, and they spent the next hour lost in each other's arms. Sometimes it felt like Ron was riding an untamed animal, trying to match her gyrations and athletic movements. It was everything he could do just to hold on. Even after all these years, she still drove him up the wall and excited him to no end.

They collapsed in each other's arms and lay there speechless for what seemed like an eternity.

Ron mumbled afterward, "Want to go again?"

Val said, "Dreamer, by the time you get it up again, we'll be in a retirement home."

"Okay. Let's go talk and eat."

Ron whistled as he marched down the hallway to the kitchen with Val following behind.

They settled in at the kitchen table each with a small toss salad, half a ham-and-cheese sandwich, and a cup of basil-tomato soup.

Ron glanced over at his wife, thinking how beautiful and sexy she looked. He was amazed that after seventeen years she still made his knees weak when she looked at him in a certain way.

After they did a practice run of Val's police interview, Val told Ron that in the interview she would inform the police that she and Steve were going to find out who was behind the panty incident. The incident must be cleared up before it became an election issue and could be handled separate from the murder. They decided to record the interview.

Ron agreed and requested that Val let him know how she would organize the investigation. They agreed that a public statement on her police interview should not be decided until after the interview.

They embraced and kissed. They cleaned up the dishes before leaving to face the challenges of the afternoon.

Meanwhile, Charles was in the war room. The campaign committee had rented space in an office building from one of the mayor's supporters. Upon Ron's reelection, there is a good possibility that rent will be waived.

Except for Charles's and Mike's office, each with a window looking out over the workroom, the war room was completely open. Phone banks, separated by partitions, could be operated without noise interference, and worktables covered by campaign material were scattered around. Beige-colored walls, dotted extensively with tacked-up campaign posters, helped brighten the room. Volunteers worked all eight of the phones.

Charles and Mike had conferred and taken assignments of contacting the media with the intention of minimizing the fallout over Amy Johnson's murder. Surprisingly, the other political camps had remained almost silent on the matter. Wilmington Brown's campaign only stated that the death was a terrible tragedy and that they would be cooperating with the police to apprehend the monster who committed this crime.

Charles looked out his office window at the bank of telephone operators working the phones on Ron's behalf. The volunteers, coordinated by Mike, were calling all registered voters with a prepared text on why they should vote for Ron. They also attempted to obtain commitments from Ron's voters and requested donations of money or time, if responses were positive. Mike had briefed them this morning on answering questions about the murder and provided each a tout sheet to assist in responding.

With the ever-expanding frontiers of telecommunications, Ron later would send out a prepared recorded telephone message for all voters.

The telephone message, plus the workers who have been lined up for door-to-door contact, would be vital to a successful election. Since these workers talk directly with voters, they usually obtain feedback on how the campaign is progressing.

CHAPTER 9

CHARLES HAD HIS EYES ON an exceptionally nice-looking woman who had been working the phones for the last two days and decided it was time to talk with her. When she started her campaign work, she had been introduced to him as Julie Carrico. He had made a point of talking with her on occasion.

Charles strolled over and asked if she would step into his office when she could take a break. Between calls, she came into Charles's office. He offered the usual thanks for her efforts on behalf of Ron and asked what kind of responses she was receiving.

While she was commenting, her beauty and sultry voice enchanted him. About five feet five, Julie had honey-blonde hair, sparkling gray eyes touching on blue, and full lips tinted perfectly to match her natural coloring, with a body to match. Well-formed breasts pushed against her silky blouse. Custom-fitted blue jeans drew one's eyes to a firm ass. He guessed her age to be around forty. She definitely was stunning. He previously had noticed a large diamond ring next to a wedding ring.

As talking progressed, Charles felt a familiar physical tugging between them. She reported receiving many favorable telephone responses and, at this time, had not received any real negative feedback over the murder. Charles was concerned about the impact of the murder.

"Good news, just what we wanted to hear, Julie. May I call you Julie?" Charles asked.

She nodded. "Yes."

Charles looked at his watch and said, "Listen, its lunchtime, and I missed breakfast this morning. Would you like to go to lunch with me? We can discuss this some more and get some nourishment."

After a slight hesitation, Julie looked him in the eye and agreed, saying her shift was about over anyway. Charles asked if she had any lunch preference, but she deferred the selection of a restaurant to him, saying she would eat lightly anyway.

Charles decided on an out-of-the-way place, one not too far from his apartment just in case something developed.

While driving to lunch, Charles found out that Julie was the wife of a family doctor and had two children, both boys and both away at a private high school. She commented that her husband spent many hours at work, even volunteering for charity medical work in the less-fortunate areas of the city. Since she had so much free time, she joined Ron's campaign and also started working on the United Way campaign.

Charles's response was to tell her that she could be a much more valuable resource to Ron than just telephoning. The campaign could work with the many community contacts she and her husband have. She indicated that might be possible.

They had an enjoyable lunch, but a sexual undercurrent definitely was there. Charles decided it was worth pursuing.

As they buckled up in the car, Charles asked if she would mind if he stopped by his apartment to pick up some papers he needed.

Julie said, "No, I don't mind."

Charles parked the car in front of his apartment and invited her up to look at a bachelor's apartment while he looked in his files for the papers.

She broke eye contact, looked away, and said, "Okay."

Charles opened the car door for her. They went into the apartment. His apartment, located on the ground floor of a three-story building in the apartment complex, presented an appealing entranceway about six feet long with rocks and plants off to the side and another door providing entrance into a combined living room and dining room. The ceiling, composed of pine beams and slats, highlighted the southwestern style of the room. Furniture completed the theme with a heavily wooden couch and chairs. Indian rugs were scattered around the hardwood floor. The dining area held a mahogany buffet, a dining table, and four chairs. A doorway led to a small kitchen. On the other side of the living room, next to a southwestern-style fireplace, a short hall led to two bedrooms, each with full bathrooms. Framed pictures and prints on white walls continued the southwestern theme.

They stopped in the living room. Charles touched Julie's arm and said, "I have a confession. I don't have any papers to pick up here. From the time you first started working at headquarters, you caught my eye. You are a beautiful, smart woman, and you bewitched me. I needed to tell you privately, and I hope you feel something for me."

"Oh, Charles, I figured out your intentions the minute you suggested stopping by your apartment, and all I can say is here I am."

Charles moved closer, placing his hands on her waist. They locked eyes, and then both responded with a long and passionate kiss. He moved his hands down and pressed their bodies together. She felt his manhood growing larger as he whispered hoarsely, "Let's go in the bedroom." Julie started to say something but didn't, and he led her into the bedroom.

There, they kissed again and he started taking off her blouse. He then unsnapped and helped her take off both her blouse and bra, exposing beautiful breasts. He kissed her breasts and teased them with his tongue until they were hard. They undressed and had wonderful sex. Afterward, they lay beside each other, legs entwined. He told her she was a marvelous lover, all any man could want.

Julie burst into tears and told Charles she and her husband, John, had not had sex in over two weeks. They used to have sex three to four times per week.

A reliable source told her he was having an affair with a young nurse at the hospital. She hastily said his affair played a little bit into her accepting Charles's offer, but she also had her needs and had felt the strong sexual overtones from Charles. Charles asked, "How long can you stay?" And she replied, "I can stay until about five."

Charles called headquarters and told Mike he would be out for the afternoon but to tell Ron that, if he was needed, he was available on his cell phone.

He then went into his walk-in closet, took out a couple of robes, gave Julie one, put one on, and said he would open a bottle of wine to celebrate the mating of two lonely people who were not so lonely anymore.

They found themselves feeling comfortable with each other as they chatted about their lives and enjoyed the wine. Julie said that she at first wanted to decline his advances, but changed her mind quickly. They later continued their lovemaking.

At five o'clock Julie said, "Oh, my car is up at the headquarters parking lot." Charles said he would take her back, but for her sake, they should give the headquarters staff time to leave.

She agreed. They arrived at her car without meeting any staff and volunteers. Julie agreed they would get together again.

After parking his car, Charles entered the war room, now silent, to catch up on phone calls. While walking to the office, he reflected on the afternoon and Julie and thought about how amazing she was. They would have to be careful. He did not want her hurt.

CHAPTER 10

L EAVING THE HOUSE AFTER LUNCH, Ron headed to campaign headquarters to report Val's decision to pursue identifying the panty-incident originator. The luncheon discussion with Val made him feel better about the whole mess. She was absolutely right—they couldn't rely solely on normal police activity. There was too much at stake. It was fortunate that Steve had investigative experience from his military service and was willing to help her. Embedding students in the other campaigns, especially in Gonzo's, should provide some leads.

Gonzo was Wilber Gonsolic. He was loud and obnoxious. He would garner a few votes but was not Ron's main concern. Will Brown was a more serious opponent. Ron found Gonzo irritating. Ron knew that Gonzo would stoop to anything to acquire votes.

Ron pulled into the campaign headquarters parking lot. It always made him relax to be there. Having all these people volunteering their time to help his campaign lifted his spirits. He entered the building and went around greeting people, shaking hands and expressing his appreciation for their efforts on his behalf. Mike told Ron that Charles was at home and asked if he wanted him called. Ron said, "No."

Ron decided to make a short speech about the murder. He asked the working volunteers to stop work while he explained something. He then told them he was sure they knew all about the horrific murder of Amy Johnson They may have seen Val jump on Amy when she handed her panties to Ron or at least have heard about it. He mentioned also that he was likely setup by a competitor.

He mentioned Val had been home alone during the critical hours and had to be looked at as a suspect by the police. She informed the police she was available for an interview but knew very little about the matter. Ron knew she had done nothing and would not do anything illegal. He joked that she wouldn't even jaywalk.

He reminded them this was a political season—as if they needed reminding—and he had no idea how the public would react to the publicity about Val giving an interview as the prime suspect. "We know she is innocent. Please continue your support as the campaign proceeds." Ron asked for and answered some questions, and they showed their support with applause when he finished.

He then went to city hall, where he was scheduled to give two water department employees citations for extinguishing a car fire and pulling the owner safely from the car.

CHAPTER 11

SIMON MARTINEZ OWNED A CONSTRUCTION company but had become involved in city politics as a member of Wilber Gonsolic's election committee. Due to his ability to raise money for Gonsolic, he was on Gonsolic's executive committee, his brain trust. Simon wanted a job at the city, and he especially wanted to be a public works director. He was working hard for Gonsolic.

Simon moved around the city, drumming up support for his candidate. Once, he stopped in at a bar called Bottoms Up. Simon had met Amy Johnson there three months ago. She was a bartender. He hit on her and she was receptive. They developed a relationship, but a discreet one, and he kept his married life as far away as possible. She, too, wanted it kept quiet, although she had never told him why.

Simon thought that he could keep his relationship with her unknown. He had to keep his role in the panty incident quiet, and he knew the brain trust would make every effort to do that. But what a ball's up it turned out to be.

Actually, when Amy had called about the incident two days before, so upset, he told her he would be right over. When Simon arrived at her apartment, she was feeling the effect of a few drinks and a couple of lines of coke and was still simmering from the confrontation with the Steadmans. She tore into him, blaming him for the whole thing. Amy told him that she was chucking it all. He had caused her public embarrassment and humiliation, and she might write a letter to the editor accusing him of setting up the trick. He told her it was just bad timing and defended the plan.

A vicious argument erupted. She slapped him, went ballistic, and tried to scratch and hit him. He grabbed her around the neck and waist. She bit him on the arm. He let go and slapped her. She picked up a glass ashtray and swung it at him, but he grabbed her arm, twisted it, and she dropped the ashtray. She swung around, and with her other arm she pulled a pistol out of a drawer. Simon grabbed the gun and the hand she was holding it with. While wrestling for the gun, it fired. Amy went limp. Holding her, he lowered her to the floor and saw a hole in her chest starting to leak blood.

Fearing that he had killed her, Simon checked for a pulse. No pulse. He sunk to the floor in a sitting position, dazed. After a few minutes of staring at the dead girl, he finally realized he must do something. He couldn't call the medics or police—he would go to jail, facing a minimum manslaughter charge, and possibly second-degree murder. Gonzo's election would be decimated, but his concern was jail.

He rose, pulled his cell phone out, and called his brother, Tomas, in El Paso. Tomas had Mexican crime cartel connections. He needed advice. Tomas quizzed Simon and then tried to calm him down. Tomas explained to Simon that Amy sounded like a loose cannon, and maybe her death would be helpful. He suggested Simon get a shovel, take the body out to a remote mesa, and then bury it. After pacing the floor for a few minutes, Simon decided to wait until late evening and drop the body off at Steadman's campaign office. He anticipated problems for Steadman.

Noting blood was creeping toward the floor, he went into the bedroom for a heavy blanket and rolled the body up in it. After dark came, he moved his pickup close to Amy's door and laid the blanket-covered body in the pickup bed, covering it with a tarp.

Simon drove home, stopping for milk and bread at the store as requested by his wife. His family had dinner, watched TV for a while, and after the kids were in bed, he said he had left some papers at his office he needed for tomorrow. He would pick them up and be back home in an hour or so. He drove to Steadman's office and saw the lights were on, so he placed the body next to Steadman's door in the alley. Tomas had requested Simon to mail him the gun so he could take care of its disposal. The next day Simon FedExed it.

He was thankful that he had not had intercourse with Amy last night. Any fingerprints missed and connected to him may have to be explained some way. Fortunately, he never had been fingerprinted.

He vowed to anyone who would listen that if he made it through this he would never associate with a cokehead or a dealer again.

CHAPTER 12

A<small>T HIS HEADQUARTERS</small>, G<small>ONZO WAS</small> holding a conference with his campaign manager and two advisors, who were on his campaign committee because of large campaign contributions and support. Both had been promised important jobs in his administration—one as water director (Johnny Bustos) and the other (Simon Martinez) as public works director. Sally Carter, the PR person, was a paid campaign employee. In the polls, Gonzo was running in third place with about 10 percent.

Gonzo said, "I don't understand why we aren't stealing votes from Steadman. Amy Johnson's blood is all over him."

Gonzo sported a shaved bullet head with sharp brown eyes and bushy eyebrows. With his six-foot-two heavyweight frame, he fit his nickname to a tee and was an imposing figure. When he spoke, he tended to lean into what many people felt was their personal space. He did so while speaking to Simon Martinez.

Simon Martinez presented a neat appearance. Of average height, with heavy dark hair and regular facial features framed in an almost-square face, he almost qualified for movie-star billing and dressed the part.

Simon was talking to Gonzo. "Amy was to leave the impression Steadman and she had an intimate relationship. The plan was a good one but her timing was flawed. She did it in front of Steadman's wife, whom she didn't recognize. Valarie made her look like a two-bit whore. Amy called me right afterward. I consoled her and suggested she go to Will Brown's office and offer to volunteer."

While Gonzo questioned the others on how to salvage something out of the mess, Simon reflected on his activities with Amy again and how he could keep his association with her private.

Sally commented, "We need to put the heat on the Steadmans. I'll put a bug in the reporter's ear. No matter how the Steadmans respond, it will still leave a lot of doubts in some people's mind."

Simon had a lot riding on Gonzo. Although making a decent living with his small construction company, being public works director would offer all kinds of opportunities to expand his income. The city annually spent millions in capital improvements.

Simon jerked himself back to the present and realized Gonzo was talking to him. "Hey, Simon, do you have anything to say? What about Brown? Is there anything we can do to swing some of his supporters? Excluding me announcing that I'm a homosexual, I'm open to suggestions," Gonzo joked.

"Maybe we can get Simon to announce he is a closet gay," Sally came back.

Simon retorted, "Screw you, Sally."

Gonzo smiled and said, "Now, boys and girls, let's be civil."

"How about we find someone who can lure Brown into an affair and catch him in the act with photos?" Sally questioned.

Bustos said, "Brown currently has a partner who has been with him for at least two years, and the relationship would be hard to breach. We better let it alone." Johnny was a small person, about five feet six inches, lean, and wiry.

Johnny suggested, "Let's try to be more green than Brown." He realized what he just said when he saw the polite smiles of the others. He followed, "So if he's brown, how can he be greener than us? Remember when Steadman and the council bought forty acres in the foothills for open space? Let's propose that we expand the acreage another sixty acres by swapping or buying from the Forest Service."

"Might be a good idea. Let's check with the Forest Service and attempt to buy more open land."

"Another environmental announcement would help. Let's think on it. Give me a call if you come up with something else. We need a spike some way. We are using up our campaign funds and will have a hard time raising any more if we don't start rising in the polls."

As Simon left the building, he was thinking about Gonzo's campaign not working out as planned. He took Gonzo's comments as a crisis point in the campaign. Without money, they had no chance. He had to evaluate his position. Should he stay with Gonzo until the end, or should he think about going to Brown's campaign? Any such move would be suicide if not timed and handled right; after all, he was involved in a murder. But what if something happens that changes the election dynamics? Steadman had 46 percent, and Brown had 44 percent in the last poll. If Brown were out of the picture, it was possible a real horse race could develop. With Gonzo taking a stronger environmental position, he might pick up nearly all the green votes now behind Brown.

Gonzo is Catholic, and Steadman's Protestant; Gonzo could get a few more points by making an issue out of abortion in the heavily Catholic precincts. He might really be able to win this thing if Brown were not in the race. But Brown was in the race. Damn it! There's zilch possibility of Brown disappearing.

Gonzo's only chance was for Brown to drop out of the race.

After making several calls, he learned Brown was a nondrinker and held memberships in the Sierra Club, Chamber of Commerce, Wild Life Federation, and Professional Accountants Association from a reply to the newspaper questionnaire. He was Evangelical Lutheran, pro-choice, and liberal in other ways. They'll have to work on a way to get him out of the election because there's nothing apparent to be used for tarnishing his image.

CHAPTER 13

VAL WAS WORKING ON AN experiment in the lab when Lieutenant Maxwell called. He appreciated Val's willingness to be interviewed and wanted to arrange a time to talk to her.

Val and Ron, while at lunch, had discussed where the interview should be held and decided Reynolds's office would be the best place. If the police did not leak the interview to the media, it could be held without publicity and fanfare. If it was leaked, there would be photo opportunities only in the parking garage. The lawyer's office being private, media people would be denied entrance.

Val informed Maxwell that she had Bob Reynolds on retainer, and it would be best if meeting arrangements were made with him, especially since the meeting would be in his office conference room.

Maxwell stated that he preferred the interview be held at the police station.

Val said meeting there would cause too many problems.

"I would prefer to have the meeting at my lawyer's office, if it's not too much of a hardship for the police. It would be extremely inconvenient and perhaps embarrassing for me to be seen at the police department," she said.

Sensitive to her being the mayor's wife, Maxwell then stated that he would call Reynolds and set it up. Val told him she had previously called Reynolds and had suggested times when she would be available. Val told him late afternoon would be best for her.

She then called Ron and told him the interview had been arranged. He asked who called and she told him it was Lieutenant Maxwell. His only comment was that he was glad Maxwell still was in control.

Steve wasn't in the lab, so she went down the hall to the employees' lounge and found him having coffee with a couple of people. Steve saw her, excused himself, and they walked back down the hall. She told him about her conversation with Lieutenant Maxwell. Steve said that it sounded good, but they ought to proceed with their investigation as discussed. Everyone knew that the wheels of justice turned slowly.

Val told him she would clear everything with Dean Lorensten. She would let him know they might be out of the lab more than usual during the day for a few weeks, but work and experiments would continue as normal.

She called the dean, and he said that as long as the work continued, there would be no problem. He said, "Good luck."

One of the advantages of laboratory work was that flexitime is almost mandatory. When an experiment was running, a person might need to be in the lab off and on every few hours all day long, but there were days where one may not be needed continually. Val was thinking about the advantage of being able to attend to other matters when needed.

Then Bob Reynolds called about the police interview being set for 4:00 p.m. in his office. He suggested she get there at about 3:30 p.m. He wanted to run through her statement one more time. The agenda was simple. Val would make a statement and then say that she would attempt to answer questions. Val mentioned to Bob she would bring a coworker with her and would explain why when she arrived.

Val finished her lab work by 3:00 p.m. This allowed her adequate time to fight the traffic downtown to the law offices and find parking. Val and Steve rode together and parked in the garage. They found it empty. Good, no one had leaked the meeting.

They took the elevator to Reynolds's offices on the eighteenth floor. Reynolds appeared in the reception area promptly after they were announced. Val had suggested to Steve that she first meet alone with Reynolds to start, and then they jointly would discuss their investigation plans with him after her discussion of the police interview matters.

Reynolds escorted Val into his office. She observed several pictures of him with political leaders on the walnut walls, even one of President Clinton and Reynolds. His law degrees and certificates of authorization to represent clients before the state and federal supreme courts were prominent. Val couldn't help but think this added to the hourly rate.

Reynolds sat in his captain's chair behind his massive oak desk. The desk was clean on top except for a small clock, writing tablet, and three pens. Again, Val, in her cynic mood, thought that no doubt the writing materials were for recording billing time. Yes, Reynolds worked in beautiful surroundings, but he earned them through winning for his clients.

Reynolds's Armani suit draped his slim figure well. Although only of moderate height, he appeared large. His hair, well styled and silver, framed a tanned, clean face with few wrinkles. Reynolds presented an attitude of being helpful, although Val could not identify how he accomplished it. He asked her to run through her opening statement again for him.

"I was at campaign headquarters," Val began.

"I show up there about once per week to meet volunteers and introduce myself around the office. Faces change, and it's good to let them know they are appreciated.

"I was standing next to Ron, slightly behind him in the open area of the office, when a woman came through the front door in a hurry. She had something in her hand and a purse hanging over her shoulder. She headed straight for Ron.

"She was a nice-looking woman with blonde hair flowing around her shoulders, dark brown eyes that were dilated, and full, smiling lips. She walked up to Ron, handed him the material in her hand, saying 'Here, these are for you.' She handed him a lacy black Frederick's thong.

"She obviously did not notice me and probably did not know me. We had never met before, as far as I know.

"Ron stood there dumbfounded with the panties in his hands. I wasn't, to the contrary. My combative instincts surged. I asked the woman what she thought she was doing by making a public scene with her daughter's private clothing since it obviously was too small for her. Then I slapped her. Essentially I ran her out."

"She didn't say anything but 'oh' and scurried out the door with me following, saying some things.

"Ron threw the panties in a trash can and commented to the people there that the previous day, the first day she worked in the office, was the first time he had ever seen her. He had never talked with her and didn't know what it was all about, but he assured everyone they would be among the first to know when the matter was cleared up.

"I turned to the people in the office and said, 'Please excuse my vulgarity in talking with that piece of trash, but I was making a point to her that had to be expressed on her level, or it would not have been effective.' That was the first and last time I ever saw the woman."

Reynolds noted that the statement was simple and direct, but the detectives would be quizzing her on her later activities and then would follow up on confirming what she told them about her activity the rest of the day. Stay consistent and stay with facts.

Before they left for the interview, Val told Reynolds another item that should be discussed. She explained Steve's presence. "He's a student intern in my lab. He will be attending the police interview. Steve has made several good suggestions and has informed me about his military service, where he had been assigned to a section in the military police as a criminal investigator for a prosecutor's office."

She told Reynolds that she and Ron had decided that the panty incident had to be investigated because they thought it was some sort of conspiracy from one of their political opponents, likely from one of the opposing candidates. Steve had driven over with her and was sitting in the reception room waiting to be called. Reynolds buzzed his secretary and asked her to send Steve into the meeting. When he arrived, Reynolds asked him to explain the investigative plan to him.

Steve told Reynolds that they had decided it would be good to plant a person in each of the other opponents' offices. This would be accomplished with a couple of students who were willing to assist and himself.

He felt that his experience might offer a chance to discover who sent Johnson over to Steadman's office. Much to their surprise, Reynolds agreed and stated that Steve might be helpful on the interview team.

They moved into the conference room, just down the hall from Reynolds's office. The room held a long mahogany table with ten chairs around it. Two walls were covered with filled bookcases, mostly law books, it seemed. One wall held a large picture window showing the mountain vista in the distance. There, on one side of the table, were four men. Val's team walked over to the other side of the table, and Reynolds introduced them.

Lieutenant Maxwell introduced himself and the other three as Detective Studdard, Detective Davis, and Assistant District Attorney Mark Bracken. Maxwell noted that all three had been assigned to the case under his supervision.

The two detectives were younger looking, probably late twenties; Studdard might be older, maybe thirty-five. Both were clean-cut, handsome men. Davis was Caucasian. Studdard was African American. They too were sturdy and strong.

Maxwell, also Caucasian, obviously worked out. About six feet in height, he had a weight lifter's body, and the sleeves of his shirt looked as if his muscles would break out at any time. His haircut was marine style, trimmed closely to the skull, his face a study of intensity, with a slightly crooked nose and a firm mouth.

Studdard, a large man both in stature and girth, was balding on top; but he had the kind of face that appeared ready to laugh at any time. His clothes appeared ruffled, and his tie was askew. Val stifled an urge to reach over to straighten it.

Davis, stocky in build, had a face so normal it was hard to describe and remember. *He is the perfect person to follow someone,* Val thought.

Mark Bracken, the attorney, had brown hair, brown eyes, and wore a brown suit. He made Val think of a cat ready to pounce.

Maxwell, taking charge immediately, asked, "Who is Steve?"

Steve stepped forward and, with his hand out and a huge smile, said, "Hi, Lieut. I'm a friend and coworker of Val's."

Maxwell looked at him coldly and said, "Mr. Janson, that's 'Lieutenant.'"

Val took one look at Steve and thought, *Oh no, here we go.*

Steve cracked another smile and said, "Sorry, sir, Lieutenant, sir."

Val noticed the muscle in the lieutenant's jaw tense. He was obviously grinding his teeth, but he just said, "Still, the question is why are you here?"

Reynolds decided to step in, and he said, "Lieutenant, sir, Mr. Janson will represent my office on some investigative work we propose to undertake. This will be made clear after Mrs. Steadman's statement and interview. Mr. Janson is a trained investigator. He was in the military for five years working in the criminal justice area. His assigned duty was criminal investigation on behalf of a prosecutor's office."

Val chimed in, "Steve knows about the panty incident and murder, and he has generously offered to assist me in clearing up this matter."

Maxwell looked again at Steve and asked, "Is there any way we can verify your investigative background? We need more than just your word. This is a murder investigation and this interview is officially a part of that. We don't want a public meeting."

Steve pulled a card out of his pocket and said, "Here is the name of my former commanding officer and his telephone number, sir, Lieutenant, sir. We have stayed in touch."

Again, the muscles in Maxwell's jaw stood out as he ground off a little more enamel, and he turned to Detective Studdard and asked him to call and check this out.

While Studdard left to confirm Steve's claim, Steve took out a tape recorder and questioned, "Sir, Lieutenant, sir, will it be okay with you if we make our own tape of this interview? I know you are taping it, and I believe we have a legal right to do so. Mr. Reynolds suggested we do this."

At this point, Reynolds piped in, "Lieutenant, I believe we are within the law in making our own recording."

Val looked at the lieutenant and figured that his back molar was about gone, but he said politely that he had no objections. Bracken's face showed his dislike, but he also said nothing.

About that time, Studdard returned and, with a look of admiration at Steve, said, "That's quite a recommendation your commanding officer gave you, Captain Janson."

Steve smiled. "That's Mr. Medical Student Janson now, but thanks for the kudos. I can use all of those I can get."

Studdard turned to Maxwell. "Max, Janson's boss said the unit never lost a court decision on cases investigated and reported by Janson."

The recorders were hooked up and started. Val gave her statement as previously reviewed with Reynolds. Then the questioning began.

"Mrs. Steadman, do you think your husband was having an affair or starting an affair with Amy Johnson?" Maxwell asked.

Val replied, "No, I don't. He wasn't and did not."

"Do you own a gun?"

Val briefly hesitated. "No, I don't own a gun. Ron does."

"What kind is it?"

"A handgun. I think he called it a Glock."

"Have you fired it?"

"Not since Ron bought it and took me out to a firing range to learn. I would say that occurred about one year ago."

"We would like to have the gun. I'll send a policeman out to pick it up."

Maxwell continued, "How long has Amy Johnson worked in the campaign office?"

"I don't know firsthand, but Charles and Ron said it had only been one day before."

"Before what?"

"Before the incident."

"That would have been Monday, correct?"

"Yes," Val responded.

"What were her work assignments?"

"I don't know specifically. Charles said she performed clerical work."

"Who is Charles?"

"Oh, Charles is Ron's campaign manager and runs the office."

During her briefing with Reynolds, he had informed Val that the police would ask questions about the incident and timing of related events. The police would be asking the same questions of other people. The questions usually served several purposes—to establish facts, to uncover inconsistencies in statements, to gain impressions about the person being questioned, and to obtain leads on solving the crime.

Reynolds said that the same questions would be asked in different ways, even to the point where the person being questioned could become unsettled and trip over himself. This might be helpful to them, as the person may say something valuable.

Val now knew why he warned her about the redundancy. She was starting to become irritated, thinking, *We are wasting time when we could be working on stem-cell experiments possibly benefiting mankind.* But Reynolds's warning helped her contain her famous temper.

Finally, after about forty-five minutes of different but redundant questioning, Maxwell arrived at the final question. "Did you kill Amy Johnson?"

Val responded firmly, "No. Please find out who did before the election."

The detectives thanked Val for her time and said they would be calling if they had any more questions.

"Fine, you have my number."

Then Val continued, "This brings us to some information you should have. We need to inform you that Steve and I will be investigating Amy Johnson for the purpose of finding out who instigated her panty incident.

"We think it was one of the other candidates or at least someone in one of their campaigns. It could be just another dirty political trick, but we need some answers before the election. We will try to stay clear of your murder investigation, but if we hear or discover anything relating to it, you will be informed immediately."

"You might pose a problem for the police if the parties start crossing paths with each other." Maxwell said, "I do not want to threaten or serve you with papers for obstructing justice or withholding information pertinent to a murder investigation."

Steve replied, "We read you loud and clear, sir, Lieutenant, sir, but this activity will not cause you any problems. The Steadmans have an election to win—and that is our only motivation. I think the possibility exists that we might uncover something relating to both the incident and the death. If that happens, you will be informed immediately, as just said."

The interview ended, and Val and Steve stood up and left. Val told Steve that it really shook her up. Reynolds and Val walked out while Steve sort of hung back.

Val said, "Bob, how did the interview go?"

He said that it went well. "You answered all questions concisely and at all times stated or implied you were telling all you know." He hoped they would be pursuing other leads more diligently now.

Later, Steve told her that he had invited Lieutenant Maxwell for a beer later that night. He also said that he noticed the men admiring her legs and ass as she walked out. "You obviously impressed those dudes."

Val giggled. "Well, at least something is positive. Women work hard to show their best side, or should I say end?"

Continuing, Steve smiled. "I told Max it's a look-only situation. I know, because I have been trying."

"I guess I'll take that as a compliment."

Val called Ron, reported everything, and suggested that they eat in for dinner. She was bushed. He said he would pick up some Chinese on the way home.

Steve and Val talked about the Amy Johnson matter on their way back to the lab.

Steve said, "It is my intention to have a serious dialogue with Maxwell while we are having a beer. I don't expect him to be forthright, but we have to show him we are leveling with him. I will preen him for any information that could be helpful."

Steve also said he had lined up a couple of friends for infiltrating the other opponents' camps.

Steve asked Val, "Which camp do you want me to take?"

Val told him, based on what Ron and she knew about the opponents, he should concentrate on Gonzo. One of the opponents, she noted, Will Brown, was a decent, honorable person and would not sanction such an incident. But he can't be completely ignored because it could be an unsanctioned incident. Another opponent, Simpson, was a possibility only because he is unknown. Every candidate should be checked. She thought Gonzo definitely was the most likely suspect, so he should be Steve's assignment.

They arrived at the lab. "The police interview just really upset me. I can't believe I am the only suspect."

Steve said that she's probably not the only one, just the first one they're checking out. "When they are satisfied with your story, they will get more serious with others."

"Well, let's hope they clear me early because I have enough worries. It's late. I'm going home. See you tomorrow."

Val was home looking at mail when Ron arrived. She jumped up to welcome him and kissed him on his cheek. She explained that she and Steve had just come from the interrogation by Maxwell.

Ron asked, "Well, how did it go?"

Val proceeded to inform him of the interrogation and how Reynolds thought it went well, but she felt uneasy about the undertones Maxwell had been digging into because she didn't know where he was heading.

Ron mixed them each a scotch and water, and they reviewed Ron's day.

CHAPTER 14

MAXWELL SUGGESTED THE TEAM GO back to his office to discuss the interview. Reynolds's office was only two blocks from the station. They had walked over for the interview and were walking back.

Davis commented, "Val's a fox and smart too."

"No wonder the mayor always appears happy," said Stud.

Bracken ruined any further comments. He said, "She still is a suspect."

The team entered the station and the homicide section. They pulled chairs around Maxwell's desk and sat down. Max asked for comments on the interview.

Stud then stated that he thought Val was honest in answering questions, but she still had no alibi. She said that they have a gun. "I'll go over to pick it up. Do we want a search warrant?" Max thought for a minute and then said, "We'll just ask for cooperation first, then if a problem can't be resolved, we'll get the warrant." Max said that he agreed with Stud. "She appeared innocent, but some people, as we all know, are great liars."

Bracken said that it appeared she had no motive. They shouldn't move her off the list but suggested that the team should look harder for other suspects.

"It's unanimous," Max stated. "I'll inform the chief, but before that, let's review what we have on the case and how to proceed."

He turned around to face his computer as he asked Davis if the file was up-to-date.

Davis said, "We still need the pathologist report and the notes from the interview."

Booting up the computer, he commented that sometimes using a PC appeared slower than pulling out a file from a drawer. Max read the file aloud.

"At 10:27 p.m., the officer checking alleys along his route from his patrol car discovered the body of a young woman behind the office building at 1714 Elm Street. She had an entrance wound in front on her chest and the bullet lodged next to the spine."

Maxwell stopped reading and said, "We need the forensic pathologist's report. Hopefully he can tell us the caliber of the bullet and any DNA results."

Maxwell continued to read, "He notified the dispatcher. Maxwell instructed her to call Stud and forensics. All arrived at the site about the same time.

"Hearing the commotion, the mayor and three of his staff, identified as Charles McKay, Mike Bronson, and Jay Barnes, came outside. The mayor identified the body as Amy Johnson's, who previously had worked in his campaign. At Maxwell's request, he furnished Johnson's home address from the campaign records.

"Estimated time of death was between 5:00 p.m. and 6:30 p.m. on the same day. The body had obviously been moved.

"In searching her apartment, check stubs from Bottoms Up Bar were found. Also found was a dime bag of cocaine in her dresser, a pipe, and a cell phone. There were signs of a struggle in the living room. Furniture was broken and a lamp had been knocked over.

"Davis interviewed bar employees, names noted here, but other than obtaining personal information about Johnson, who was a bartender, no leads have developed. One waitress, Tillie Maes, was off work and had not been interviewed. People interviewed knew little of Johnson's personal life."

Looking up, Maxwell delegated the following: "Stud, I want you to assign a tail on Simon Martinez. I will hold some discussions with Janson, mainly just to check him out. Why don't we both go for a beer." Maxwell continued, "I want 24-7 surveillance on Maritinez. Also, Davis, get a detective and go back for another run through Johnson's apartment. Check again the names of associates, and look through her financial records. Check with the guys canvassing the neighborhood for any leads. We need a lead bad. I'll go locate Tillie, the waitress, for an interview.

"Before that though, Davis, write up the reports, and, Stud, let's go see the chief and then we'll have that beer with Janson."

Bracken said, "I'll be in the DA's office if needed." And he left. Max and Stud followed him out and went upstairs to report to the chief.

CHAPTER 15

THE COCKTAIL HOUR WAS AN established routine when the Steadmans were home for the evening. Normally, Val would jokingly ask, "Well, what will we discuss tonight? Garbage or sewage?"

In actuality, these two operations formed the basis of their discussions occasionally. The water department had operational problems at the sewage plant off and on. When a sewage problem occurred, it usually resulted in a serious odor problem for people living close to the plant. On the other hand, garbage trucks operated on the streets and sometimes let waste papers fly around in the wind. Some even escaped from the landfill.

People become upset at bad odor or trash flying around. If they were upset, sometimes the mayor got upset too.

The cocktail-hour drinks helped the Steadmans unwind. Tonight there would be no discussion about actual trash—just election garbage and Val's police interrogation.

Ron asked Val to review her police interview in more detail, and she told him the police would now likely expand their investigation. She couldn't say the police would eliminate her; they probably wouldn't until they found someone else.

The chief had reported findings to Ron, and he related it to Val, who had read the situation correctly. He noted the issue would hang out there as an election issue until Val was cleared. Ron was most interested in learning the results of Steve's discussion with Maxwell, and they speculated on what might develop from the meeting. They then discussed their agenda for the rest of the week and how to offset her police problem.

They reviewed three important campaign events. Ron was to speak at a Rotary lunch the next day and at a prayer breakfast on Friday morning. Ron was a strong Christian and took the prayer breakfast seriously. A candidate debate was set for Sunday afternoon at the university. Prior to that debate, Val had arranged an informal reception for Ron with university officials and friends.

Previous municipal elections experienced low voter turnout. They knew they had to get their supporters out to vote. The Steadmans expected strong support at the university from faculty and students, and they wanted them to vote.

Normally, the Steadmans didn't talk much about stem-cell lab work during cocktail hour. It was too technical for Ron, who leaned toward people matters. They sometimes discussed people dynamics at the lab. Val had found this helpful in her work.

Scientists are like everyone else. Ego stroking works wonders. Being highly educated, scientists' egos may even be bigger. Val worked on maintaining good relationships with coworkers, and discussions with Ron on this subject sometimes were amusing but always beneficial.

Going to the table for the Chinese food, they ate all they wanted and placed the leftovers in the refrigerator. Ron opened a fortune cookie.

Val opened hers and asked Ron, "What is your fortune?"

Ron read, "Good luck is smiling upon you. What does yours say?"

Val pretended to read, "Sex will carry you over the moon tonight. It appears this is your lucky night. I'm going to take a shower. Want to join me?"

Ron questioned, "Hot or cold water?"

"You always pull that! It's still hot water," Val replied as she headed for the bedroom.

As they entered the shower, Val said, "Everyone should have a large walk-in shower with the master bedroom, if anyone asks."

Afterward while they prepared for bed, Val stated that she looked forward to tomorrow. Stem-cell research was fun and rewarding, but investigating a murder, especially with Steve, was a whole new ball of wax.

CHAPTER 16

I T WAS 8:30 P.M. WHEN Steve drove to Fourth Street Bar, where Maxwell suggested they meet. Steve figured this place would be an off-duty police favorite.

Steve speculated on how things might play out over a beer. Was Maxwell all business all the time?

He parked his car and entered the bar. Like most bars, Steve felt like he was entering a cave or dark room after leaving bright sunlight. He walked into a short entryway. Steve moved slowly so he would not bump anything. The hallway led him into the main room, which was more long than wide, with a bar on the far side. Dim lighting made it difficult to recognize other patrons.

Steve listened to the low buzz of voices while his eyes adjusted. Spying Maxwell and Studdard over in a corner booth, he joined them.

Before Steve could ask, Maxwell noted, "Davis is writing up the day's events, and Bracken returned to his office."

So Steve asked, "How do you determine who gets the report assignment?"

Maxwell responded, "Davis is the junior member of the team."

Everything is the same everywhere, Steve surmised.

"I thought your interview with Val was professional and all encompassing. I hope you got what you needed to conclude that a flare-up from Val toward the murder victim did not constitute a stronger motive than responding to an obvious action aimed toward embarrassing Ron."

"Motive is not always necessary for a crime," Maxwell said. "A person can just kill because he or she loses control or because it is in his or her nature. We'll keep working the case and go where it takes us."

Taking a sip of beer, Steve responded, "That's wise, but all of the Steadmans' arrows right now are aimed at the election. Neither would jeopardize Ron's reelection by taking any action against Johnson. Besides the fact that they would not murder anyone. Let me inform you of something. When Val came back to the lab after the panty incident, she confided in me. But she had already begun to analyze Johnson's motivation. She surmised it was a deliberate act determined to embarrass Ron.

"Val and I discussed further how we could conduct an investigation aimed toward uncovering the conspiracy, and what I want to relay to you today is the basic plan we developed."

"Well, we are all ears, but the admonition stated at the interview still holds. We are conducting an officially sanctioned investigation into a murder, and we will not allow any interference."

Studdard chimed in to say, "That is about as clear as we can make it."

Steve proceeded, "I will reveal our basic plan for you. It's simple, and I believe when you hear it you will see it is possible we could supplement your work if we handle it right and keep you informed. Simply put, we will insert interns in the other campaigns. Their mission will be information gathering.

"Our interns will gather information by talking to other people working on the campaign. People tend to chat and talk, and there is a free flow of information. Intelligence tidbits, which when put together, sometimes can be revealing. I am sure that has been your experience. I need to clear up one thing before we go further. Do you prefer I call you 'sir, Lieutenant sir' or 'Max'?"

Both Max and Studdard laughed, and Max said, "Oh, just call me Max, but do it reverently, if you can."

Studdard said, "Most people, including women, call me Stud, for two or three obvious reasons."

"Is that a double entendre?" Steve asked.

"How the hell do I know? I don't speak Spanish."

"Forget it. Val and I think the Gonsolic campaign is the most likely source of the Amy Johnson panty incident. We know that Brown and Simpson are decent people, and Simpson seems to be a nonentity in the election. A couple of my medical school friends will take Brown and Simpson, and I will infiltrate Gonsolic's group. You may not be aware that medical school is more than a full-time occupation, so we face the question of how much time we students can allot to this. We may not turn up anything, but I owe it to Val to try. She's the greatest person I've ever met."

Max said, "Sounds like love to me."

"I am motivated," Steve said.

They drank their beers, watched the interplay around the bar, flirted with the waitress, and discussed sports trivia.

Steve said, "This was my show, I'll buy."

As they walked out of the bar, Max commented to Steve, "I've ordered complete background checks on several people in each of the candidates' campaigns."

"That's good. If you let me see anything of interest to our investigation, I'd appreciate it." Steve noticed that Max did not respond, so he did not pursue it.

Changing the subject, Max invited Steve to go with him to Bottoms Up Bar to find a waitress who might know something.

"Bottoms Up Bar—now that is a double entendre. Let's go."

CHAPTER 17

CHARLES HAD RISEN FROM BED at 7:00 a.m. the next morning thinking about the afternoon he spent with Julie, noting his usual morning erection and waiting for it to go down so he could use the bathroom. The phone rang and he picked it up.

"Charles, this is Julie."

"Good morning, Julie. What a pleasant surprise."

Julie said, "Yes, here is another surprise. I am just leaving the house to come over with breakfast. Do you have time? You missed breakfast yesterday."

"Yes, but that was all I missed, and I'll give breakfast up anytime for you."

Julie said, "John told me last night that he is assisting in surgery this morning and left about thirty minutes ago. You can have me and breakfast too."

"I'll be waiting for you. I haven't showered yet. Maybe we could take one together. It's a walk-in shower," Charles suggested.

"Sounds great. I'll be there is a few minutes."

Charles pumped his fist in the air as his loins tingled. He started straightening the bed. Charles threw all loose clothing in the hamper. He decided a Bloody Mary would be nice as a welcome, with coffee and breakfast to come afterward. He brushed his teeth and shaved and waited for her "I'll be there in a few minutes." only his pajama bottoms.

The doorbell rang, and Charles quickly opened the door. Julie stepped in with a sack in her hand. She stuck the sack out. Charles took the sack and, in the same motion, took her in his arms and kissed her passionately.

"Um, you smell good," he said as he came up for air. Charles had one hand on her rear, rubbing softly, holding the sack with two fingers.

"Can you tell that I don't have on any panties?"

"Now that you mention it, yes," Charles whispered. "You have a great butt either way."

Charles closed the door, and they went into the bedroom. He placed the drinks on an end table and set the sack there. He picked up the drinks, handed her one, and said as they sipped, "I want to watch you undress." He sat down on the side of the bed.

Julie set her drink on a table, slowly unbuttoned her blouse, took it off, and tossed it at Charles. She had not worn a bra. Keeping her eyes riveted on him, Julie eased out of her shoes and shimmied out of her skirt, moving slowly toward Charles. Charles dropped his pajamas, and they started kissing while joining their bodies.

Afterward, they were spread out on the bed. She had one arm around his neck with her head resting on his shoulder.

After resting a few minutes, he got up, picked up the Bloody Marys, handed her one, and sat on the bed looking at her over the top of his glass. He said, "That might just have been the best sex I ever had. Even better than yesterday, and yesterday was great."

Julie smiled. "I agree."

"We better rest a few minutes before we take our shower. Let me recover," Charles said.

They sat on the bed with their bodies touching but each in their own thoughts. After a few minutes, Charles asked, "Have you ever taken a shower with a man before?"

"Yes, I have, but I've never had an affair before."

"Let's go try it."

Charles turned on the water and adjusted the temperature. Standing to one side, he waved Julie to enter. She stepped under the water stream, making sure that her hair was above the flow and stayed dry.

Charles stepped into the shower with two washcloths and handed one to Julie. Charles squirted soap on his cloth and washed her back, her rear, and her legs. He then asked her to turn around and he washed her breasts. He kept washing downward and arrived at his destination. Her hair became drenched. She didn't notice.

After Charles finished, they hugged. She then washed him. Charles kissed her and recited Tina Turner's song title, "What's love got to do with it?"

As they stepped out of the shower, Julie said, "Now you have earned breakfast, unless you have another adventure planned."

Charles said, "What did you bring?"

Julie laughed, "A fast-food gourmet dish—sausage and egg biscuit."

They moved into the kitchen.

Julie took a glass of orange juice and poured a cup of coffee. While sipping the juice, she watched Charles warm a biscuit and start eating.

"That was the most intense lovemaking I ever experienced," Julie said.

"There is no question that it was special for me," Charles responded.

"What did you mean when you quoted the song title?" Julie asked.

"Oh, nothing, it just popped out."

"It struck me as a strange thing to say."

Charles agreed, "Yeah, now that I think about it, it was a strange thing to say. I don't know why I said it though."

"Well, maybe we should refer it to Dr. Ruth."

Charles laughed, "The sex expert on TV? Let's do it, but I really don't know why I said it."

"It hardly qualifies as an original in some situations, but it is unusual in the setting we were in."

Charles changed the subject. "There is something else hardly hard right now, and it likely won't meet expectations for a while. Are you tied up for lunch? We could have a bologna sandwich here."

"I'll skip lunch. There are some things I need to do today, and my hair is a mess," Julie replied.

"Just a minute," Charles muttered as he went into the bathroom, took a hairdryer, brush, and comb out of a drawer, and came back saying, "I'll help you with your hair."

He moved a chair over in front of a mirror. She sat down.

"You have beautiful hair, wet or dry," he said as he ran the hair dryer over her hair. He kept brushing and drying.

Julie watched him work. She said, "This is strange. Here I sit with a lover doing my hair and my existing world crumbling. It's falling apart. My husband is going down a path that has to lead to divorce. The young thing has him wrapped around her fingers by now and is, I'm sure, pressuring him to marry her. He is treating me as if I am not there, so a divorce is imminent."

Charles asked her whether it was too late to confront him with her knowledge about the affair and then suggested she ask her husband if he wanted to salvage the marriage.

"Charles, where is our relationship going?"

Thinking that the relationship might go down the tubes if he answered wrong, Charles carefully said, "I hope our relationship can be kept separate from your marriage problems, but maybe that is too much to expect. If you reconcile with John, then I assume you will leave me. If you don't reconcile with John, I hope we continue as we are."

"Then I look forward to continuing our relationship."

Charles had an extraneous thought. *Is this what all hairdressers go through?*

Charles continued, "Let me make one thing clear. Our first time in bed was a pure animal reaction. However, I couldn't continue this with you if I didn't have feelings for you. I do have those feelings. I admire you and care deeply for you. I don't want you hurt. I don't know if it is love yet because with our short time together I'm not able to distinguish between love and my desire for you."

Julie said, "We better leave it at that. I am becoming confused."

"Well, how does your hair look to you?" he asked. "It is dry and floats around your face and shoulders in a sexy, becoming way. Maybe I ought to become a hairdresser in my next life."

Julie shrugged. "Looks nice. I'll let you know about tomorrow. I take your remarks to mean we shouldn't fall in love. Maybe time will help you clarify our relationship. I'll be volunteering this afternoon and will see you then." Julie gathered her purse and left in a huff.

Charles thought, *Damn, I wish I hadn't mentioned the song title.* He dressed and left for the war room.

When Charles arrived at campaign headquarters, he and Mike reviewed the workers and assignments for the day, and Mike handed them out to volunteers.

Charles made some phone calls and checked on the financial status of the campaign. Everything looked right. Based on the bank balance and pledged contributions, the campaign should have enough money to respond to any last-minute attacks.

Picking up the phone, he called Julie. "Julie, this is Charles. Sorry I caused confusion this morning. Let me explain how I feel. I'm concerned about where my feelings are taking me because of the uncertainty facing us. I believe we shouldn't rush into anything. We need time to see where all this is going. I'd like to continue the way we are until we see what shakes out. I want to continue seeing you."

"Oh, Charles," Julie said, "that makes me feel so much better. With all the other stuff in my life right now and with the great time we had together, I just couldn't figure out what you meant this morning. Let's figure on lunch tomorrow at your place. I'll see you this afternoon. I'm scheduled to work on the phones."

Charles thought as he ended the conversation that the relationship is back on track.

Charles mentioned to Mike, "Julie Carrico, one of the people working phones, is the wife of a well-known doctor. I'm thinking we could use that relationship someway. What do you suggest?"

"What about a letter from him to all the doctors who are registered city voters? We could compare our voter list to the doctor registration list, if he is willing. In addition, perhaps he and his wife could host a coffee or cocktail reception somewhere."

"She is scheduled to work this afternoon. We can talk with her at that time," Charles commented.

That afternoon Charles and Mike discussed the ideas with Julie, and she agreed to ask her husband if he was willing to get involved.

After Julie left, Mike commented that she certainly is attractive.

"The understatement of the day," Charles replied.

CHAPTER 18

A T GONZO'S HEADQUARTERS, GONZO TOOK a call from Johnny Bustos. "Chief, I have an idea for a new environmental issue. All the city buses run on diesel. I was just following one. The buses puff out black smoke and stink up the air. Why not propose all buses be converted to propane? Propane would be cleaner, burning with fewer emissions, maintenance costs would be reduced, and pollution would decrease. In addition, the life of the buses will be extended. The calculations show conversion costs could be amortized in five to seven years. A more detailed analysis could be performed before going public."

"The figures would stand up to any questions. I ran through enough calculations to know the idea is fiscally sound."

"Johnny, I'll get some people on that right away. Great idea," Gonzo stated.

Sally appeared at the door and said, "A Steve Janson is here to see you."

"Did he say what he wanted?" Gonzo asked.

"No, just that he would like to talk with you."

"Okay, send him in."

Steve walked into Gonzo's office and introduced himself. He said, "Mr. Gonsolic, I'm a medical student at the university. Although I really don't have much spare time, I want to get involved in this election, primarily just to learn something about politics and help a candidate. I would like to work on your campaign."

Sitting behind the beat-up desk in a relaxed posture, Gonzo said, "Have a seat. Why did you decide to select me?"

Sitting down in the hard-backed chair in front of the desk, Steve, with a broad smile, said, "I did some background reading on the candidates. I agree with most of your positions on issues, and frankly, it appears you need more help than does Steadman and Brown. I went by their offices and they have more people than you do."

Gonzo snapped, "There's already an opportunity for you to learn something about politics. Number one, don't be so damn frank." Gonzo smiled.

"Just like medicine then, I'll have to use my best bedside manner," Steve bantered.

"But you're right, young man. We can use help. What did you have in mind? Anything in particular?"

"I would like to contribute as much as I can," Steve replied.

"Young man, you are a quick study. You made an intelligent comment, but you didn't commit to anything. You have the makings of a politician. Yet I think I understand what you might have said or intended to say. Why don't you spend some time on the phones? I'll check with Sally about you moving to other things, perhaps sit in on a strategy session, if you have time."

Steve reflected on the conversation. *That ol' boy is quick. That was a fun conversation, except I'll waste my time on the phone. I need to get into conversations with the players, such as Sally.*

Entering the work area outside the office, Steve noted two people, both women, making phone calls. Four phone booths were not occupied.

Steve glanced back into Gonzo's office as he headed to a phone station. Sally and Gonzo were conferring. About him? Probably.

He decided to work the phones for forty minutes or so and then find Sally or go to the table where three women were folding brochures and help there. The women were chatting away. Sally's desk, located next to Gonzo's office, was covered with all kinds of campaign literature. Maybe he could slip a glance at some of it.

Steve sat down at a phone, took the prepared script, and started calling. He had a list of names and phone numbers, plus a note sheet that categorized responses.

After forty minutes or so, he noticed Sally at the worktable handling some papers.

He walked over to her and said, "Hi again. Did Gonzo talk with you about me?"

"Yes, he told me to take you around the different workstations and answer your questions. He likes you, by the way."

"Always glad to hear that," Steve said.

Sally presented an air of competence. About five feet six inches, with platinum-blonde hair, wide-spaced brown eyes, attractive features, a slim and athletic body, and nice-looking legs, she turned heads, especially in the matching tan jacket, short skirt, and dark-brown low-cut blouse that showed some of the cleavage between her breasts.

As Sally was giving Steve the tour, he asked her how she happened to be in Gonzo's campaign.

Sally told Steve that she had been working the city beat for Channel 12 as a reporter when she ran into Gonzo. They meshed and started dating. Gonzo decided to run for mayor. She quit the station and joined the Gonzo campaign. Although her title is public relations officer, she also managed the office. As Sally spoke, she flipped her hair back with her head and pushed the hair slightly with her hand.

Steve had decided long ago that when a woman did this, it was a preliminary flirting move. That was okay with him because he was between girlfriends at the moment, and she would be a good information source.

After finishing the tour, Steve said, "Why don't I join the people at the table for a while. I can get to know them and help. It is close to five o'clock. Would you like to go for a beer or drink afterward?"

Sally said, "Sure, and I can fill you in on some things we are working toward. There is a strategy meeting tomorrow with the brain trust. I believe you are invited. I'll give you a briefing."

"Who is on the brain trust?" Steve asked.

"The members are Gonzo, of course, Johnny Bustos, Simon Martinez, and me."

"What do Johnny Bustos and Simon Martinez do for a living?"

Sally replied, "Johnny is a partner in a surveying company, and Simon owns a construction company. Johnny would like to be the water department director, and Simon wants the public works director position."

"How interesting," Steve commented.

Steve walked over to the table and started folding mailers with the three women. He introduced himself. One asked about Steve's background, and he mentioned that he was a medical-school student.

After a few minutes of satisfying their curiosity about school, Steve found out that the three women spent time most every day helping in the office. Continuing discussion led to his learning that they were relatives of Simon and Johnny. At other times, they brought friends or relatives with them. Steve thought they were acting similar to a sewing circle and would be a good source of gossip.

At five o'clock Steve and Sally walked to a nearby bar, seating themselves in a cozy corner booth. The booths were on one side and the bar on the other. It was relatively empty and quiet.

To Steve, Sally certainly looked sexy in the dim lighting, especially with her blonde hair reflecting what light there was. He told Sally she looked pretty, and Sally smiled and thanked him with a sexy little wink.

Sally ordered a vodka martini and Steve a draft beer. The thought occurred to Steve that spying could get expensive and might make a dent in his bank balance. He hoped it would not get to a point where he would have to mention this to Val.

Steve said, "I found the campaign office work interesting. A tremendous amount of effort and work goes into a campaign. It looks as if you have the work well organized."

"It's an ongoing task to keep it that way," Sally said. "My main job, public relations, is much more exciting. So many things happen, many outside our control. It is a constant challenge. I love it." As she was talking and drinking, Sally felt Steve's sexual magnetism. She found him handsome, obviously smart, and going to be a doctor. Had she guessed wrong about Gonzo? The campaign was not drawing new supporters. Gonzo was becoming difficult, nervous about the campaign probably. Maybe something would develop with Steve.

Sally smiled at Steve. He asked, "Is something funny?"

Sally said, "Oh no, I am just enjoying our discussion, and I smiled."

"Good, you have a beautiful smile." Steve said as he waved at the waiter to bring another drink. He thought she seemed to be feeling the first one.

"I'm ordering another drink for you, but I'm the designated driver, so I'll nurse this one beer. Sally, what are your thoughts about Johnny and Simon?"

"They seem to be strong supporters of Gonzo and have been helpful in the campaign. Gonzo has decided to emphasize his green credentials, and Johnny came up with a proposal to convert city buses to propane fuel. The conversion figures show an operating savings enough to be economically feasible. Gonzo will hold a press conference tomorrow to announce his findings. We need to spike our campaign and get momentum. Simon's dedicated to Gonzo and has raised most of our funding, but I believe he's made all kinds of promises to people, probably difficult to meet. Gonzo has braced him on that a couple of times. Still, Simon seems to listen, then proceeds as if he didn't hear a word."

Sally hesitated and then said, "I hope Simon does not become a loose cannon. He can become emotional over issues. Simon's so serious. He never sees the humor in anything. He has a temper, and it regularly flies off."

"Wow, loose cannons can be dangerous," Steve exclaimed. There was a lull in the conversation as Sally worked on her second drink.

After some moments, Sally said, "Gonzo has coffee scheduled at a friend's house at seven and wants me to attend. We must do this again sometime."

Steve walked her back to his car at Gonzo's office and opened the passenger door for her. He took the driver's seat, started the car, and casually asked, "Are you and Gonzo an item?"

"Yes, for now. However, we have our differences and, sometimes, disputes. This election is changing him. I'm keeping my options open."

"May I buy an option?" Steve asked.

"Steve, you certainly can," she replied and leaned over to brush her lips on Steve's cheek.

"That is good to know," Steve responded with a pat on her thigh.

"Will your schedule allow you to come into the office tomorrow?" Sally asked.

"I have to hit the books hard tonight and don't know if library time will be required. I guess it will depend on what I accomplish. I have two classes tomorrow. How about I call you in the morning?"

Sally asked Steve for his cell phone and then programmed her number in it.

Steve stopped in front of Sally's apartment; she opened the car door, saying she would wait for his call tomorrow.

As she entered the house, glancing at the time, she noted that she had about an hour before Gonzo arrived. That would give her time to shower and change clothes. She thought, *I'll have Gonzo drop me off at the campaign office to pick up my car after the coffee.*

Steve drove off, reflecting that, all in all, this had been a most informative day. He looked forward to reporting his findings to Val and Max but definitely would not mention his being an "option" for Sally. They would have too much fun at his expense.

He could picture them saying, "Tell us about it, Mr. Option. Run that by me again, Mr. Option. I wish you were my option, Mr. Option." No way would that happen.

CHAPTER 19

FIRST THING THE NEXT MORNING, Steve stopped by the lab and gave Val a report on his meeting at Gonzo's office and his discussion with Sally. He mentioned the bus conversion news conference and reported he had been invited to Gonzo's brain trust meeting being held later that day.

"That's interesting. We can use the info on the buses," Val said. "Another thing, have you wondered why they didn't check your background before taking you into their confidence?"

Steve smiled. "It's probably my enticing personality and smile. No, just kidding. I hadn't considered that. My guess is Gonzo's campaign is hurting for money and supporters so bad they are happy to see new recruits."

"Could be, but I guess it's not our problem," Val said.

Val then called Ron at city hall and told him about the bus conversion news conference.

Ron told her that Carson, the transportation director, already had been working on the conversion for about a month. He would call Mike at the war room to have him get together with Carson.

Ron briefed Mike and told him, "I would like to undercut Gonzo's news conference but in a way that it appears to be a coincidence."

Mike called Carson in his office. After brainstorming several ideas, Mike said, "Doesn't Andy Stricker usually stop by for coffee in the cafeteria midmornings, Carson? Why not join him and mention the conversion project when Andy asks you what's going on in transportation?"

Carson said, "That'll work."

Mike reported the solution back to Ron, noting his anticipation for the news conference where Andy would either ask Gonzo if he was aware the city already was working on the project or would report it when he wrote his newspaper column tomorrow.

Later in the morning, Carson reported to Ron that he had had an interesting conversation with Andy Stricker while having coffee. Stricker asked several questions about the bus conversion project. One question was to find out when it would be sent to the council. He told him that they planned on council introduction in two weeks.

Lupe informed Ron that the water department director, Sam Hopkins, wanted him and Art for a short discussion with a Frenchman who had an interesting proposal for the city. She had set up an immediate meeting.

Sam entered with Charles Laurent. Introductions were made. Sam mentioned that Laurent was a landowner's representative for a large, undeveloped parcel of land, about eighty thousand acres, sixty miles south of Centerville. The land nestled in the high desert, bordering the east side of the Rio Grande River and Elephant Butte Lake.

According to Laurent, the owners believed the soil and climate to be perfect for growing wine grapes. They proposed to sell off one-hundred-acre parcels to European wine growers.

Successful completion of the project required a guaranteed source of water not currently available at the site.

The owners proposed that the city lease sixteen thousand acre-feet of surplus water to them. Sam pointed out that city policy encouraged such leasing because the water was stored in lakes when not used, and considerable amounts were lost to evaporation. Elephant Butte Lake near the proposed site held about fifty thousand acre-feet of city water.

Sam requested the mayor approve negotiating a contract containing provisions for a twenty-five-year lease, with two five-year renewal options. These terms had been discussed and agreed to by Mr. Laurent.

Ron stated, "There is no question that this type of clean industry is desirable, and I'm giving it my enthusiastic approval."

Mr. Laurent and the mayor then held a short discussion about the wine business, with Ron asking questions. Mr. Laurent informed Ron he currently has twelve wine growers interested in the project and believe four more will be buying land. Mr. Laurent said that in Europe, the growers expected production of about four thousand bottles of wine per acre, and he would expect a similar production level here.

After the meeting, Art could tell the mayor was pumped up.

With little urging, Ron told Art, "That kind of thing is what makes this job great and fun. We will be at the starting line of a completely new industry in this state. I know there is not one commercial winery in this state right now. In ten to twenty years, New Mexico will be competing with Washington and Oregon in the wine business. Of course, catching California is another world away."

Ron left for the campaign office with a bounce in his step. Things were looking good for a change.

CHAPTER 20

C HARLES WAS ON THE PHONE when Ron arrived at the campaign office but concluded his conversation. Mike, working at a table, saw the mayor arrive and joined them.

"I had our favorite bond consultant on the phone, Mayor. He added five thousand dollars to our account," Charles said.

"Well, that'll help the cause," Ron responded. "I came by to discuss our final mail-out. The other night we laid out our plans—first, to contact every organization, company, and group who endorsed us and obtain their agreement for inclusion in our full-page newspaper ad and our letter to voters and, secondly, to draft the letter."

Mike said, "Mayor, I completed the draft and will give it to Charles today for his review. We should have the final draft for your approval by late today. I have three people calling all those who have endorsed us. The response has been positive. Most volunteered to share in the cost of the full-page ad. The newspaper illustrator designed the page layout."

"Good, everything sounds right." Ron said, "I have a prayer breakfast in the morning, and many of our big contributors will be there. By the way, I am using the Twenty-Third Psalm for the prayer. That's different from what I usually do."

Charles said, "Great selection. It says it all."

CHAPTER 21

STEVE CALLED SALLY ON HIS cell phone the next morning. "I'm on my way to class. What time is the brain trust meeting?"

"It will be about 3:30 p.m., depending on how long the news conference lasts."

"Right now it looks as if I can make the meeting but cannot attend the news conference," Steve said. "You will be busy anyway. I'll check with you about getting together later."

Sally said, "Fine, we will be able to plan something by then."

Steve then called Max. He reported on his afternoon at Gonzo's headquarters. Max said that his team had interviewed Gonzo and his three main people the previous morning but learned very little. Max expected background reports on them this morning. Steve suggested a cup of coffee after lunch, and Max agreed to meet at the police department. Max had decided Steve's participation in the investigation had some value.

After his first class, Steve talked with the students who had agreed to assist in the panty incident investigation about starting.

They agreed to start but protested again that they would not have much time to spend on the investigation. Steve said that he understood but would appreciate it if they could spend as much time as they could. Carlos took Brown, and Harold took Simpson. Each agreed to compare notes with Steve on Saturday.

After lunch, Steve and Max met at Max's office. Steve brought him up-to-date, including his session with Sally.

Max smiled. "It's a small world. I went out with Sally a few times back when she was reporting for TV. She's a pistol. We had some fun, but I didn't see much future for us, so we broke it off."

"Well, if she and I get something going, would that cause a problem with you?" Steve asked.

"Not at all. Sally and I are history," Max said.

"Is there anything interesting from the background checks?" Steve asked.

"Steve, I can't leak anything from those. They are confidential, as you must know," Max said. "However, I will share some general impressions. Amy was just a fun-loving girl. At the time of her death, she was working as a bartender at Bottoms Up. Not a dive, but not first-class either. Being a divorcee, Amy was known to date, probably some men she met at the bar, but did not have a serious relationship going currently, according to one of her friends. Amy had a few 'just among us girls' conversations but really did not open up with the other girls as some women are known to do. We're going back to the bar to do some more snooping. Are you ready? I owe you a beer."

"Sure, I know better than to say no to a cop, especially when he offers to buy me a beer."

"Well, I may be tight with money, but you will find that I am a magnet for women. You will never have it as good as you do when I am with you. I may have a run at the mayor's wife." Max followed.

Suddenly, Steve became very quiet and was no longer smiling. Max, realizing his mistake, immediately said, "I'm sorry, that was way out of line. I know that you're trying to make a move on her. Let's go get that beer. Hell, I'll even drive my car and use my gas."

At that, Steve smiled. "Dude, you must really be sorry."

"Let's go."

When they arrived at Bottoms Up, Max said, "Okay, just follow my lead."

A cute and scantily clad waitress seated them in a booth. Her nametag said Matilda, but Max said, "Hey there, Tillie. My friend is going to buy me a beer, and he'd like to buy you a drink if you can join us."

"Well, so much for paybacks," Steve said. "That's one of the shortest repentance times I ever witnessed."

Tillie brought the beers and her drink, saying it was vodka—but Max figured it was probably water—and joined them. Max introduced Steve as Dr. Steve Janson, and Tillie immediately gave Steve much of her attention.

They chatted a while, and then Max asked Tillie if she had thought about anymore guys Amy had been seeing. Steve and Max really came to attention when she said, "Well, I now remember there was an old creep who said he was a good friend of an upcoming mayor."

Casually, Max asked, "Can you describe him?"

Tilly could and did.

Steve exclaimed, "Bingo! That's a perfect fit for our senor Simon Martinez, who's on Gonzo's election committee."

Max said with some irritation at Steve's violation of interrogation procedure, "Whoa, let's not jump to conclusions here. I will set up a meeting with him for tomorrow to explore any relationship."

Steve said, "Are you going to do that right now?"

"Not after two beers. Tillie,bring us two more and one for yourself."

Steve said, "You are something else, Max. What a cheapskate. All right, Tillie, bring another round for you and Max and be sure to bring me the tab, right, Lieutenant?"

Steve and Max finished the beers and left. Max took Steve to get his car. On the way, they discussed the case.

"I think this pretty much tells us who set up the panty event," Steve said. "But it really doesn't tell us much about the murder. Such things are not necessarily related."

Max said, "You're right, Steve. We have a lot more work to do on that angle, but this does give us a connection between Simon and Amy. I appreciate your help so far. Without telling you more than I should, I can tell you we have found some noteworthy unsavory relatives in Simon's family. I would like to keep you in the loop. Anything that you discover about the incident, let me know, and I'll take it from there. By the way, we examined the mayor's gun, and it had not been fired recently. We fired it and checked ballistics. No match on anything. Tell the mayor we'll return the gun."

CHAPTER 22

THEY HAD ARRIVED AT STEVE'S car. Steve said that he would be in touch, and Max pulled out. Steve called Val on his cell with the good news. Val was elated and said that she'd inform Ron immediately. Then Steve called Sally to see if he could set a time to meet.

He was anxious to quiz her about Simon. His gut feeling told him that she knew more than she had told him previously. Besides, the combination of beer and the female companionship at the bar made him want more female companionship. He felt better since he had cleared things about Sally's relationship with Max but wondered if he could use that information to his advantage. He let his thoughts return to Val but then remembered what his grandmother used to say—"if you cannot have the thing you love, then love the thing you have." So here's to Sally!

Sally didn't answer her phone. Later he found out why when he and Sally got together before the brain trust meeting. It seemed that Andy Stricker had arrived for the press conference a few minutes early and asked Sally about the subject of the conference. Sally told him about the bus conversion, but Andy had asked her if Gonzo was aware the city transportation department had that study almost completed.

Sally had immediately called Carson and confirmed Andy's comments. When told, Gonzo instructed Sally to cancel the news conference and put out a news release that Gonzo had checked the city's findings on the conversion, agreed with them, and, when elected mayor, he would give priority to the project.

Meanwhile, Val had called Ron immediately with the information about Simon Martinez and Amy Johnson. She ecstatically stated that the connection proven between the two was adequate to conclude that Gonzo's campaign was behind the panty incident, even though the evidence was not conclusive that Martinez had set it up.

Ron told her that he would check with Charles and Mike on how to best use the info.

Ron called Charles, explained the findings, and requested he and Mike start kicking around ideas on how to proceed while he was driving over to the war room.

By the time Ron arrived, Charles and Mike had concluded that since there was no proof that Simon Martinez had set up the incident nor was there proof that Gonzo sanctioned it, the mayor should call Gonzo, report the discovery of the connection, and ask if he had approved the plan because they were considering going public with an accusation that his campaign was behind the incident.

Ron called Gonzo, who at the time was berating Johnny for almost embarrassing him with the bus conversion issue. Ron stated that he was considering a public statement on the panty incident and accused Gonzo of orchestrating it.

Gonzo denied approving the plan and also denied knowing of the Martinez-Johnson relationship. He said he would fire Martinez, if Martinez confirmed the information.

Ron said he would hold off a public statement on the matter now but might later clarify the incident with a news release.

"Okay, fellows, we will see how Gonzo handles this shot over the yardarm. I would prefer he handle his problem rather than us, since we don't have actual proof against Martinez. An accusation without proof could backfire. Steve had said he would keep on top of the matter. Some leaks on our findings to date wouldn't hurt. I leave that to you, Mike. Val and I have a political meeting tonight. I'll suggest she drop some comments about dirty political tricks there."

CHAPTER 23

BETWEEN LEAVING MAX AND LEAVING for the brain trust meeting, Steve reviewed materials for Friday's classes. Friday was a light day for him. He had two morning classes but was free afterward, if he delayed his library time. Tonight would be a good time to ask Sally out, if she were not tied up with Gonzo or his campaign. Drinks, dinner, and whatever would make for an enjoyable evening. He headed out to Gonzo's brain trust conference. It would be his first meeting with Martinez and Bustos.

Steve arrived a few minutes early. Looking through the office window, he could see Sally and Johnny Bustos with Gonzo. They seemed tense, the way they were gesturing and talking loudly. Steve figured something had gone wrong. *I'll find out shortly.*

The preconference broke up. Bustos left. Sally came out the door, went over to her desk, picked up a legal pad and pen, and said as she walked past Steve, "Let's get this over with."

Sally and Steve sat down with Gonzo, who said, "Steve, we are having a rotten day. First, I had to call off the press conference because the city staff already had the proposal almost completed on the bus conversion. Then I had a call from the mayor. He claimed that Simon set up his panty incident and accused me of being a part of the conspiracy."

"I denied that, of course. But when I discussed the matter with Simon, I didn't like his answers. We ended up arguing, and he is now no longer associated with the campaign."

"It hurts. I've lost a valuable supporter. We will charge on, but our meeting is being canceled. I'm going to the weekly poker game. Maybe my luck will change. At least I can down a few beers with my friends."

As they walked out, Steve said, "Sally, looks like Gonzo will not need you tonight, and I'm free also. Let me exercise my option—let's go out for drinks and dinner."

"Fine by me," Sally said. "What time?"

"I'll come by your apartment about seven, if that's okay."

"Looking forward to it. Steve, see you then."

CHAPTER 24

ARLIER THAT DAY, BEFORE TALKING with Sally and Steve and after Ron had called Gonzo, Gonzo had called Simon. He said that something urgent had come up, and they needed to meet immediately. He would be waiting for Simon in front of the headquarters.

Simon pulled up in his pickup and Gonzo jumped in. He said, "You can drive or park." Simon found a parking place. He turned off the motor, turned slightly, and asked, "What's up? Must be bad. You're upset."

Gonzo told Simon about the mayor's call. Cursing, Simon said, "That is bad. That bastard, I hate his guts. This puts me in a hole, a deep hole. What are you going to do?"

Gonzo said that the worst thing they could do is just sit on it. He mentioned he had told the mayor that he was unaware of the plot, let alone that one of his people was involved. The mayor seemed to accept his comment and said he would not be publicizing his findings right now. "I think we should announce you have left the campaign," Gonzo told Simon. "You need to make some statement to the effect that it has been too time consuming and you have neglected your construction business. I'll tell the press I regret your resignation, because you have been a great help, and we'll miss your sound advice.

"But just between you and me, our agreement still holds. When I'm elected, the public works job will be yours. For now, you can continue to raise money and work in the background. We can continue. There just won't be an official connection, so work on covering your tracks."

Simon was quiet for a moment and then said, "I probably can't do anything else to move us out of the mess. Screw it. Go ahead and have Sally prepare a press release for me and send it out."

Simon then took Gonzo back to headquarters, dropped him off, and drove away. Gonzo entered, told Sally what had happened, and asked her to prepare the statement for distribution the next morning.

Simon drove around for a while, trying to come up with some trick to get Brown out of the race but kept coming back to one thought. Brown won't get out unless he has some kind of accident and becomes incapacitated. Simon remembered well the mayor cutting him out of a big-paving contract with the city. The selection committee had been ready to award the contract to him, when the mayor presented information that Simon's company had overbilled the city on another contract, and claimed it was deliberate. One of Simon's former disgruntled employees had blown the whistle on him, and his company was disqualified until the matter was resolved. It was a two-million-dollar contract the bastard made him lose, and he wasn't going to forget it. Now the mayor knew his connection to Amy and the panty incident. He will never be awarded any work as long as Steadman was mayor.

CHAPTER 25

R ON AND VAL HAD MET at the house to prepare for the AAUW meeting, where Ron was the scheduled speaker. The American Association of University Women was a civic group of women college graduates. Most of the members are voters. Val is a former president of the group. She felt that unless Ron talked himself out of the votes, he should be in good shape with the group. Ron had informed her he would emphasize the point that the city truly is an equal-opportunity employer. Women were in supervisory positions, and they made the same pay as men who are in similar positions. He supported city intervention in lawsuits against employers who do not provide equal pay for women and men. This would include intervention in cases before the equal rights commission, as well as court cases.

Another good thing about AAUW is that they take care of business and hold short meetings. Val and he would be home before ten thirty with a pocketful of votes.

Ron and Val mingled with those in attendance. He made his speech and they left. Everything went as planned.

CHAPTER 26

S TEVE ARRIVED AT THE APARTMENT he shared with two other medical students. He showered and shaved while he thought about the successes of the day and then started thinking about his date tonight. His thoughts were interrupted when it occurred to him that since Simon knew he had entered the Gonzo organization, if he appeared with Max at Simon's interview, his cover would be blown. Tomorrow he'll call Max to drop off the interview team.

Harold, one of his two spies, caught up with Steve as he was leaving. He reported contacting Mr. Simpson and offering to help his campaign. Simpson stated his appreciation but said he was withdrawing from the race. The announcement had been released to the media.

Steve drove to Sally's apartment in his 1999 Toyota. He promised himself someday, not too far down the road, he would own a good car, like a BMW or Lexus. Even though he had money in the bank, he did not intend to use it before starting his practice.

He knocked on the door; Sally opened it, greeted him with a quick kiss on the cheek, and said, "Fix us drinks while I finish putting on my makeup. Vodka tonic for me." She disappeared into a bedroom.

Steve looked around the room, thinking Sally had a comfortable apartment. The hallway opened into the living room, a large room with functional leather chairs and a sofa. End tables and a glass coffee table bracketed the sofa. A north-facing skylight offered buffered light, and off-white walls enhanced the lighting. Prints of famous Renaissance paintings stood out on the walls. A large television faced the seating area.

A small dining/breakfast area joined one side of an open kitchen counter. The kitchen cabinets were maple. A coffee pot sat on the granite counter and a skillet was on the stove. Bottles of vodka, scotch, and bourbon, a pitcher of water, empty glasses, and cans of diet tonic water and Coke sat on the counter.

Steve prepared the drinks—vodka tonics for both—and yelled, "Your drink's ready. Do you want it in the bedroom?"

"Just set it on the coffee table. I'll be right out." In a few minutes, she came out in a grayish, light-blue suit that matched her eyes. A white ruffled blouse and stylish blue shoes completed the outfit.

Steve handed her the drink and said, "You look ravishing."

"Well, I am moving up in the world, going out with a future doctor, and want to look it. Tell me, can a doctor still tell a maître d' that he's a doctor and obtain special treatment for dinner reservations?"

Steve laughed, saying that he didn't know but was willing to try. "And that brings up the question, where do we eat? I'm ready for anything to please you, but it occurs to me by eating at one of the restaurants nearby, we can walk, and I can drink without worrying about a DUI. Are any of them worth trying?"

"Two or three are acceptable. Morries has a nice bar and restaurant atmosphere, and the food is pretty good. A reservation won't be necessary. We could go there."

"Easy enough. That's good for me."

They finished their drinks and walked toward Morries, about a block away in a strip shopping mall. Steve had his arm lightly around her waist while he told funny stories about people working in labs at the medical school.

They were escorted to a table in a relatively quiet area. The maître d' had greeted Sally by name, so did the waiter.

"This is one of my hangouts," Sally said.

After ordering drinks and receiving menus, Steve said, "Tell me about the blowup. I'm really curious about what happened."

"Oh, sure," Sally said, "I mentioned that Simon could be a loose cannon. He apparently sent a girlfriend over to the mayor's campaign office, where she handed the mayor her panties, a thong actually. The purpose obviously was to embarrass him. But his wife was there and embarrassed the girl, Amy Johnson. She's the one who was murdered. The mayor called Gonzo with the message that he had found out Simon was behind the failed trick and threatened to go public. Gonzo had to remove Simon from the campaign committee. Simon has been sacrificed."

"Had Gonzo agreed to the trick, or did Simon act without consulting him?"

"Although Simon has acted on his own some, it is possible Gonzo sanctioned this one. I shouldn't say he did, because I'm not privy to any discussions on the subject."

The two ordered dinner with wine and enjoyed each other's company. Sally had several funny stories about TV-recording foul-ups. She previously worked at Channel 12 TV, in the news room.

Steve paid the bill, and they went back to Sally's apartment, where Sally invited Steve in for a nightcap. Steve mixed the drinks, felt her presence, turned around, and saw Sally was standing close. She looked kissable. They had a long passionate kiss. As they separated, she said she was going to change into something more comfortable and went into the bedroom.

A few minutes later he heard the toilet flush, and she came back in a light-blue silk robe. He stood up; they embraced and kissed. She had nothing on under the robe and smelled wonderful. He suggested they go into the bedroom. They did, and somehow he lost his clothes before they went to bed. He noted the bed was queen size. Later, he commented, "If I spend the night, I definitely will not get a DUI."

She agreed. "A DUI would ruin a wonderful night."

CHAPTER 27

FRIDAY MORNING, RON AND VAL were up early because of Ron's prayer breakfast. Ron had a glass of orange juice and a cup of coffee and asked Val what she had planned for the day.

Val said, "Well, I have a ton of catch-up to do. Steve is off today playing detective, so I will have to divide the cells, feed them, yada, yada, yada."

"Good enough. I'm off to my breakfast," Ron said.

Val drove slowly to the lab, mentally making a list of all the things she had to do.

When she arrived, the first thing she saw was a huge pile of unopened mail and a pink telephone slip telling her to call the dean, ASAP.

Val decided the dean wouldn't be in this early, so she started on the mail.

The third letter she opened was the one she had both dreaded and had most wanted. She started reading and then started whooping and dancing around the lab, singing, "I can't believe it! Holy cow, I can't believe it! I gotta call Ron and Steve."

She called Ron; his voice message came up, so she left a message, saying, "Call me as soon as you can. It is good news." Then she pushed her cell phone button and called Steve. It was early but it was worth it.

Steve answered somewhat groggily, "This is Steve, I think."

"Steve, we did it! We did it," Val said, practically screaming in his ear. "They funded our grant, the whole thing, Steve, the whole bloody thing. For five years at our full funding request. Can you believe it? Can you frigging believe it?"

After a couple of silent moments, Steve let out a thunderous, "Eureka! Hold everything, and as soon as I get dressed, I will be there. Uh, I didn't exactly sleep at home last night, but I am just a short way from the lab."

Val could hear a feminine voice in the background, and Steve said, "Just a second, and I will tell you."

Val said, "Steve, I am really sorry I called like this, but I was so excited and didn't think you might not be home."

Steve just laughed and said, "I'm on my way." He explained to Sally that his boss had made a breakthrough at the lab, and needed him.

Val had finished the mail and was getting ready to call the dean when Steve burst through the door. He picked Val up and spun her around and around the room until they were both dizzy. When he stopped spinning, they realized they were locked together, and then Steve kissed her. It wasn't a quick peck. Val felt herself responding in a way she hadn't responded to a kiss in a long time. Steve finally pulled away and said, "I didn't mean to do that, but boy, am I glad I did." Then he gave Val another huge hug and said, "Now let's see what the monster man wants."

Val, a little out of breath, dialed the dean's number. His secretary said that the dean would see her as soon as she could get downstairs. Val told her Steve was with her, and the secretary told her to bring him along.

The dean stood as they walked into his office. In Val's world, with Ron and Steve as examples, most people were tall. Dean Lorensten wasn't much taller than Val. He had dark hair, a dark complexion, and moved somewhat jerkily. His dark mustache and neatly trimmed beard hid some of his mouth. He walked around his desk and shook hands with Val first and then with Steve, congratulating them on the grant funding.

He had them sit down and said, "I have some outstanding news for you both. The National Institute of Health has telephoned me to see if our lab complex can be expanded into a national laboratory for retesting stem cells for purity and safety after they have been tested in their own laboratories. I know at least one such facility has been operating in Germany, but the government feels we need our own American facility. The significance is that instead of you soliciting work from outside laboratories, we would be the designated federal laboratory validating work of other labs."

Steve and Val just looked at each other, and this was the only time since they had met that Steve was speechless. This meant money would be flowing into the lab for expansion and operations of the facility, higher salaries, and additional employees.

Continuing, the dean handed Val a list of laboratory requirements for a national laboratory. Glancing at these, she realized that many tasks had to be completed in lab improvements and expansion before operations could be optimized.

The dean turned to Steve and asked him what would be needed to persuade him to reverse his school program where he would obtain his PhD degree before his MD. By this time, Steve had recovered from his shock and suggested that having all his student loans paid off would be a good start. The dean was famous for his lack of humor, and he didn't find this amusing. However, Val did and had a hard time keeping a straight face.

"Well," said the dean, "your school costs can be placed in the new lab budget and you will receive a pay raise and the amenities of a full-time employee. Of course, you will want to continue your class work."

The discussion concluded with the dean setting up a meeting for early Monday morning with all of the necessary people. At that time, they would begin detailing the proposal. A short discussion resulted in the dean heading the Architecture Committee with Val and the chairman of the Cellular Biology Department as members. Val would chair the project committee, with two appointees to be made. Placing Steve on the committee required discussion with the dean, who expressed reservations.

"Well," said the dean, "you know how people are going to react to an intern on the committee. All of the PhDs in the department are going to argue they deserve it more than a medical student with a BS."

Val immediately responded that this was one point that could not be negotiated. She pointed out several people working there who only had BS degrees, and some were much more valuable than some of the faculty with higher degrees. She said that she was sure the Human Resources Department could come up with something to placate the PhDs. Steve had provided valuable assistance in writing the original grant application resulting in the grant. He should be included as a main contributor in any further reports and papers, especially since he had agreed to change his career path.

At that point, Val had a feeling the dean might excuse her from the position of project leader, but she couldn't back down. Everyone who has ever dealt with the politics born and bred in a university was aware they are much more cutthroat than anything you find in the real world, such as a mayoral election.

The dean, although somewhat startled by her outburst, said, "Very well, we will see you both on Monday. Please arrive with improvements, acquisitions, and a budget for us to consider."

As Val and Steve were walking back to their lab, Steve was absolutely in stitches. Val didn't see anything that funny until Steve said, "I really wanted to say, 'For God's sake, don't hand her your undies, because that really makes her come unglued.'"

The remark brought Val back down to earth, as Steve's comments often do, and upon arrival, each went to work drafting proposed lab improvements.

Val's phone rang just as she was organizing her thoughts. It was Ron. Val quickly brought him up-to-date and told him the university would publicize the grant award. She told him this was sure to cause some political grief. His challengers had little to attack and exploit so far for their political advantage.

After word came out that the rigged panty incident was a dirty political trick, an attack issue was needed. Val said that she was concerned the cell farm lab might be the hot-button social issue Ron's opponents had been looking for. The anti-stem-cell radicals certainly would come out in droves to fight the new lab. A likely approach might be an attempt to fight through the use of city and state politics, and through those paths, try to change the decision of the university in accepting the national laboratory designation.

Val told Ron that if he wanted, she could turn down the assignment of leading the proposal team. That ultimately could cause her to lose the lab director position, but it would remove her from being the lightning rod and prime target of stem-cell study opponents.

Ron said that there is a limit to what one does to win an election. "You will not turn down anything that promotes your career. We can fight the political battle and win anyway."

"Ron, I can see that, but let's meet at lunch and discuss this further."

"Who is it that said, 'There's no free lunch'? But I'll take a chance."

"I'll stop by the war room on the way home and spend a few minutes with Charles and Mike. We wouldn't want them surprised by the lab announcement if it leaks early. Expect me shortly after twelve."

Smiling, Val muttered to herself, "No question about it, this is my day."

Before leaving for the war room, Ron phoned to make sure that Charles and Mike were there. Upon his arrival, they met in Charles's office with the door closed. Ron yelled, "Hello, everyone!" He moved through the workers in the office. Most responded with their own greetings, but some just waved.

Ron quickly ran through the situation with Charles and Mike. They were sincerely pleased for Val's good fortune but agreed that, at the least, this was a blip on the radar. At the most, the issue could be a major distraction that could alienate some voters. These voters would be sure to vote for anyone that opposed the lab.

So one question remained—would any candidate oppose the lab? The issue could cause lost votes more than gained votes, assuming most people would be in favor of the lab. If no candidate comes out in opposition to the lab, voters opposing the lab may not even vote.

Mike suggested that Val meet with the medical school dean to define who would assume the role of public spokesman for the new lab. He suggested that the dean assume the role since this would require such a large effort by the medical school. Of course, the dean would brief the university president, who might also want a major role in support of the lab. The program would need someone with clout to back up the public affairs person as spokesman. Her suggestion should include development of a strong public relations program by the university under the dean's and president's leadership. Val should suggest that she remain a background figure and advisor. Ron said he would broach the idea with Val.

Ron started home. Val was making sandwiches in the kitchen when he arrived. He kissed her on the cheek while greeting her. This turned into a longer kiss. She obviously was on a high because of the good news, and the mood carried over into the lovemaking. Both were most energetic and had great sex.

Back in the kitchen, they sat around the table while Ron reported the conclusions of Charles and Mike regarding the public relations program for the university. Val listened and then said, "What they conclude makes a lot of sense." She said she still would have to be available when the dean requested. Ron agreed.

CHAPTER 28

O N FRIDAY MORNING, MAX, STUD, and Davis were reviewing the information collected to date on the Johnson murder. They agreed that the Johnson-Martinez connection offered the best lead. Max assigned Davis to further check into Simon's background. Max and Stud would take Simon's statement that morning. Steve had informed him he would not attend the meeting, which satisfied Max because he felt he had made a mistake in asking for Steve's attendance. He called Simon, who agreed to meet with them right away. The meeting would be at Simon's office in his construction company yard.

While driving over to the meeting, Max said, "Let's forget about good cop/bad cop in this interview, Stud, unless the interview leads us that way. Then you act the bad cop.

"We know this guy lied to you in your first interview by denying he knew Amy. We know they had some kind of relationship and it had gone on for months. That is reason enough for you to question any statements he makes today. What do you think?"

"I think I would like to make him for the everything, including the murder, that's what I think," Stud said. "He not only lied, but he also managed to be rude. I even picked up some racial vibes from him as indicated by his tone and body mannerisms."

"Well, in that case, start out as bad cop if you want. We don't put up with that shit. We know that our objective is to get him to tell the truth about the relationship and see if we can make a killing. We could use his attitude problem to build toward self-incriminating comments. We know he inherited a small construction company and built it up. He thinks that makes him hot stuff. As the chief is always saying, we go with the flow."

As they drove up to the Martinez Construction Company site, they noted a large yard, completely fenced. The large entrance gate held the company sign. Max exited the car to open the gate. The large yard, about four or five acres, had all kinds of construction equipment and debris scattered around. Some of the equipment appeared to have been abandoned, but most were in good shape. Stacks of pipes, wood, and discarded items, such as old air air-conditioners, stood sentry. Knee-high native weeds and crabgrass stood out around dry, sandy areas.

The office was a dirty-white modified mobile home structure. The sign on the building stated Martinez Construction Company Office. They drove to the front of the building.

Stud said as they exited the car, "My detective instincts tell me we are in the right place. This sign validates the fence sign."

"Detective instincts are good. Glad you brought them," Max said.

"Where is the junkyard dog? Everybody has one," Stud followed up just as they heard a growl. They both jumped back in the car and slammed the doors. A huge dog ran around the car, growling, with fangs showing.

Stud said, "Damn, I hate dogs. When I was a teen breaking into places like this, they always were a problem. I was severely bit one time."

"Why would you break into construction yards? Nothing but junk here."

"Copper, aluminum, other metals could get us enough cash for a Big Mac."

"I am sure you are aware this confession is no good. The statute of limitations obviously has expired," Max said. "You are free to go, young man. Find us someone else to arrest."

"First, let's take care of the damn dog. You want me to shoot him?" Stud asked.

"No, but it obviously would be self-defense. I'll blow the horn. Someone will come out."

The horn brought Simon to the door. He yelled at the dog, took him by the collar, and chained him to the side of the building.

Simon apologized, saying that he thought the dog was chained. They only let him loose at night after closing.

Stud did not verbalize his belief that the dog was loose on purpose, but he filed the thought. Another mark against Mr. Martinez.

As they entered the office, Max looked around and noticed a beat-up desk with papers covering the top, a decent chair for the owner, and two hard-backed chairs in front of the desk.

A Playboy calendar hung on the far paneled wall. A fluorescent ceiling light provided the necessary light and a soiled tan carpet muffled their footsteps. A small dirty table next to a sidewall held a partially full coffee pot and unused plastic cups. Gray metal file cabinets sat off to the side.

Simon offered coffee, but the two policemen declined. Stud tried to set the tone of the meeting by saying, "Mr. Martinez, we have a problem. You caused it. The problem is we have conflicting information about whether or not you knew Amy Johnson. You responded to a direct question by denying you knew Amy. We have two witnesses who say you had a relationship with Amy, for at least the last two or three months she was alive. One person said Amy personally informed her it was a close relationship."

Simon hesitated a few moments and then said, "I made a mistake. I should have mentioned that relationship to you, but I had what I thought was a good reason for keeping it quiet. I have been active in the mayor's race on behalf of Gonsolic, as one of his two top assistants. Since the girl was murdered, the relationship could have been embarrassing to Gonzo and harmful to the campaign due to the panty incident.

"Even so, there was a murder, and I should have mentioned the relationship. The irony is it was all for naught. Mayor Steadman discovered the relationship and accused Gonsolic of masterminding the incident. Now I have been kicked off his committee."

Stud said, "Tell us about the relationship. How close was it? How long had it been going on?"

"I was in the bar, oh, less than three months ago. Hardly anyone else was in there. I remember two guys playing liar's dice at a corner table. Amy and I got to bantering with each other and enjoyed the give-and-take. Although I am married, I asked her about getting together, and we did. We tried to keep it quiet because I told her about being married and not jeopardizing my marriage. We had an intimate relationship, but I did not attempt to stop her from seeing other men, and I believe she was."

"Do you have a name or two?"

"No," Simon said. "Being married, I thought it prudent not to be nosy."

"When did you last see her?"

"Let's see, I think it was before she went to the mayor's headquarters. We were in her apartment. That's right. She said she was going to play a trick on the mayor. I asked what trick. She laughed and said I should read the newspaper. It should help Gonzo's campaign by embarrassing the mayor."

"So you are saying she did this on her own," Stud queried.

"That's right."

"Why were you at the apartment?"

"We had finished sex, and I was telling her of Gonzo's election problems."

"Did you kill her?"

Startled, Simon looked at Stud and said, "No, certainly not. We had a great relationship."

"Do you have any idea or names of persons who may have killed her?"

"Unfortunately, no."

"Do you have the full name of her ex-husband? Did she ever discuss him?"

"She never mentioned anything about an ex-husband or other men. I know I have to be a suspect. I hope you find the person who did it."

"Thank you, Mr. Martinez. Next time tell us the truth first," Max said. "We usually get there anyway, and it saves time. If you think of anything that might help us on this, please call us. We likely will have more questions for you as we progress with our investigation."

Stud said, "If we come back we want that dog chained. I would hate to shoot your guard dog."

"I apologize again. He'll be chained," Martinez responded.

The cops drove off while Martinez stood by the office door, thinking it went all right. They seemed to buy it. He would call Gonzo to tell him he presented the incident as Amy acting out her own idea.

"Stud, what do your detective instincts tell you about all that?" Max asked as they drove away.

"My detective instincts, vibes, and commonsense experience all scream out the bastard's still lying."

Max said, "We have enough to keep us working. A wiretap likely would give us the info needed to solve this case, but there's not enough evidence to get court approval. We have to keep digging until we get enough to lasso him. There was or wasn't a connection between the panty incident and her murder. A connection reduces our investigative work by about 50 percent and presents a known suspect."

Max pulled into a parking space at the police department. "Let's give the chief a status report. He wants to be kept up-to-date more so than usual on this case. Remember, he likes the facts summarized and then starts the speculation."

The chief was in a conference about some traffic division matters. His secretary said she would buzz them when the meeting broke up, so they proceeded to their desks in the detective division.

Stud started writing the report on the Martinez interview and had barely sat down when the chief's secretary informed them that the chief was available.

They trudged back upstairs. As they walked in the office and sat down, the chief said, "Make my day. Give me the good news, guys—you've solved the case, and the perp is not the mayor's wife."

Max crinkled his forehead. This was not starting as expected.

"You nailed it, Chief. Only one problem—we don't have enough evidence our perp did it, just our detective instincts."

"Never had a district attorney take a case to court on detective instinct," the chief said. "In fact, she's most happy when she has a confession. Keep that in mind."

"Our suspect is Simon Martinez, owner of a construction company and, until today, a chief assistant to Gonsolic. Frankly, Chief, this is going to be a tough one if turning over rocks or receiving a tip from someone doesn't give us something. We should have a lab report waiting. Hopefully there'll be something good in it," Max said.

"Keep pushing it. This Martinez guy may make a mistake under pressure. Keep the heat on, and maybe you'll get a break or just get lucky. Keep me informed," Pirwarsky said as he picked up some telephone slips and turned to his landline phone, effectively ending the session.

On the way back to their desks, Stud said, "We need to find that murder weapon."

The chief called Ron to give him a status report on the case.

CHAPTER 29

CHARLES LEFT THE WAR ROOM to meet Julie at his apartment. She arrived there shortly after him. They made passionate love. While resting on the bed, Julie said that she had made some personal decisions. One was she was not comfortable having an affair while married, so she was planning to file for divorce. Second, while proceeding with the divorce, she and Charles should place a hold on their relationship. She had no other lovers.

Third, she hired a private detective this morning to catch John in his affair. When she had the proof, she would file. After the divorce, she would be free from any guilt feelings, and if Charles and she were still interested, they could resume where they left off, with certain understandings.

Surprised, Charles stammered that he understood but hated her solution because they would be the ones penalized for John's affair.

Julie replied, "Yes, you may be correct, but I have to live with myself." She arose from the bed and started dressing.

Charles watched, trying to think of some appropriate remark but couldn't say anything, except, "I admire your resolution to your problem, but have a hard time accepting it because . . . I think I love you."

She leaned down, kissed him, and said, "Thank you, Charles, for everything. This may not be the end." She left.

Charles started back to the war room in a daze. What started out as a great afternoon had been flushed down the drain. At first, he mulled over the separation scene, but finally he started relating Julie's action to the overall picture of the election.

She and John had promised to hold an event for Ron, and it appeared they had only a few days to arrange the event. He would call Julie when he arrived at the office to find out when the reception could be held. It should be held at the hospital on a workday, probably from 5:00 p.m. to 6:30 p.m. in the hospital training room. He'd try for next Tuesday. Wednesday was bad because many doctors take the afternoon off.

At the office, he called Julie and suggested Tuesday for the reception. He suggested Julie hold off separating from John until after the reception. She sounded a little put off by the comment but agreed to the suggestion and would reserve the room. Charles then asked her to provide a list of all the doctors and office staff to be invited and told her that the campaign office would prepare invitations for mailing.

He also suggested that she allow Mike to handle the event. He then brought Mike up-to-date and gave him her telephone number, saying he was not sure Julie would continue working at the office.

CHAPTER 30

MAX CALLED A PLANNING MEETING to review all the case information accumulated to date and make assignments. A lab technician had brought the lab report over, but little had been found at the crime scene except for random fingerprints. The estimated time of death was between 3:00 p.m. and 6:00 p.m. Max asked Stud if his notes reflected where Simon was during that time. Stud said that Simon stated he was at his office until five and then headed home. He stopped by the grocers as requested by his wife and arrived home about six. Max then asked Stud to call Martinez to come in for fingerprinting and DNA testing. He pointed out that Simon's reported activities allowed time for the murder. With cell phones, calls now could be received anywhere. Evidence against Martinez kept building, but they were nowhere near having the case; it was all circumstantial with some speculation.

Max told them that he had, a few minutes before, received a call from Steve Janson, during which he accused Simon Martinez of arranging the panty incident. The possibility exists that Gonzo knew of the plan. This was contrary to the statement Simon had made that morning when he stated Amy Johnson acted on her own.

The team agreed that Simon's lies made him their prime suspect. Why else would he be lying? The problem basically was the difficulty of obtaining hard evidence short of obtaining a confession.

One decision was that Stud would keep placing follow-up calls to Simon. Also, Stud would talk again with Simon when he came in for fingerprinting.

Occasionally, Davis or Stud would follow him when he was driving.

Max would invite Steve back to Bottoms Up Bar for further discussion. Max had decided Steve could be an asset in the investigation and planned on him being fully involved. Not only could he use his investigative skills, but using Steve would also show the mayor that he would not embarrass the mayor or Val.

Max had the background checks he requested. He began reading out loud. "*Wilber Gonsolic*—social security number, home address, parking tickets, misdemeanors, but nothing substantial. *Simon Martinez*—home address, social security number, suspected in criminal suit involving extortion, money laundering, and bribery. Charges dismissed."

"*Toxicology report*—the victim. Her BAC was approximately .0246 percent and found traces of $C_{17}H_{21}NO_4$, or benzoylmethylecgonine (INN). It is a crystalline tropane alkaloid that is obtained from the leaves of the cocoa plant. The victim was definitely using cocaine."

"We need to find her supplier, guys," Max interjected.

"*Pathologist report*—found abrasions on right cheek and light blood clotting. Root cause—blunt force trauma. Bruises around throat and both wrists. Entry wound consistent with that of a nine-by-nineteen bullet. Confirmation of 9 mm. Photograph is enclosed."

Max said, "Ballistics and photographs of the 9 mm bullet removed from the victim's chest have been sent to the Santa Fe Department of Public Safety Forensic Laboratory, Forensic Firearms/Toolmark Unit. The Integrated Ballistics Identification System (IBIS) is a computerized database system whereby digital images of markings on bullets and cartridge cases recovered in criminal investigations and those test fired from recovered weapons are compared with ones from other states in our region."

CHAPTER 31

FRIDAY AFTERNOON, RON WENT TO the war room to make contributor calls. Mike thought another $10,000 should be spent on newspaper ads.

Julie called Charles, informing him that the hospital training room had been reserved for a Tuesday meet-and-greet with the mayor and hospital staff from 5:00 p.m. to 6:30 p.m.

Val headed for the medical school where she intended to discuss publicity control of her stem-cell research with the dean.

In a jovial mood, he greeted Val warmly. Val returned the warm greeting and then asked the dean to please help her in solving a problem. She explained that her husband's race for mayor was going extremely well, but one thing could possibly cause some grief. Her involvement in the stem-cell project could cause a fallout in Ron's election. Val reminded the dean that just a few days ago the environmental group Greenpeace had filed a lawsuit that had resulted in the European Union decision that scientists cannot patent stem-cell techniques that use human embryos for research. She felt this just emphasized that many groups were out there looking for excuses to stop the research.

Val said Ron would drop out of the race before he would let her give up the project, so they had discussed the possibility of the dean and the president making all official press releases and public statements. She requested that the dean be in control of all public announcements and releases as head of the project. She felt the NIH committee would approve the decision. The dean quickly agreed. Indeed, he was pleased with the thought of all the press coverage and national exposure he would accrue. His work would result in the addition of his name to research papers as an author.

Val then obtained approval for her and Steve to fly to Washington on Tuesday, where they would meet with the NIH committee on Wednesday, make a presentation to clear up remaining operational questions and details, and then return on Thursday. The dean approved the trip. Val thanked the dean for his excellent advice and help. She was glad Steve wasn't there to make one of his caustic comments, like, "Just who is doing whom a favor here?"

Val returned to the lab, called Ron to tell him the results of the meeting, and suggested that maybe they could meet for one of their noon lunches. Ron said he would clear his calendar and meet her.

Val and Steve went to work on their presentation for the committee. It seemed to move quickly. There was no doubt that they make a good team and really work extremely well together. In no time at all, it was noon.

Val said, "You can keep working if you want to, but I have a lunch date. I will see you back here about two o'clock."

Ron's car was in the driveway, so he was home. She entered the house cautiously. When Ron didn't pop out from the closet, she proceeded to the bedroom, and there was Ron snugly waiting for her under the covers. She quickly undressed and pulled the covers down and gasped. Ron was dressed in the Superman costume he had worn last Halloween.

"Hi there, I'm Lois," Val said. "Ah, the man of steel—"

"Join me and hopefully we can go up, up, and away," Ron said.

And that's just what happened.

Later, they adjourned to the kitchen and discussed the stem-cell solution approved by the dean. Ron said, "In retrospect, I feel there will be little political fallout. Any extremist group here in Centerville would be small, but I'll go over the matter with Charles and the election staff so they are prepared."

Val said, "I hope you are right, but some people already have seen some signs saying Baby Killers, Life Destroyers, and other things."

The candidate who was running closest to Ron, Will Brown, had already come out as a firm supporter of the new president's decision to back fetal stem-cell research.

Since Simpson had withdrawn from the election race, there was only Gonzo left to worry about. They both agreed that he would probably try almost anything for votes but that they had covered almost all the loopholes.

Val, placing dirty dishes in the dishwasher, said, "I'd better get back before Steve finishes the whole thing without me. He's certainly proving to be an outstanding scientist, as well as a real asset in public relations."

Ron said, 'Well, I have always said your taste in men is impeccable, and here I am to prove it. But let me point out that you caution me about the danger of sexual infidelity in political life constantly. You should have the same concern. A good example is Steve. From my viewpoint, it appears he would like to replace me in your life. I know you have the greatest respect for his intelligence and personality, but he might present the same danger to you and me as any bimbo might to you and me. I like Steve and know what a great job he does for you, but he looks at you in a way that bothers me. He's probably in love with you. It certainly is more than respect. Just as you rely on me keeping our vows, I also rely on you."

"I don't think you should compare Steve to a bimbo," Val said.

"Didn't mean it that way, but is this a sensitive subject for you? Maybe I should start worrying," Ron said.

"No, you shouldn't worry, even though I know how Steve feels. It is sensitive in that I work with him daily and sort of enjoy his personal remarks, but I haven't reciprocated. We all like to be admired."

Ron said, "Life is tough, isn't it? We both are worried that the other will be liked too much. If we control our emotions then we don't have to worry."

With that comment, they went back to work—Val to the lab and Ron to city hall.

CHAPTER 32

As Ron walked by Lupe, she said, "Sam has a report for you and Art on the wine growers."

"If Art is available, have him come in, and tell Sam to come up."

As Ron was signing various papers presented to him with explanations of what they contained, Sam arrived. Ron told him to have a seat.

Sam reported that contract negotiations with the wine growers had moved rapidly. Laurent requested Sam to fly to France for a meeting of the growers. The landowners and growers were ready to sign purchase agreements, but before signing, the growers wanted a city official to personally appear before them to provide assurance that the city would provide the water for the project. The growers couldn't come here because it was harvest time.

Sam stated he could go and had money in his budget but was concerned about the political ramifications of a city official flying to Paris. Newspapers always jumped on such activity as a waste of city money. In addition, those articles reflected the feelings of many voters. With the election less than a month away, the trip could become an issue. Sam said that he did not want to cause any election problems, that such things are unhealthy for long-term employment.

Ron smiled and said, "Sam, as long as you continue analyzing decisions in this manner, your long-term employment looks sound to me."

Art said, "Mayor, we have good relations with the state. Why don't we have Sam visit with the director of economic development to see if they will fund the trip's cost? Maybe it is time to bring the state into the picture anyway. The land is in another county, and we anticipate that wine growing will have a large effect on the state's economy in the near future."

Sam said he thought this an excellent idea. He knew Bill Ransome, the economic department director, well. He thought Bill would approve financing the trip. Making the trip a joint decision of the state and city removed it from election politics.

"I like it," the mayor said. "It also saves our money. Go see the director, Sam. Tell him we need his help. We anticipate wine-grape growing becoming a multimillion-dollar business in the state."

Sam said he would try to see Bill before the end of the workday and would report to Art.

Right before city hall closed for the weekend, Sam notified Art by phone about Ransome's approval financing the trip. He would fly to Paris on Monday for the wine grower's contract meeting. His understanding was that the meeting would be held on a wine farm in the Champagne region of eastern France on Tuesday.

CHAPTER 33

O N FRIDAY AFTERNOON, STUD CONTACTED Martinez, asking him to come down to the police department for fingerprinting. He explained that five sets of fingerprints had been found in Amy's apartment. One set, of course, was Amy's. They wanted to see if any of the others were his. Simon expressed his reluctance to come to the police department. Stud finally convinced him it was better to fingerprint at the department, saying, "We do not intend to arrest you. Don't you want to help find Amy's murderer?" This convinced Simon to come down to the station.

When Simon showed up, he obviously had nipped a few beers but was coherent and in control of himself, but there was no question that the request had irritated him.

Simon's comments ranged from "I'm being harassed" to "Why don't you look for the killer?" After he left the police department, where he'd almost panicked, Simon entered his car and tried to settle down and think. What did he have to worry about? They had no evidence against him. If they did, they would arrest him. He just had to keep going as he was. But everything was lost if Gonzo did not win. How could people support that homo Brown over Gonzo? Simon wanted him out of the race. He called his wife, told her he'd be home late, and started making the rounds. See what pops. Might find a new girlfriend.

Max called Steve to invite him for a beer at Bottoms Up. Steve said, "My boss just piled a ton of work on me. We were notified today we're receiving federal funding for expanding our lab. But it's time for a break. After all, it is Friday. Since I'm anticipating a big raise, let me buy the beer. Need I ask if that's okay with you?"

Max got the message but didn't respond.

Steve and Max met at the bar, but the waitresses were too busy with the large Friday crowd to spend any meaningful time with them. They rode each other hard, Max really laying it on Steve when he found out Steve had spent the night with Sally. Steve said that he and Sally were going to the zoo Saturday afternoon, and Steve hoped the day would last all night. After beers, Steve stopped by the lab on the way home, and Max went straight home.

CHAPTER 34

AFTER A QUIET DAY TAKING care of household and personal affairs, Val and Ron joined their attorney, Charley Barnes, and his wife, Sissy, for dinner at one of their favorite steak houses. Although they had been seated at a corner table out of restaurant traffic, some people stopped by to say hello or visit shortly with the mayor. Ron made it a point to stand up, shake hands, and introduce Val, Sissy, and Charley. This interrupted their conversations somewhat, but after their food was served, people left them in peace.

Charley asked Val how her police interview went and then asked how the investigation was proceeding. Ron said the police had a suspect they were investigating but apparently had not developed hard evidence. He said he didn't have a name.

Ron told Charley that the Gonzo campaign had organized the panty incident and related his phone conversation with Gonzo. Charley wondered why Ron had not told the news media. Ron said he had, but the incident did not get the news media play he anticipated, probably because the murder had become the news. Sometimes it is better to let a matter lay dormant.

Val was able to change the subject to Charley's funny courtroom experiences, like the time the opposing counsel informed the witness that it was necessary all his responses be oral. When asked, "What is your name?" Response, "Oral." "Where did you go to school?" Response, "Oral."

Then there was the time a policeman was testifying. The question was, "Officer, what led you to believe the defendant was under the influence?" Answer. "Because he was argumentary and couldn't pronunciation his words."

Then there was a woman testifying, who was asked, "Did you spend the night with Mr. Jones in Denver?" She answered, "I refuse to answer that question." "Did you spend the night with Mr. Jones in Santa Fe?" She answered, "I refuse to answer that question." "Did you spend the night with Mr. Jones in Phoenix?" She answered, "No."

The Steadmans and Barnes always enjoyed their nights out.

CHAPTER 35

AL AND RON WERE UP early Sunday and discussed the afternoon university reception. They mentioned names to each other of people who would be there. This helped them refresh their memories of names and faces. Neither had the ability to remember people forever, like some politicians can. Ron was aware "Happy" Chandler, a Kentucky governor of past years, knew twenty-five thousand people by name. Ditto for Bruce King, a recent governor of New Mexico.

Since Ron could not do this, Val and he agreed that Val would concentrate on remembering women's names and Ron, the men's names.

The reception was held at the student center in one of the large meeting rooms. All kinds of university people showed up—the university president, several vice presidents, deans, professors, and some students.

Ron and the university president McKinzie held a discussion about operations where the university and the city had overlapping problems, such as traffic control, parking, road improvements, etc. They agreed that each would assign staff to jointly work on such problems.

Val and Dean Lorensten continued their discussion of the new grants and lab expansion. As planned, President McKinzie and Dean Lorensten took the opportunity to announce the funding for stem-cell research. As soon as word spread about Val's assignment as director of the new lab, she became the focus of attention of many of the faculty, especially those of the medical school. In fact, the purpose of the reception was almost lost until Ron made a campaign speech that included lighthearted remarks about being the husband of such an outstanding university scientist. Remarks such as his marrying an intelligent person like Val showed his sound judgment in selecting people and his ability to work with them for a better city and university. Ron and Val graded the event with five stars. Hopefully the people who were there would get out and vote. Charles had a register all attendees had signed, and they all would be contacted for the get-out-the-vote drive.

CHAPTER 36

O N Sunday afternoon, Simon was driving around the city alone, giving serious thought to what he considered the Brown problem. He had worked toward a final solution and was considering how to accomplish it. He had already discarded several methods to dispose of Brown because they could be tied back to him. He had to be clear at the time of death because he already was the prime suspect in Amy's death.

The police would come at him hard if Brown were murdered. Simon finally decided it had to be a hate crime, based on Brown's homosexuality. He telephoned his brother, Tomas, in El Paso. After checking on the health of family members, Simon said, "I have a problem up here that needs a specialist. I think a specialist from out of town is more likely to be successful in solving the problem. Do you have someone you can recommend? I need a competent professional, who can come here, take care of the problem, and leave."

Tomas said, "Yes, a couple of people come to mind. Let me do some checking and get back to you. When will you need him and how much is the job worth?"

"I plan on paying the going rate, plus travel and incidental expenses, and I need this done as soon as possible. It would be good if the person could come here tomorrow. We could meet, discuss the details, see if we get into agreement, and plan the job."

"Okie dokie, I'll call back with a name and phone number. You take it from there, and we will forget about this conversation. It never occurred."

Later, Tomas called with an El Paso phone number and instructions to ask for Roberto.

A small town called Stanton is located about thirty miles south of Centerville. By phone, Simon arranged to meet Roberto at the main street coffee shop on Monday morning about eleven. Not knowing each other, they arranged for Roberto to wear a blue Windbreaker and Simon a red one.

CHAPTER 37

T HE PREVIOUS DAY, SIMON HAD noticed a car following his car around town. So when he headed for Stanton, he carefully took some detours until he was sure he was alone. When he entered the coffee shop in Stanton, a man in a blue Windbreaker was sitting at a table with a cup of coffee. Roberto appeared to be about five feet eight inches tall and stocky. His face matched his body—sort of round, with fleshy cheeks and heavy black eyebrows. His brown eyes were puffy, as if he had not slept well or had drunk too much. Heavy black wavy hair covered the top of his head and appeared to lower his forehead. In addition to the blue Windbreaker, he wore blue jeans and cowboy boots. Roberto's facial structure and coloring made Simon think he had some Indian blood.

As he sat down, Simon asked, "Are you Roberto Olivas?"

Roberto said, "I am. You are Simon Martinez? You have some landscaping for me?"

Even though no one was close by, both talked low and soft. Simon told Roberto who the target was, his home address, what he looked like, and then mentioned that he had a companion with him often. Both may need to be taken out. Roberto said that was no problem, but the price doubles to $14,000. They agreed on seven thousand up front, with half the money to be wired today to Tomas and the rest to be wired no later than the day after the job. Tomas would hold the money for Roberto. This arrangement gave Simon a reason why a large bank account withdrawal happened at this particular time. He could claim he had loaned the money to his brother.

Simon explained the hit had to look like a hate crime, with a note saying something like, "Gays should not run for mayor."

Roberto said he would scout out potential sites and would make the hit Tuesday night. He suggested Simon have an alibi from 7:00 p.m. until late that night. Simon gave Roberto a partial Brown itinerary for Monday and Tuesday that he had been able to obtain from Brown's political office.

Roberto said that he would leave immediately after the hit for El Paso. He would make sure the gun was destroyed. Simon told Olivas to phone him after the hit, so he would know it had been successful. When Simon answered, Olivas should say, "Sorry, wrong number" and hang up, if successful, and "Bill here," if something went wrong. They left the coffee shop and separately drove to Centerville.

While driving back to town, Simon reminded himself that the plan was set, and there was no turning back now. His future was in Roberto's hands, and also a substantial chunk of his money. When Simon arrived in town, he stopped by the bank and Western Union, wired the $7,000 to Tomas, and called him about the arrangement.

CHAPTER 38

R ON AND VAL WERE STILL emotionally high from the university reception when they were having breakfast Monday morning. While Val cooked an egg omelet, Ron brought in the morning paper. Over cups of coffee, orange juice, omelet, and toast, they carefully read the headline story.

In large, bold print, the front-page headline announced, "university medical school selected for nat'l stem cell certification laboratory."

The initial paragraphs stated,

At a large university reception in the student center yesterday, President McKenzie and medical school dean Dr. Rafer Lorensten announced that the university has been selected by the National Institute of Health and the Federal Drug Administration as the site for a national laboratory whose purpose is to certify stem cells for purity and health.

A medical committee, headed by the dean, would oversee the planning for lab construction and lab operations.

The dean stated that this would be the only laboratory in the nation where stem cells could be certified for use in experiments in other laboratories around the country.

"Certification labs primarily are located in Europe currently," he said. "After President Obama announced the federal government will support stem-cell research, such a lab is necessary to assure stem-cell quality control."

He noted that Dr. Valarie Steadman was instrumental in obtaining the grant and would be laboratory director.

The article went on to review the history of stem-cell research and the advantages of such research in finding cures for several diseases.

After finishing the article, Ron said, "Well, at least you are buried in the details of the article, and perhaps for the first time, you are not identified as the wife of the mayor. Your reputation has come from your own efforts, and you will be known for such. I think you are to be congratulated." He gave her a kiss.

After breakfast, Val left for the lab and found that she was there before Steve. She set out the scientific articles she had reviewed previously, reread them, and highlighted the pertinent sections.

Steve came in at around ten, and Val started with "A diller, a dollar," but quickly stopped as Steve gave her a look to kill.

"Bad night, huh?"

Steve grimaced and said, "Actually, too much of a very good night." And with that remark, he started in on the papers. It wasn't a very pleasant task because the papers were reports of stem cells gone maverick and its terrible effects. Val and Steve discussed several of the experiments, starting with some early studies with mice that had been helped or cured with the stem-cell injections only to develop tumors in one to five sites away from the targeted area. Finally, they read articles performed on humans and were particularly upset by one of a ten-year-old boy, apparently cured of his initial problem, but who five years later developed five tumors in other parts of his body away from the injection site.

Val said, "We will redo our presentation to include a website where all investigators must report all of their results and the time frame involved. This would be a secure site but would give the programmer the opportunity to compile statistics of the cell line involved, the age of the cells when injected, how many injections the patient received, and hopefully material from the laboratory. This would allow the new national lab an opportunity to study the cells for any changes that had taken place. These studies might pinpoint the culprit causing these cells to keep proliferating instead of shutting down.

"If the trigger could be found, it could be isolated, purified, and identified. It might then be possible to prevent such cells from being used for human experiments or to modify them in a way their proliferation is stopped," she said.

Finally, they were satisfied they had covered this subject thoroughly, and after agreeing to meet at the airport on Tuesday, they compiled their papers and divided them into stacks for each to review. Val took hers home. She had laid out her Louis Vuitton bag for the trip and remembered Steve's smart comment about taking his Sunday best backpack. Val had promised him that if all continued to go well, she would see to it that before the next trip he would have a briefcase by Coach.

CHAPTER 39

MAX ENTERED POLICE HEADQUARTERS AND headed directly for his desk in the detective division, only stopping to pour a cup of coffee, noting that it appeared fresh for a change. Someone was to be thanked. Stud and Davis were at their desks, also with coffee.

In keeping with his rank, Max's desk was located in a small office. Stud's and Davis's desks were outside his office, pushed up against each other. Other detective desks and several filing cabinets filled the large room. All desks and filing cabinets were gray metal, probably military surplus, but who knew since they had been there much longer than the detectives had. The room, with a worn tile floor and pale-green-painted walls, defied description except for two words—bland and sickly. A whiteboard hung on one wall, noting the statuses of active cases. Posters of wanted criminals were tacked on another wall. Computers sat on the desks, reasonably new. They had been purchased with federal grant money.

Max looked at the piles of papers and folders on his desk. He picked up one pile, carried it out to Davis, dropped it on the desk, and said, "I'm tired of looking at this pile of shit. It's been on my desk for at least two weeks. See if you can do something with it."

Looking over at Stud, Davis said, "Stud, I believe we have a bull by the tail today. Max appears ready to go. Now is he going to lead us to glory or down to the pits of hell?"

"Do you mean a tiger by the tail or a bull by the horns?"

Davis said, "I mean what I said. Cops are bulls, not tigers, and we certainly don't have Max by the horns."

"You have a point. You also raised the prime question. I'm going to write it on the whiteboard so we can be reminded of it and reflect on it all day. Personally, I would like to head down the glory road."

"All right, guys," Max said, "I got the message. But I am frustrated. We lack evidence on the Johnson murder, and I don't know where we are going to find some. We know who did it. I need ideas from the superlative detective team on where I am to lead you."

Stud said, "Spoken like a true leader. Just tell me where to go, and I will lead you. Davis, you started this. How do we find the glory road?"

"Shit, Stud, just like always. We pound the pavement, dig in the garden, and mow the grass. I think you know what I mean."

Max said, "I have the privilege of presenting some breaking news to you. The chief is swearing in the mayor as a policeman, and he is joining our Johnson team. We don't know who will be in charge, and no decision on the communications network was decided. I don't want any questions, just accept it and see what develops."

"Wow—no, double wow!" Davis exclaimed.

"Well stated, my feelings also. All right, let's go over what we have, see where we stand, and then decide what we do today."

"We could rework everything," Stud said, "redo all the interviews, but we have our man, and we know it. Let's review everything on him. Then do you think we will be ready to Miranda him and formally grill him?"

"I'm not sure about that," Davis said.

"Stud, you have the file on Martinez and the complete Amy Johnson file. Let's go to work," Max directed.

Stud began to read, "The body was found at 10:14 p.m. in the alley behind the Steadman campaign headquarters, located at 2007 Locust Street. The coroner placed time of death between

4:00 p.m. and 6:00 p.m. The site of the murder has not been determined, but most evidence indicates the murder occurred somewhere else, probably her residence, but not confirmed. Size of the entrance wound suggests a 9 mm or .38 caliber."

Max questioned, "Has the coroner said anything about estimating the size of the hands causing the bruises? I haven't seen anything on that in his report. Make a note to check on that, Stud."

"I think she had to be standing up, facing her murderer, when it started. The coroner agrees. It would be difficult for someone to cause those kinds of neck bruises from the side or back. There are few bruises other than the ones on the neck, so there was not an extended struggle," Stud surmised. "I'll ask the coroner about the hands."

They worked on the case until Max said, "Let's take a break. I think we can stop the paper review right now. We have a major suspect and we should go after him. Stud, call Bracken to see if he is available to sit in with us. I'll call the chief and the mayor to invite them. We may need legal advice on how far we can go when we bring in Martinez. I think Bracken will advise that we call him a *person of interest*."

Stud said, "He and that dog certainly have my interest."

Bracken showed up in short order. The mayor and chief stated they had conflicting commitments and wanted a report on the meeting. Bracken advised telling Martinez that inconsistencies in his comments have to be cleared up. He should be requested to come in voluntarily, but a subpoena can be obtained if necessary. Advise him he may want to bring his attorney.

"I want the pleasure of calling him," Stud said. He called, informed Simon that he was a person of interest, and that there was further information the team needed from him. Stud told him he would be making a formal statement, and he might want to bring an attorney.

Later, an attorney, Jason Knott, called Stud and told him he was Simon's attorney and was willing to arrange a deposition time for Simon. Stud gave him Bracken's phone number. Later, Bracken informed Stud the deposition would be given at 3:00 p.m. in the DA's offices.

CHAPTER 40

WHEN RON ARRIVED AT HIS office, the normal Monday frenzy existed. Three people were in the reception area, apparently waiting for him.

Art came up as he entered his office, saying, "Mayor, I have a couple of updates for you. Sam is on his way to France with your letter designating him as your official representative to the wine growers. Andy Stricker had already nosed out the trip and seemed disappointed that economic development was financing the trip. We probably ruined his story and one or more editorials. Also, I never had the opportunity to report on the city council public hearing last Thursday."

Art then related an amusing story about the interruption of the hearing to remove a guy testifying. He had escaped from a mental hospital. Afterward a listener had called in to say that he was the only one making sense.

"Art, you have made my day already. Now stay away if you come up with any bad news," the mayor said.

"No real problems facing you to my knowledge. The article on the reception yesterday was positive. Pass my congratulations on to Mrs. Steadman."

"Yes, I told her she no longer has to be Mrs. Mayor," Ron replied. "She is Dr. Steadman now."

Art left for his office. Ron asked Lupe about the people waiting to see him. After listening to their matter of concern, a zoning dispute, he referred them to the zoning office.

CHAPTER 41

R ON CHECKED IN WITH CHARLES at the war room. Charles was upbeat about the Sunday reception and the reports in the paper, radio, and television. Mike was following up with news releases about the Sunday event.

Charles said, "Let me make you aware that we received four irate or rude calls about the use of stem cells in science. The claim is such use is blasphemy and contrary to God's will."

"It started already?" asked Ron. "We weren't expecting such quick reaction from that element. Val and I discussed the possibility of such opposition, but we both feel this can be such a boon to mankind. Political fallout must be accepted, regardless. I respect other people's opinions even when we disagree. For example, Will Brown's a fine person. We just disagree on how to allocate city resources. I believe he likes me personally also. But acceptance like this is alien to extremists. This might get nastier. We'll have to see what develops.

"I just checked the political schedule. Looks free today. I'll take the opportunity to catch up on city work but will try to make a few phone calls. Val is being sent to Washington tomorrow to justify more grant money from NIH, as I mentioned. She will return Thursday. This means I will go to the hospital reception tomorrow without her. You might let our hosts know."

"I'll do that," Charles said. "Also, you may want to alert Val that she should continue efforts to keep Steve's name out of the papers. Sally or someone over at Gonzo's might pick up on that and blow his cover. If his cover is blown, he may want to keep some distance from Gonzo. He might get bloodied."

CHAPTER 42

ON TUESDAY MORNING, AFTER HIS usual huevos rancheros breakfast, Roberto Olivas drove his rented van, first to the residential address noted on his tout sheet as Brown's home. Observing the home and grounds carefully, he noted a large tree with foliage around it close to the side of the garage and near the door. Since in February, darkness arrived before 6:00 p.m., this could be the best place. He then drove to the address of Brown's campaign headquarters, noting the openness of the parking area and traffic passing by as a negative. Next, he went to the Carpenters' Union Hall. Brown was scheduled to meet the union board Tuesday evening to solicit their support. The hall was a large metal building, primarily aluminum, but with steel supports and a metal roof. A sloping roof easily drained rainwater. The building faced a large fenced parking lot, with room for fifty to seventy-five vehicles.

There were only three vehicles, two pickups, and one SUV in the lot. This was another possibility for the kill, but the fence and gate could be a problem. Also, one or more of the board members might go out to the car with Brown. If that occurred, this site would not be acceptable.

Roberto decided that the best site for egress and regress was Brown's home.

With the site selected, he decided to have a couple of beers and drove downtown looking for a bar. Finding an acceptable-looking one, Roberto parked, entered, and sat down on a barstool. Ordering a draft beer, he glanced around the room, hoping to see an unattended woman. He saw a typical bar, with booths along the walls and tables filling the middle area. One wall pictured a mural of settlers and a wagon with animals, obviously taking the advice of Horace Greeley, given long ago.

The other walls were some kind of darkly stained wood. Small tin lamps provided some semblance of light for booths. Overhead florescent lights flickered on the tables. One booth and a couple of tables were occupied but not with unattended women. When his stomach growled, he realized it must be time for lunch. Roberto hadn't realized time had passed so quickly.

Unknown to Roberto, the three men at one of the tables were Drug Enforcement Agency agents. They worked out of El Paso but were in Centerville for a conference.

They had just completed the morning session and gone out for lunch. One of them noticed Roberto enter and recognized him. In a low voice, he said, "Don't look now, but that guy who just entered is Roberto Olivas from El Paso. I took a picture of him going through customs a few months back. He is in the cartel and is known as a major hit man. Wonder why he's up here? Whatever it is, it won't be good."

The other two agents made a point of catching a good look of Roberto without his noticing. One said that since the DEA El Paso director would be speaking this afternoon, he would mention Olivas being in town to him.

He said, "He'll want to know. What's the name of this bar anyway? I didn't notice when we came in."

"Happy Hour," one said.

The other two laughed and one asked, "Do you go into bars often?"

"No, my wife doesn't approve," he answered.

The third officer said, "Happy hour is when the bar has discounted drinks. The name of the bar is The Embassy. We'll check out the street name as we leave.

"When I get back to the office, I'll draft a report for the El Paso Drug Task Force. The report, of course, will be routed to the Centerville Drug Task Force. I like our setup for communications between the law enforcement agencies. The report goes to every agency represented on the task force.

"Centerville has three officers for their police drug enforcement section of the task force. The sheriff has two officers assigned. FBI assumes the role of coordinator for all task forces. By the end of the week, every law enforcement office in the region would know Olivas was in Centerville today."

The sighting was reported to the DEA director after he spoke. He said that they would check lodgings to locate him and set up a surveillance team. The director thanked them for good work and said, "Add the cost of the beer to your expense accounts."

"We should have had two beers," one commented.

Back at the bar, Roberto had a beer and then ordered a boilermaker (bourbon and beer), downed it, and ordered his lunch. After eating, he stopped by a convenience store, bought a six-pack of beer, took it to his motel room, drank it, and then took a short nap.

CHAPTER 43

THE DETECTIVES, BRACKEN, AND SIMON Martinez and his attorney met in a district attorney conference room as arranged. Simon introduced his attorney, Jason Knott. Max mentally observed that Knott was a small dapper man with a face featuring a prominent nose and a receding hairline. He wore a nice-fitting black suit with a white shirt and gray tie.

Bracken laid out the ground rules for the interrogation and after performing the reading of the Miranda warning, and obtaining Simon's signature that he heard and understood his rights, the questions started.

The detectives had previously agreed that Stud would lead the questioning. He'd be hard-nosed. The others would jump in when appropriate.

Stud began, "Before we start recording this interrogation, let me mention, Mr. Martinez, we interviewed you twice, the second time because you had lied to us the first time. We obtained provable information from others that contradicted your statements to us the second time. It is possible we will charge you with the murder of Amy Johnson, depending on what you say today. We want the truth. Cut out the bullshit. At a minimum, you have impeded our investigation. That itself is a chargeable offense. You currently are a person of interest."

Knott asked that he and Simon be allowed to confer. Knott said that he and Simon had not conferred in detail before arriving, and he needed more information from Simon before proceeding. The detectives, Bracken, and the stenographer left the room.

Simon asked Knott about his rights. Knott informed him that he did not have to answer any questions. He pointed out that Simon had not been subpoenaed. He also could state that he refused to answer by saying, "My answer may tend to incriminate me."

"I recommend you say you are refusing to answer questions right now because we have not had time to confer and suggest another time for the interrogation be established. As your attorney, I need more information from you on what happened previously before we proceed with the police, if I am to advise you effectively."

When the detective team returned, Knott said he had just advised Mr. Martinez to respond to every question, except his name and address, by saying he will not answer because his answer may tend to incriminate him. He told them he and Simon needed to confer extensively before the interrogation. "I suggest we be allowed to confer tomorrow morning, and be available tomorrow afternoon for interrogation."

The faces of the detectives showed their displeasure, but Stud suggested 1:30 p.m. tomorrow in this conference room. That settled, Simon and his attorney left.

Afterward, Max said, "What a smooth exit. Simon appears to have a good attorney. He saw his client starting to freeze up and got him out of here. I will report to the chief and mayor and meet with you back at homicide."

He caught the chief headed for the tunnel to city hall and gave him a brief report, saying, "Chief, we are sure we have the right guy for this, but it appears he has a good attorney, and I doubt he will let Martinez say anything helpful to us. I'll report to the mayor."

"Keep it going," the chief said. "Something may pop. When it does, jump on it and keep me informed."

CHAPTER 44

AFTER HIS NAP, ROBERTO DROVE to Walmart to purchase scissors, glue, paper, and thin plastic gloves. Back in the motel room, he put on the gloves, started cutting letters out of the morning newspaper, and glued them on the blank sheet of paper. The letters soon read, "No gays will become mayor." He placed the note in his Windbreaker pocket. He drank beer while working.

He broke down his .22 target pistol, obtained especially in Juarez for this job, and carefully reassembled it and then added the silencer. He checked proper operation by pulling the trigger a few times before loading it with a clip of 9 mm hollow-point bullets. Now all he had to do was wait. After showering and dressing, he sacked all his garbage, checked out of the motel, and drove toward Brown's campaign office. The drug enforcement people located Roberto's motel only after he had checked out.

Brown and his partner, Jamie Torres, were in the office along with one other person. He settled down to wait. Later, Brown and the two people left the office and proceeded to a restaurant. Roberto watched them be seated and order, and then drove to a Burger King close by and ordered a hamburger and fries for himself.

He drove back to keep Brown under observation in the restaurant while he ate his burger and fries. After Brown's party finished eating, he followed them back to the office where the third person was dropped off. Brown and his partner then drove to Brown's house. They drove into the driveway, opened the garage door by remote from the car, and drove into the garage. They then exited the car, hit the close button, and the door started down. Roberto watched these actions carefully as he drove slowly by. Now that Brown's routine was known, he thought it would be timely to do the job after Brown's meeting tonight. He decided the best approach would be to hide behind the tree and foliage close to the garage door, step in the garage when they had pulled the car inside, and do them.

Apparently, Brown and his partner had gone in to prepare and wait for the union board meeting they were to attend that evening.

Rather than wait in this quiet residential area where he might draw attention sitting in a car, he drove to a bar where he could nurse a beer while waiting. Later, he drove to a parking lot across the street from union hall, scooted down in the car seat, and waited. Right before 8:00 p.m., Brown and his partner arrived at union hall. They parked their car and went into the hall.

Roberto drove back to Brown's house and drove slowly by the house to check it out. It appeared empty. He drove about two blocks away, parked the car on the street, and walked back to Brown's house, where he hid in the foliage next to the tree. In the darkness, he was sure no one would see him, especially since he had dressed in all-black clothes and wore a black balaclava. He sat down on the ground to wait.

Shortly after 9:00 p.m. Roberto saw car lights coming down the street, and the car turned onto the driveway. The garage door opened, and the car pulled into the garage. Roberto entered the garage before the door closed.

As Brown exited the car, Roberto stepped up, and shot him point-blank in his head. He quickly ran around the car. Torres was crouched next to the car. Torres said, "Please don't" as Roberto shot him in the head also. Both men were down. He checked the pulses in their necks and could not find a heartbeat. He thumbtacked the hate note to Brown's chest and left, leaving the garage door open.

As Roberto walked back to his car, he removed his gloves. He was sure no one had heard anything, because the street was empty and he heard no ruckus. He entered his car, drove a few blocks before pulling over, called Simon with the "sorry, wrong number" message, and headed south, throwing the gun minus the silencer in the river as he drove over the bridge.

Turning onto the interstate, he set the speed control at 70 mph, 5 mph under the limit and turned on his CD player. All his CDs were country music. George Strait belted out "All My Ex's Live in Texas."

CHAPTER 45

A T 1:30 P.M. ON TUESDAY, Simon and Knott arrived at the DA's office for the interrogation. The detectives were waiting. Stud started the proceedings with the same comments made the previous day. He then went on record, stating the date and time, those present, and the purpose of the interrogation.

Stud said, "Mr. Martinez, please state your name and address."

Simon did so.

"Are you involved in the mayoral election officially?"

Simon said he had been but no longer was directly involved. He had left the Gonsolic campaign committee.

Stud asked, "Why did you leave the committee?"

Simon said that the committee was taking too much of his time away from his construction business.

"Did you know Amy Johnson?"

Simon answered, "I refuse to answer on the basis my answer may tend to incriminate me."

Figuring Simon would use the Fifth Amendment on all questions about Amy's murder, he asked, "How would your answer tend to incriminate you?"

Knott jumped in immediately, "Mr. Martinez, the question requires the same Fifth Amendment answer." From that point on, Simon refused to answer any further questions, pleading the Fifth.

After trying several questions about Amy Johnson and Simon's relationship, Stud asked one final question. "Are you going to plead the Fifth when I ask anything relating to Amy Johnson?"

Simon responded, "Yes."

Stud asked his last question, "Did you kill or participate in killing Amy Johnson?"

Simon responded, "No, I did not." Realizing he just violated his previous comment, he gave a wry smile.

Stud shut down the recorder and said the meeting was over. Simon and Knott left the room and a disappointed group of law officers.

Bracken said, "Martinez might not be the killer, but he is involved up to his neck. Nothing in the interview would help in putting together a case against him. We need more evidence. We can't go to court on the scraps we have."

Max agreed and said they would keep digging. "We need a break. We do have him tied into the panty incident as one of the originators and in a relationship with Johnson. We need to crack his alibi for the time of the murder. He originally claimed he worked at the construction yard until slightly after 5:00 p.m., he had a beer, fed and let the dog loose, and locked the gate as he left. He said he went straight home and met his wife there about five thirty. I checked with his wife, and she confirmed he was home about that time.

"To check times, Stud drove the shortest route from his construction yard to his home, and it took almost fifteen minutes." Max continued, "The questionable time is four to five. Simon was by himself and claimed he made no phone calls during this time. We have been trying to find someone who saw him away from his office or even at the office but have struck out so far. We will keep working on breaking Simon's alibi and pursue any lead showing promise."

Max followed by saying, "Stud, you and Davis go back to the Gonsolic office, interview Gonzo, Johnny, and Sally again. Without saying so, let them know our focus is on Simon. Shake the tree, see what falls out. I'll go see the chief and the mayor. Mark, any suggestions?"

"Yes," said Bracken. "I will see about a court order for a DNA sample, a cast of his hands. If I get it, you can measure them and see what the coroner can do with them."

"Good thought. I am feeling better about this. Maybe something will break for us."

Max and the chief reported the Martinez interview to the mayor, who said it was too bad nothing developed, but he agreed they had the right person.

CHAPTER 46

RON HAD OFFERED TO DRIVE Val and Steve to the airport. When Steve entered the car, a ping of jealousy struck. He recalled his admonition directed to Val, but still wondered about the relationship.

Ron took care of his mayoral duties after seeing Val and Steve off. He left the office early to stop by the house to change into fresh clothes for the Carrico hospital reception. He checked with Charles on the need for any special remarks, but Charles said, "Just be your usual charming self."

The hospital had a large training area, about a thousand square feet, but portable screens were used to separate the area for the reception. Charles introduced Ron to John Carrico, and Ron gave Julie a peck on the cheek while thanking them for sponsoring the event. He offered apologies for Val, explaining why she could not attend.

The Carricos had seen the papers about the new lab facility and seemed impressed by Val's work, commenting how wonderful it would be to conquer some of these diseases.

Ron also thanked Julie for her efforts on his behalf in the war room. Ron made the rounds, introducing himself or saying the right things if he already knew the person.

At the proper moment, Ron made his campaign speech. He could tell that this particular group was for him by the way his remarks were received.

As he and Charles left, Ron said, "Let's stop for a drink at the Hyatt bar, if you would like." Charles said that he would meet him there.

Ron arrived first at the bar located in the hotel lobby. Huge pillars cut up the large area. A recessed area located in the lobby center with a railing around it presented an airy feeling. Several tables were interspersed with foliage growing out of large pots. A small water fountain and sculptures added to the décor. A three-story atrium rose out of the bar center, expanding the open feeling.

Charles sat down, commenting on how well the reception went. As the waiter arrived to take drink orders, Ron said, "I think so too. The Carricos seem like very nice people, and that Julie is really a striking woman. Although she is beautiful, I think it is her bedroom eyes that grab you. She obviously is intelligent and the complete package."

They both ordered scotch with water in tall glasses.

"Her eyes certainly do. I have some gossip. Julie and I had lunch the other day. She confided that she is divorcing John. It seems John has a serious affair going with a nurse, and Julie is upset about it. She even hired a private detective. I asked her to wait until after the reception before telling John about the divorce. I suspect they will be having the conversation tonight or tomorrow, but I'm just speculating."

"That's too bad," Ron said. "I feel sorry for Julie having to go through the divorce. I'm told that it is a traumatic experience. I hope I will never have to experience that." For just a moment he thought of Val and Steve in Washington. He dismissed that thought and instead thought about how honest and trustworthy Val had always been.

Several election campaign matters were discussed, including the appointments for the remainder of the week. The drinks finished, they went home.

CHAPTER 47

RON PREPARED FOR BED AND thought about Julie and her divorce. She might be looking for something to keep her busy. Maybe he'd discuss a job at the city for her after the election. She would make a fine assistant, and with shorthanded staff, there was plenty of work. She had a nice personality to go with her looks, and those attributes were helpful in public life.

He took a shower, put on his pajamas and robe, and went into the kitchen to find something to assuage his hunger. He found some ham slices, made a small sandwich, poured a glass of milk, and listened to his message machine. Mrs. Perkins, his neighbor on the west side of his house, had called again about the terrible noise created by the garbage collection trucks. This happened almost every week, because she was home most weeks during the pickups.

I will kid her out of her complaint when I catch her out sometime, he decided. Like maybe offering her a ride in the truck. Some skill is required to align the garbage bins with the bin catchers and then dumping without spilling garbage everywhere. The lift machinery is loud. Muffling the noise would add to the cost of the trucks. At times people ignored the fact that most improvements cost money. The improvements can raise taxes or fees; only so much can be absorbed as additional costs. Most people would prefer to live with the noise rather than have garbage fees go higher.

The second message was Val reporting they had arrived in Washington and had checked into the Adams Hotel. Her room number was 1102.

His emergency phone broke his reverie. The police chief had requested he have a phone installed with a direct line, so he could be reached at home at all times. The ring shocked him. This phone had never rung before, and for a second he considered not answering it.

He hustled over to the phone and answered, "Yes, Chief?"

"Mayor, we have two more murders. We have cars and forensics people headed to Will Brown's house. He and his partner have been killed. A neighbor walking his dog discovered the bodies. He saw the bodies in the garage and called 911. They apparently were shot. That's all I have right now."

A few seconds of silence ensued. The chief asked, "Mayor, are you there?"

"Yes, sorry. Just in shock, I'm overwhelmed. Why Will? Everyone likes Will. Even those people who did not agree with his environmental positions treat him with respect. Chief, I will need a little time to absorb this and the complications. Where are you?"

"I'm at home, getting ready to go to the scene."

"I will meet you there, Chief. It'll take me a few minutes to get going."

Ron went into the bathroom, freshened up, and started dressing. His thoughts jumped all over the wall. *Settle down. I'm glad I had only one drink. Even so, better wash my mouth out.*

A guy, a nice guy, running for mayor got killed. Does it have to do with the election, or is it something else? Running for or being president is one thing, but being a mayor? Was there that much there? His thoughts continued. Sure, there was some power and glory involved in being a mayor, but no one he knew about had gone in office poor and then walked away from the job wealthy or with the background to claim $100,000 per speech. He knew of a past mayor who started driving a cab after being in office. Will, although picking up some voters, was down in the last poll.

Sure, a threat was always there, but only a long-shot threat for election. If this had to do with the election, then someone was not thinking clearly. How come the poll leader wasn't the first selection for a target?

Maybe this had nothing to do with the election. In any event, the chief had better talk about some protection. This is unreal.

Ron grabbed a cup of coffee as he went through the kitchen. He entered his car as the garage door went up, backed out, hit the remote to close the door, and started over to Will's house, which was only about fifteen minutes away.

When he arrived, he observed controlled bedlam in and around the garage, but with several people standing around on the street outside the crime scene—mainly neighbors, he guessed, but media people also. The lights on four police cars were flashing.

The garage lights glowed, as well as a yard light. Even so, the police had rigged an extension cord with a strong light for the garage. Evidence search parties of three police were carefully searching the ground and shrubbery around the garage. The coroner was working over one body. Ron found the chief in the garage after working himself through the police gauntlet. He first identified himself to one of the police protecting the crime scene perimeter and said he wanted to talk with the chief. He then had been allowed through the cordon. Ron met the chief and asked, "What do we know?" The chief caught Max's eye and motioned him over. The chief said, "Let's step inside, and Max will give you a report."

They went inside to the kitchen and stood around a butcher table rather than sitting. Even though there had been a murder, Ron felt as if he was intruding on Brown by standing in the kitchen, but he said nothing.

Max reported, "This is what we know. Two 9 mm casings were found, one by each body. A neighbor found the bodies while walking his dog shortly after ten. He quickly called 911 with the report. One of our patrol cars, the closest, arrived first, followed by an ambulance with med techs, the homicide detective on duty, and a fire truck. The detective secured the scene with the help of the patrol right after he called the coroner. After he identified the body of Brown, he then called dispatch and directed her to call me and the chief.

"After a preliminary exam, the coroner stated that one fatal bullet wound to the head was found on each body. This likely killed them, but an autopsy must confirm this. A note was found on Brown's body stating, 'No gays will become mayor.'

"Our initial investigation of the scene showed foliage next to the garage door had been disturbed. From those facts, we surmise the perp waited for Brown to return home while hidden by the foliage. When Brown drove into the garage, the perp stepped in before the door was closed and, as Brown and his partner stepped out of the car, likely shot Brown first, walked around, and shot the partner. He then left. We assume his car was close by, or he had a driver pick him up. Most likely, he acted alone. We will see if the bullets match. If they do, we have one killer, as we surmised. The disturbed foliage indicated one person.

"The note indicated either a hate crime or a copycat crime made to look like a hate crime. It seems we always find evidence leading in more than one direction. We will work first assuming the validity of the note but will keep in mind the possibility it was a setup to lead us in the wrong direction."

The chief said, "Good report, Max."

Ron thanked Max, who then went back into the garage. Ron, still in a state of shock, said out loud but more to himself than the chief, "There are some rewards for being mayor, but something like this makes me wonder if they are worth all the other crap."

"I understand your feelings," the chief said. "We have the extremes in the police department all the time. From the low of a policeman killed or injured to the high of a successful crime-prevention operation or capture of one or more vicious criminals. During the lows, I want to chuck the badge, but then something good happens and I realize the merits of the job. We do society some good, Mayor. That one reward keeps us going."

Ron replied, "You're right, of course. I'm going home. Who is my escort? Make sure Gonsolic also has a bodyguard."

"Already done, Mayor. Officer Collins over there by your car is your bodyguard."

As Ron was walking to his car, he was recognized by a TV reporter, who shouted at him and ran over, her cameraman following, asking for a comment.

The mayor said, "Excuse me, I am in shock. A fine, outstanding citizen and friend had his life taken this evening. I will have more comments tomorrow when we know more."

CHAPTER 48

VAL AND STEVE'S FLIGHT TO Washington was time-consuming but uneventful, and they arrived at the Adams Hotel late afternoon.

Both didn't feel like changing out of their casual clothes, so they decided to eat at the hotel coffee shop. Thinking that fish would be good, they both ate the special fried catfish while discussing their forthcoming meeting. Then they opted for an early bedtime and retired to their respective rooms.

The meeting was to start at ten on Wednesday morning. Reviewing herself in a mirror the next morning, Val felt good in her DKNY charcoal suit, Bandolino shoes, and her Dolce and Gabbana purse.

Buzzing Steve on the phone, Val asked if he were ready, and he said, "Let's go." Meeting Steve in the hall, Val thought he looked perfect in his slightly worn Western Wrangler jeans, button shirt, and his tassel loafers without socks showing. Of course, Steve had to make a remark about how Val looked and then topped it off by announcing loudly in the elevator that she sure looked different without her pajamas, referring to the disposable suits they wore at work. The people in the elevator, much to Steve's amusement, took it another way, showing wry smiles.

Well, the meeting started on time and went well. Val and Steve took turns presenting the different sections of the proposal.

Val concentrated on the setup for the scientific specifications while Steve did most of the physical plant requirements and lab equipment. An estimated project cost for improvements seemed to be acceptable. The presentation took about one and a half hours—almost to the minute as had been rehearsed. The committee asked Val and Steve to step outside for a latte or coffee and Danish. Although it seemed like a lifetime to Steve and Val, it was actually only forty-five minutes.

When the meeting reconvened, there seemed to be a relaxed and pleasant atmosphere, and Steve gave Val one of his special crooked smiles.

The chairman had them take a seat and informed them that the committee was in total agreement with the proposal as written. The chairman congratulated them.

At the proper moment, Val tapped Steve on the shoulder, made the appropriate signal, and they left feeling good.

Back in her room, she kicked off her Bandolinos and immediately called Ron and the dean to report the good news and to tell the dean that the chairman of the NIH committee would be calling him sometime today to finalize grant details.

Ron startled Val with information on Will Brown and his partner being murdered the night before. He reported what details he had, including the hate note.

Val asked him if the murders were election related. He said he was not sure. "It is a possibility." She told him to make sure he has police protection the remainder of the election, and he said a patrolman was with him now. Hanging up; it took Val a few minutes to digest the information. She buzzed Steve on the phone, told him of the murders, and stated she was concerned that Ron was in danger. Steve tried to downplay that concern, saying he thought the note made it a weirdo slaying.

Shortly afterward Steve knocked on Val's door. She looked through the keyhole and then opened it. There he stood with a bottle of champagne and two glasses. Val waved him in. They discussed the murders. Val still was upset, perhaps because she had known Brown well, but part of it was likely because of concern for Ron.

After assuring Val that all efforts would be made for Ron's protection and Val could do nothing until she was home anyway, Steve suggested they celebrate their grant victory.

Val said, "You're right. Let's be happy and reward ourselves."

He popped the champagne cork and poured two glasses. They touched glasses and smiled at each other. After making small talk and two glasses of champagne, Steve took their glasses and set them on the desk. Then as if preordained, he took her in his arms and kissed her gently while caressing her lower back. He raised his head, looked at Val, and said, "Should I stop?"

Val simply stood on her tiptoes, put her arms around his neck, and kissed him gently on the forehead.

Steve smiled and said, "That's a no, isn't it?"

Val returned his smile and answered, "Your move was a surprise, Steve. But it was very tempting, and you should know that. I like you a lot, but I'm not sure about how much right now. I'm not turning you down forever, and I'm not saying it will never happen. Ron and I have something special, and I'm not prepared to give it up."

Steve stepped back, turned, and picked up the champagne. "Val, let's drink up and go for lunch. I love you, so I'll wait, but rejection is never fun."

She grinned and said, "There is one favor. Last night, a great band played in the dining room. If they are playing now, how about going dancing? You dance wonderfully, and people watching will think Fred and Ginger are back. Besides, a diversion would be healthy."

After a wonderful meal of scallops in a tomato cream sauce over pasta, they danced everything, even tried the Argentina tango. It seemed that Steve had once dated a lady from Argentina and had learned the dance. Val gave it her best but ended up laughing so hard she almost made them fall during one of the maneuvers. Steve said, "Let's have a Bloody Mary for two reasons—a toast to you for being a great boss and lady and for your common sense. Please don't ever tell my buddies, but my feeling is you were right to turn me down. You are one foxy lady and we are going to set up and run the best stem-cell laboratory in the USA. After that, I will try you again."

CHAPTER 49

B OTH VAL AND STEVE, TOTALLY exhausted, slept all the way to Centerville. Ron met them at the airport, hugged and kissed Val, and shook hands with Steve. Val, elated over the trip's success, followed the welcoming kiss with a long hug. After congratulations, Ron summarized the Brown situation. He introduced them to his current bodyguard, Luis Sanchez, and brought them up-to-date on the campaign. Ron noted that the campaign dynamics had changed now that there were only two candidates. Both he and Gonzo had to go after those voters who had been backing Brown. Charles was working on a strategy to accomplish that. He asked Val and Steve if they could attend a meeting to review Charles's work.

Steve declined because of class work, and Val said that she would have to report to the dean.

Ron dropped Steve off at his apartment, Val at home. Val told Ron she wanted to freshen up before she met with the dean. After a thorough review of her meeting in Washington, Val decided a good shower and nap would help. Val woke up feeling refreshed, unpacked, and threw dirty clothes in the washer, all the while thinking about dinner but with flashbacks of the hotel room scene with Steve. He didn't know how close she was to submitting. Thank God, it didn't happen.

She decided on lamb shish kebab for dinner, a favorite of Ron's. They could make a big return-home evening of it. She selected a bottle of 2006 Gruet New Mexico Pinot Noir.

Then she gathered all the ingredients needed for the dinner and started cooking.

To Val, this was the part she liked best about her marriage. She and Ron would have good wine, gourmet food, and stimulating conversation. Then go to bed and have good sex. Ron came in a few minutes later and was all smiles when he saw the dinner selection. He opened the wine and poured two glasses. The conversation while cooking was on the murders. Ron said nothing new had turned up, but he was sure it was connected to the campaign. With another glass of wine, they sat down to eat and discussed Val's Washington trip. Ron said that he had worried somewhat about a relationship between Val and Steve. They see so much of each other, and she was always singing his praises. Val said that's true. He's a remarkable person, and she liked him, but no sex happened in Washington and had never occurred. Ron said, "That's good, and I trust it never will."

Changing the subject, Val said that tomorrow, the dean's press conference purpose was to report the feds' commitment to the national lab. Ron thought that the campaign would take a little heat, but the heat would not stand up to the good publicity.

Later they went to bed and did just what Val said. They had good, rewarding sex. Thinking that it's always good to be home, Val slept with her head on Ron's shoulder.

CHAPTER 50

V AL AWOKE EARLY AND DRESSED for work. The dean's press
conference was set for ten o'clock, and she wanted to
be early. The press coverage was complete with all three
local TV stations and both newspapers represented. Some local
protest groups attended but for now were quiet.

To Val, nothing new was presented. The dean reviewed new
job figures and requested Val to discuss how several months ago
the university advertised a job for a professional cell-care person
and the status of recruitment, with additional explanations of lab
programs.

Val noted that four candidates would be interviewed, and
the final selection would be made today. The search produced
extremely qualified candidates.

She outlined the research she had performed for the original
grant and emphasized that research would continue, making the
new national laboratory a part of their continued studies to find
new ways to safeguard the use of the stem cells.

Overall, the press conference went well, and the dean was
pleased.

Val found it amusing that the university president and dean
were interviewed while the press had little interest in her. Oh
well, that was what the campaign wanted. She realized a lot of

plain luck and timing set up the grant, but the result was that her new job now was firmly secure and she had risen in the ranks.

Two PhD-tenured professors stopped her after the press conference to express their displeasure about an intern, Steve, being selected for the Stem Cell Committee over more senior staff, just as the dean had predicted. Knowing nothing would mollify them, Val expressed her belief that Steve Janson would be a most valuable member of the committee. They walked off obviously still angry.

As part of the interviewing committee for the new stem cell assistant director position, after lunch Steve and Val returned to the dean's conference room for interviews.

Three of the four candidates were women, pleasing Val. Interviews were held with each committee member making evaluations. Steve's grading system was unique. The first candidate graded "doable maybe," the second a definite "absolutely not doable," and then Annie Kim was graded "totally doable." She was by far the best-qualified candidate, and the committee voted for her unanimously.

It so happened she was Asian, quite striking, with obviously a mixed heritage. Her hair was shiny black and hung down to her waist, and her oval eyes looked velvety black.

She showed the whitest teeth possible and had a body to kill for. It was obvious that she not only worked out at gym but also probably ran two miles to get there. Val was attracted to her both professionally and physically.

Val found her ultimately qualified, poised, and, although a youngish twenty-eight, completely at ease with herself. With assurance that Annie would be hired, Steve was already singing her praises.

Val pointed out that it was time to perform their primary mission—lab work.

Their work started with the cells they had last checked, and by the time she and Steve finished it was almost midnight. They locked up after notifying security they were leaving—a new rule implemented because a woman had been attacked recently.

They walked to the parking lot. Just as they came up to Val's car, three masked men jumped out of the shadows on them.

One shoved her against the car, shouting, "Baby killer." Steve tried to pull Val away from the man, trying to protect her, but he was slammed hard to the concrete by one of the other men. Val started screaming, "Police, police" as she was thrown down on the concrete.

She felt dazed, with pain from both elbows and knees. Fortunately, security guards were close enough to hear the yells and came running, shouting, "Police, stop now and raise your hands."

Of course, the assailants didn't. One nastily said to Val, "This is only a warning. Close the lab." They took off running back into the darkness, still yelling, "Baby killers, baby killers!"

A security guard called the paramedics and then reported the incident to the dispatcher.

The other assisted Val up, asking if she was all right. The paramedics arrived and determined they had no serious physical damage other than cuts and bruises. The medics asked Val several questions trying to determine if she was in shock. Apparently, they determined she wasn't but tried to talk both Val and Steve into being checked at the hospital. Both said that was not necessary; they would rather go home. The medics treated the cuts. Realizing she wasn't going to the hospital, one guard informed Val he would escort her home. Val knew that the media listened constantly to the police radio frequency, and the incident would be publicized. Luckily, it was late and would not make the morning papers, but she expected coverage in the morning TV news shows. This was what Ron's campaign people had hoped to avoid.

One security guard called Ron to inform him of the incident and then followed Val home. Steve left without an escort, having declined one.

Ron and his guard were waiting in the house driveway. He asked how she felt. She said, "Sore and stiff. All I want is a hot bath, Band-Aids, and bed."

The phone rang a few times, until Ron disconnected it. The calls likely were from news media.

Even though it was late evening, Ron called Charles and Mike. He then called Chief Pirwarsky, who said he would radio the policeman assigned to watch our house to be extra alert for intruders.

The next morning the alarm rang at 5:30 a.m. Val had forgotten to turn it off. Val remembered last night's conflict when she tried to get out of bed. Wow, she was sore. Concrete does not have much give to it. She had Band-Aids and small bandages on her knees and elbows and some bruises on her body. *No work today,* she thought as she walked painfully to the shower.

As she waited for warm water, Ron stuck his head in the bathroom and asked how she felt. Val said that she felt just the way she looked. He said he had juice and coffee in the kitchen, plus an Alka-Seltzer if she wanted it. Also, he had the TV on news programs, and said, "You now are becoming more famous by the minute. Perhaps you will make *The Today Show.*"

"If they call, tell them thanks but, no, thanks."

When she arrived in the kitchen, the TV anchor was reporting, "Dr. Valarie Steadman, director of the new stem-cell research laboratory and wife of Mayor Steadman, was attacked last night, along with her assistant, by three masked men in the medical school parking lot. The three attackers fled when university security personnel appeared on the scene.

"Fortunately, according to reports, Dr. Steadman and the assistant received only cuts and bruises and went to their homes after on-site treatment by EMTs. A guard commented that he thought the attackers were right-to-life jerks."

Val said that the hot shower made her feel better. Ron walked over, gave her a hug and kiss, and said, "You are really pretty all wrapped up in white."

"I don't know how to handle all this sympathy," Val said.

"Val, I am so relieved you are okay. I don't know what to say. How do you spell 'relief'?"

"Go back and stop with the word 'pretty,' or you may be wrapped in bandages yourself."

Feeling better and having second thoughts, Val decided she would go to work. The day originally had been planned with Annie, the newly hired cell technologist, to establish work priorities and familiarize her with lab procedures. Annie had said previously that she would be in the lab even though personnel had not finished processing her.

Val appreciated her attitude and wanted to encourage it.

Val was a great proponent of stem-cell research, but sometimes the speed in which the field had progressed scared her. This whole business had only started in 1998, when James Thompson at the University of Wisconsin reported he had succeeded in removing cells from spare embryos. Then he established the world's first embryonic stem cell line. In just over a decade some diseases were being treated with stem cells.

When Val arrived at the lab, Annie was reviewing scientific journals. Val suggested that she and Annie discuss the status of existing research projects and what she sees in store for Annie's lab in the near future. Val said Steve would join them soon.

After getting a cup of coffee for each of them, Val began to detail the status of projects and their purpose, as well as the objectives and goals for the newly established lab.

Val anticipated Annie's question about a student intern being in a de facto position of authority in the lab, so she explained Steve's deep involvement and his plans for obtaining a PhD.

She explained that Steve's research projects were with adult stem cells, not embryonic stem cells. They already had three patients on treatment, and one of them had exceeded the time limit he had been expected to live.

The process used removed bone marrow from a patient, which was then treated appropriately, and then infused back into the patient. This eliminated the dreaded body rejection, since these were cells from the host himself. The newly expanded lab would be concerned with research using stem cells from three sources.

First, induced pluripotent stem cells (iPS cells). These cells, brought back to their immature state, can become any cell. Steve's project was an example of their use, but many labs were actively pursuing studies in this area. Labs were already testing these cells for type I diabetes, red blood cell diseases, and retinal cells for molecular degeneration and many other studies.

The second, Val explained, were adult stem cells. These cells were easy to harvest from the skin, heart, and bone marrow. Other sources were being studied because these cells had limited potential and were prone to grow into tumors throughout the body. Labs were working on solving this problem.

Embryonic stem cells make up the third source, by far the number-one choice of all research scientists but also the source of ongoing ethical debate. Fetal cells are the building blocks for 220 cell types found within the body. Studies were underway all around the world, in legal and illegal laboratories, by renowned scientists, as well as those new to the field. Also, scam artists have apparently appeared. They have been quick to latch onto a quick and sure source of income. These people rely on people panicking when told there is a health crisis, such as cancer.

Studies were being conducted on possible cures for congestive heart failure and blood vessel failure, on growth of new vessels, bone disease and replacement, the immune system, multiple sclerosis, melanoma, new heart muscle to replace worn-out hearts, spinal cord injury, and many other tissues.

In addition to these studies, new research was being conducted to find ways to program adult cells to repair and rebuild old tissue, using iPS cells to track the progression of a disease, to test drugs, to control proliferation and differentiation of cells, and methods to explain birth defects and how cancer cells are formed and encouraged to grow and multiply.

The NIH kept up-to-date on all these activities and was aware of the dangers if a disaster were to occur at any lab facility. These comprised the criteria for setting up their laboratory.

The university lab would be the watchdog of all stem-cell research. Every lab connected to NIH in any way, and hopefully all other labs, would keep their lab informed of both successes and failures. It was going to be a tremendous undertaking, and Val told Annie she did not envy her job, but there was no doubt that Annie would be successful.

During the period the United States had its hands tied by the government's ban on stem-cell research, UK, China, Korea, and Singapore had forged ahead to become the epicenters of stem-cell research. During the hiatus, many USA scientists had gone to these centers to continue their work. Most had now returned.

Now scientists generally concede that the United States will again be accepted as the leader in scientific research and likely would become the hub of most upcoming important discoveries.

CHAPTER 51

VAL ARRIVED HOME AND WALKED around the house trying to decide what to fix for dinner. Nothing sounded good at home, so maybe they would go out. She really needed to vent about the attack, the new laboratory, and the campaign. She wanted an update on any fallout from the press report on the attack. She started thinking about Mexican food, green-chili enchiladas in particular. That decided, she picked up a book and sat down to wait for Ron. Ron agreed to go to Renaldos, their favorite Mexican restaurant.

Ron mentioned it would not be easy to talk in Renaldos, as it was always crowded and noisy. Val said she would ask for a back table and they would be okay. At Renaldos they were seated and munching on warm, homemade tostadas and salsa while Ron quickly brought Val up-to-date on the campaign. Some way or another, the Gonzo campaign obviously had not picked up on Steve's name being publicized as her assistant.

The campaign kept heating up. His committee agreed that Ron had to make a definitive statement about the stem-cell lab. Ron suggested that Val just start explaining lab work on stem-cell research. "I guess I have to know enough to talk with people who don't know anything about it," he said. That only drew a smile from her. It wasn't good enough for a laugh.

When dinners were served, they immediately started in on the blue corn enchiladas and chili rellenos and went on with their discussion.

Val said that the most important thing about stem cells was endless potential. At the present time most countries were trying to establish regulating bodies. The Human Fertilization and Embryology Authority (HFEA) regulated the embryonic stem-cell research in the UK. Germany also had set up some controlling factors. A stem-cell registry already existed, providing ethical guidelines, stem-cell education, and training sites. Not all provided support. Research and Health Care, a national organization for protecting human life, opposed stem-cell research. The Vatican had come out in opposition of stem-cell research, as well as several other conservative religious organizations.

"We face the dawn of regenerative medicine," Val said. "Instead of insulin pumps, new insulin-producing cells would be used, real cartilage would replace titanium joints, and maybe even spinal cord patients will walk again."

She noted that, of course, there were downsides. A young boy who had been cured of his disease had several months later grown tumors at some five sites away of the targeted area. A fifty-eight-year-old with congestive heart failure had shown only 30 percent improvement instead of complete recovery. This, of course, indicated the cells were not predictable in all cases, and for some reason, certain cell lines failed to do what they were programmed to do. It seems in some cases there is no guarantee that effects are lasting.

Val went on to say that technical problems had cropped up. Websites had started advertising stem-cell replacement that would make a person healthy and take thirty years off life for only $30,000. If the first treatment doesn't work, the second would be performed for only $12,000. Most of these operations would be investigated by appropriate regulatory agencies, and those not meeting qualifications in the United States would be changed or shut down. Val was convinced that the pros of stem-cell research outweighed the cons. She felt scientists could control the negative factors, and people all over the world would benefit from this exciting research.

Citing one last statistic, Val said that the general scientific consensus for embryos was that they turned into a fetus at eight weeks. The sticking point has been the disagreement on when life begins. Does life begin at eight weeks, or does it begin when the egg is fertilized?

Ron told Val he really had benefitted from her information and felt he could now formulate his remarks. He ordered some bread pudding and asked if he could use Val as a sounding board for expressing a position.

"My political position is simple," he said. "I'm not going to change the way extremists feel about stem-cell research. No matter if the main purpose of the lab is to certify the stem cell as being usable without defects or other problems. The extremists will fight to close the lab. It was exactly like *Roe v. Wade*. There was no middle ground. I strongly support the university's efforts to establish and operate a national stem-cell lab.

"As for the election, we face one opponent now, Gonzo." Ron pointed out that Gonzo had not stated his position on stem-cell research. Ron suspected that either his position would be against it, or he would state that further study needed to be performed before he could take a position. The latter position seemed the most likely. It had the advantage of keeping those against stem-cell research leaning toward him, since Ron's position will be well-known, but will not harm him with the other voters.

Turnout is light in municipal elections. All the extremists would turn out. Fortunately, there were not many extremists, probably 2 percent of the total public. Ron said that they just have to concede that vote to Gonzo. They will win by explaining to the public the advantages of having a lab to the city and use a little scare tactic of the possible dire consequences of not having the lab in operation. They have to get more of their voters to the polls than Gonzo's voters. That's just organization and why they have Charles and Mike on their side. They are their insurance for a win, unless Ron screws up, but he said he won't allow that to happen.

Val said that she thought statements made along the line he presented would be received favorably by the public.

Ron paid the bill, left a generous tip, and they left for home. Working his way out, he shook hands or waved to other diners.

CHAPTER 52

MAX, STUD, AND DAVIS HAD spent the rest of Tuesday night at the Brown crime scene. After the coroner left, the bodies were bagged and tagged and carried away by ambulance to the morgue. Davis had rousted a judge and obtained a search warrant for Brown's house and property.

They first searched Brown's office, located in an alcove next to the living room. It contained a desk and two file cabinets, each having two drawers, along with a comfortable chair. A landline telephone and stacks of file folders were scattered on the desk. Most of the folders contained lists of voters, campaign material, and news clippings. The top of the desk held financial records, insurance papers, and contracts. A tree of life Oriental carpet covered the wood floor. Brown had been a financial advisor and consultant.

A thorough search of the other rooms in the house had not been completed that evening, so it continued this morning. Daylight seemed to work better for searches, even though adequate light could be set up at night; the detectives did better in daylight.

Frustration from lack of evidence in the house increased until the search moved outside in the area where the perp had waited. Clothing fibers were found on two thin limbs of a sickly looking bush. These were bagged and taken to the lab. Four messages were found on the phone recorder, but all were related to election matters.

A few items and files were bagged and tagged for later review, but crime-scene evidence, except for the fibers and two 9 mm bullet casings, proved nonexistent.

After returning to the station, the team discussed the scene and the crime. Davis remarked, "The simplicity of the murder, the lack of evidence, and thoroughness were more like a professional hit than an amateur. I guess it could have been a smart amateur, but not likely." This made sense to the team. The lack of evidence could be considered evidence of a professional hit.

Following normal routine, Max assigned Stud and Davis to trace the activities of Brown the last few days, and each assumed certain interview assignments. Fortunately, Brown was well organized. His scheduled activities were noted in his daily and weekly calendars, with names and phone numbers. Additional officers had been assigned to canvas the neighborhood to ask residents if anything unusual, such as suspicious cars or people, had been observed recently. Nothing was discovered.

Max reminded Stud that pressure needed to be kept on Simon. Stud asked that another person be assigned to the team for at least a few days so that the momentum on the Johnson case would not be lost because of the Brown case. Max agreed to ask the chief for someone.

CHAPTER 53

A T THE CHIEF'S OFFICE, MAX brought up the request for an additional detective, pointing out that Brown and his partner made three murders in less than two weeks under investigation, plus two others that have been under investigation. The homicide division needed more manpower. Overtime would eat up the budget and result in worn-out investigators. The chief asked some questions and then finally asked where Max would find a qualified person who could be brought up to speed quickly.

Max suggested asking the sheriff about loaning a detective. The chief said that he preferred keeping complete control of his department. Max then brought up Steve's name as a temporary employee and outlined his qualifications and activities closely related to the Brown murders. He requested that the chief authorize approaching Steve with an offer as a temporary, restricted detective. No gun, just the badge. The chief agreed.

Max telephoned Steve. "Ace, how would you like to be an investigator with us? I'm talking about being a sworn officer. We need another one, and the chief has authorized me to offer the temporary position to you. I am aware that spring break has started and you are busy with the lab, but you deserve to have a little fun also. Besides, you can learn how real detectives work."

At first, Steve was hesitant, but he thought about it. Val had requested he investigate, but to date, lack of credentials, such as a badge, had hindered him. He accepted.

Now that he worked in Annie's lab, he took the matter to her. She raised several questions about how he would handle his lab obligations while expanding his investigative work. Steve pointed out that he now mainly supervised two of the new lab assistants performing the experiments. He would continue monitoring their work and perform detective work without interruption. After he pointed out that the detective work was temporary, Annie agreed. Val concurred, of course.

CHAPTER 54

MAX HAD ASKED STEVE TO come down to be sworn in and sign his employment papers. After he had completed the process, he and Max entered the detective quarters and met with Stud and Davis.

They discussed assignments, and Max stated that he would take the lead on the Brown case, with Stud concentrating on the Johnson case. Davis and Steve would work as assigned, which would depend on developments. There were two other cases, but they were at a point where they could be placed on hold for a week or so. The mayor would work with Max.

The grunt work, as Davis had previously described it, was attacked with vigor. Later that day, while checking messages, Max saw a phone message from Don Delaney, one of three city policemen assigned to the Centerville Drug Task Force.

In an effort to assure coordination between law enforcements related to drugs and drug gangs in the district along or near the Mexican border, the federal government, headed by the FBI and DEA, had formed task forces of law enforcement organizations in certain areas, such as Centerville and El Paso. Two task forces existed because Centerville was two hundred miles north of the border.

When he returned Delaney's call, Delaney informed Max of Roberto Olivas being in town the previous day. He identified

Olivas as a drug cartel hit man out of Juarez/El Paso and suggested Max pull up his file.

According to the report from the task force, the feds had tried to place Olivas under surveillance but had lost him. He had checked out of his motel before they could set it up. Even so, Max put a secretary to work checking motels for a person registered as Olivas, making sure he had not reregistered. Later, she reported no luck.

Since Delaney had mentioned that Olivas came from El Paso, Max started thinking there were too many coincidences popping up between Johnson and Brown. Like most policemen, Max did not believe in coincidence, but he had confidence in his hunches, and for him, Olivas became a hot lead.

Stud had arranged a meeting with Simon. He would review his movements yesterday. He drove out to Martinez Construction Company, parked next to the office, withdrew his .38 special, and exited the car. The dog was on his chain on the far end of the building, so he holstered his weapon.

Stud skipped greetings. "A murder occurred last night. I need to know where you were between eight o'clock and ten o'clock last evening."

Simon reported, "Well, I took the wife and kids up to Santa Fe to visit with her sister and family. We visit each other frequently. It's only an hour's drive. They are quite close, and I get along with the husband well. We hunt elk together each year. We arrived back home about eleven."

As he drove back to headquarters, Stud decided that it all sounded too good. Probably planned. Checking further with Simon's relatives, he confirmed the alibi.

Stud decided to carry out a search warrant for Simon's office and house and asked Davis to go with him. They started with the office first. While reviewing Simon's financial records, they discovered two $7,000 bank withdrawals. When questioned, Simon said he loaned the money to his brother, Tomas, who had a financial emergency of some kind, probably gambling.

Stud reported the results of his search to Max, who called for a meeting with the mayor, chief, and the homicide detectives. He noted the possible connection of the two murder cases through

Simon. That is, Simon had a relationship with Johnson, and he had sent money to his brother in El Paso. A hit man from El Paso had been in town the day of the Brown murders and left that day. Delany had informed him Simon's brother was drug cartel connected.

The mayor asked for the brother's name.

"Tomas," responded Max. "He's with the Lopez-Carbona cartel. Another cartel was trying to move into their territory. Blood has been spilled big time. Tomas's position in the cartel was unknown, but task force reports stated he wholesaled drugs and laundered money. This case could balloon into other crime areas, such as drugs. DEA and even FBI may become involved and possibly slow things down. Of course, the vast resources of the feds should help us.

"After reviewing the reports, we may need a trip down to El Paso. First, we need to discuss the possible directions this case may take."

He asked the chief to contact Chief Sedillo in El Paso to make sure they did not surprise him when his El Paso Task Force representatives briefed him

"God, I hope we don't have to take on a whole cartel to get this bastard, but we will get him, regardless."

Steve asked what role Max wanted him to play.

Max responded, "You be Cool Hand Luke. I don't think you can handle Dirty Harry. But seriously, I think we need another look at the material taken from Simon's office. You might find something our astute detectives missed. Actually, that's unlikely, but it needs to be done. We need a trip to El Paso."

When Ron was notified of the Juarez hit man development, he said he would go with Max to the task force meeting but could not stay overnight. He pointed out that his FBI contacts may prove helpful. The chief said he had conflicts and could not go.

The chief called Sedillo, visited a moment, and then outlined his case. Sedillo offered cooperation and said that he would have a packet of information put together as well and have it faxed to Centerville.

Pirwarsky thanked him and said he would reciprocate if ever needed. As he arose from his chair to leave, Max said, "Chief, I think we are on the way to solving this thing."

CHAPTER 55

D ELANEY, AT MAX'S REQUEST, FAXED Max all the task force reports on the Carbona cartel and Olivas. While reviewing the reports, Max learned that the Carbona cartel was the oldest of two in Juarez. Turf fights between the two caused one or two murders daily. Olivas was heavily involved. The reports did not list individually how many people he had killed, but they estimated over fifty.

The reports included photographs and resumes of known cartel members, including Tomas Martinez and Roberto Olivas. Martinez was listed as an El Paso drug wholesaler and Olivas as enforcer and assassin. Olivas also had been extorting protection money from businesses along Juarez streets. For now, cartel murder apparently remained on the Mexican side of the border. Federal agencies kept close watch on such activities because strong organized cartel fights could easily spill across the border. Many Juarez citizens were moving to El Paso as a safe harbor from all the violence in Juarez.

Delaney noted that the FBI in El Paso had concurred with his request for studying the potential connection of the cartel and the Centerville murder. RICO may apply. He had pointed out that RICO, the Racketeer Influenced and Corrupt Organization Act of 1970, existed as a tool to prove an organization existed primarily for criminal purposes. Conviction of persons employed in such organizations can be and are given jail time. A known killer, such as Olivas, may be subject to the death penalty if convicted of murder.

When Max reviewed this information, he was relieved to see more manpower apparently being assigned to the case. He happily reported the FBI activity to his team. He noted that the FBI had a reputation for taking control and ignoring local law enforcement agencies, but in this case, with both national and international implications, he welcomed FBI control. The mayor can help keep cooperation under control. He instructed Steve to contact Delaney to inform him that Centerville police would send a report to the FBI outlining the status of its investigation and then prepare the report for his review.

"Write it, leaving out all your medical terms 'cause no one will understand them," Max said with a smile.

The task force information listed Olivas as an American citizen who had numerous Mexican relatives. He qualified as American because his mother was in El Paso when he was born. He happened to be the only one of his siblings born in the USA. Dropping out of school after six grades, he joined a gang. One of his sisters had murdered another woman in Mexico two years ago and was serving a life sentence in a Mexican prison. His mother was upset over her prison term.

A noteworthy item in the report was the fact that it originally was impractical to try to insert an undercover agent in a Mexican cartel because the cartel, when established, was composed of close families, going back for generations in some cases. Information was gathered through cartel members who became disloyal for many reasons, such as personal slights or insults, lover spats, fear, jealousy, or ambition. Cartel growth in recent years had brought in members not family related. Other interdictions come from drug buys made by the DEA and other undercover agents. Another interesting item in the report noted that a DEA office existed in the American embassy in Juarez. No incursions into El Paso for murder had been identified. At this time, the cartels had kept their fights in Mexico.

The leaders apparently tried to avoid encountering the vast arm of US law enforcement. The question was will this attitude change in the future? Will the crime fight spill over the border now that it appeared a cartel member killed in the United States?

Max was impressed by the amount of information compiled by the FBI task forces. He foresaw the advantage of working within and through the El Paso task force in bringing Roberto Olivas and Simon Martinez to justice. It now was imperative, he decided, that he ask for help from the task force.

He started with Delaney, asking him to arrange the meeting. Delaney called back with a proposed meeting in El Paso, at the DEA offices on Monday at 11:00 a.m. Proposed attendees were the DEA, FBI, El Paso police, El Paso County sheriff, Juarez police, Centerville police, and Immigration and Customs Enforcement (ICE).

Max phoned the chief to tell him the meeting in El Paso had been arranged. The chief called the mayor, gave him the information, and the mayor said that he and Max could fly down Monday morning. Max would have the lead in presenting the city's case, and again mentioned that he would use his FBI connections. The chief concurred, called Max, informed him of the mayor's trip, and suggested Max ask Lupe to arrange the trip, airfare, and one night's lodging for him. The mayor asked Lupe to schedule a late-afternoon return flight.

Max, Stud, Steve, and Davis brainstormed the presentation, and Max prepared an outline for his remarks.

He went over the outline with Delaney. Delaney noted that the El Paso Task Force chairman was Josh Thompson of the FBI, and he was a friend of the mayor.

The agenda was approved and routed to task force members. Max then updated the chief.

Later that afternoon, Max and Steve went out for a beer. Stud and Davis, who had personal matters to attend to, had gone home.

After sitting down in the pub, Steve ordered a fresh beer.

Max asked, "What is a fresh beer?"

Steve said, "I thought you would never ask. A fresh beer is one that gets you smacked."

Max groaned, "Ace, my love life sucks. These murders have taken so much time that I barely have the energy to crawl in bed for sleep, and Barb, my girlfriend, may be looking for someone who has time for her. I haven't even talked with her since last Monday."

"The same for me. I did call Sally to let her know I am back from Washington, but that is all. Listen, Max, I have a problem. Apparently, Sally hasn't found out I work for the wife of the mayor. It's surprising she hasn't found out. A couple of newspaper articles mentioned my name in reporting on the new lab. When she finds out, she will remember comments she has made to me that could have been harmful to Gonzo's campaign. She will be pissed. I mean, really pissed."

"Wow," said Max. "From what I know about Sally, I would not want to be around when she first finds out, but, Ace, what is your reaction to our murder cases and the turn they have taken?"

"I think this kind of thing is what makes your job so interesting, Max. Look at what happened. You start out with a common murder situation, a likely lover's quarrel getting violent, and you now have the complete law enforcement community for a large area ready to come to your aid. It's as if the cavalry were riding over the hill, charging into battle. If Custer had this kind of backup, he may have won at Little Bighorn."

"Yeah," Max said, "with the number of people scheduled at the Monday meeting, all we will need would be the horses. One of the things I wonder is whether the cartel will hear about the meeting and results. Juarez police also attend some of the task force meetings, I am told, and some of them likely are on the cartel payroll. I would hate for Olivas to get word and disappear."

Steve responded, "Why not discuss your concern privately with the chairman?"

"I'll try to do that, maybe before the meeting."

"Now who is going to pay for this beer?" Steve questioned, laughing and taking out his billfold.

"See you tomorrow. Sally and I have a date. Good luck on yours."

Steve and Sally were returning to her apartment after a nice dinner and movie. They discussed the pleasant evening, and Steve had managed to avoid disclosing the real reason for his

Washington trip by saying he was looking into employment possibilities there. He planned to look into employment at several places over the next year. After arriving at the apartment, Steve said that he needed to catch up on his drinks and poured a strong scotch on the rocks. He fixed Sally a drink. They snuggled together on the couch with their drinks, and all was well in their world.

CHAPTER 56

WHEN GONZO HEARD ABOUT BROWN'S death, he made a public announcement similar to the mayor's. He lauded Brown as an honorable person, noted the similarity of his and Brown's campaign platform, deplored the violent act, and stated he would be in touch constantly with the police chief to assure that the killer is apprehended.

He immediately called his committee, now composed of himself, Sally, and Johnny, to plan capturing Brown's supporters. Steve had not been invited. At Sally's suggestion, Gonzo telephoned the chairman of Brown's campaign, Wes Benson, to request a meeting in the afternoon.

Gonzo, Sally, and Johnny were greeted by Benson and the four people who comprised his committee.

Gonzo made his proposal. "We all admired Will Brown, a great and good man. He was running an excellent campaign. Our platforms were so similar I found it difficult to question and attack him. This similarity even hindered promoting my message. With such similarities, we should join our campaigns. Even prior to Will's death, I was considering this since it appeared to be the only way Ron Steadman could be unseated. A new poll showed Will with 42 percent, me with 10 percent, and Steadman with the rest. Together, we have a better chance. I am willing to sit with you, learn your concerns, and make suitable changes in my campaign platform. I see no major changes since our positions are so close."

Benson stated, "I agree that your platform and promises are close to Will's. We have a little over two weeks before the election. How can we effectively promote the merger in such a short time?"

Gonzo was ready with his answer. "We go out on two fronts. The first is a media blitz with a theme of keeping Will's promises alive, and I am the only option available to do so. The second is a strong message of my mayoral qualifications, especially in the environmental arena." Gonzo hoped his comment about the second front would be the cincher. Benson appeared receptive.

Benson said he and his committee needed to discuss the proposal privately. Since time was so short, they would give Gonzo a decision within one or two hours. "If we come in, you have to accept we will be major role players in the campaign and in the new administration."

"No problem there," said Gonzo. "Sally can meet with you at any time to review your suggestions and make necessary commitments."

In the car driving back to his office, Gonzo said, "I think they will buy the package. Sally, start planning our new campaign, and think about what we can afford to give up in a merger."

Before the two hours expired, Wes Benson called to say the committee agreed to merge but would release all individuals who had committed to Brown, so they could decide for themselves whether to support Gonzo.

Gonzo said he would have Sally work with Benson to iron out details and develop the new campaign.

Benson continued, "The merger is approved on the condition that the Brown organization will be given the selection of the new planning and zoning director and the first three positions that open up on the Planning and Zoning Commission. The Brown people also want veto power over the parks and recreation director appointment. If this is acceptable, we have a deal."

Gonzo was somewhat shocked with the demands but saw no alternative. He accepted the conditions. "If you agree, Sally will call you to set a time for a joint news conference to announce the merger."

"That's fine," said Benson. "Let's hope the tide will turn."

Gonzo took Sally and Johnny out for a drink to celebrate and hinted that Sally's company would be welcome that evening. Expecting Steve to call, she pleaded a previous commitment. He instructed her to set up the joint news conference for the next afternoon, timed for the five-o'clock news shows.

Sally went home to wait for Steve's call. Turning on the TV for the five-o'clock news, she saw the newscaster announce that the new laboratory director for stem-cell evaluation at the university medical school will be Dr. Valerie Steadman. Steve Janson, a doctoral student, who also was Steadman's lab assistant, had assisted Dr. Steadman in obtaining the grant expanding the lab. He would continue in that position. Several new lab positions will be created and filled.

Sally was utterly shocked. She collapsed on the couch. After a few minutes, she collected herself but felt her temperature rising.

"That son of a bitch! He treated me like a fool or a puppet on a string." But Sally then admitted to herself she had been foolish by not checking Steve out. This made her angrier.

Pacing her living room floor, Sally tried to calm down. She started mentally reviewing some of the conversations she and Steve had held and considered only one or two comments that could have been detrimental to the Gonzo campaign. One was identifying Simon as the panty organizer. Since Simon was gone, that didn't hurt anything. The other was the bus conversion program, and if Steve had anything to do with the city's announcement, it still worked to the advantage of the campaign, preventing a possible campaign gaffe.

Her anger diminished a little but came back strong when she connected her sex life to the campaign. She had slept with the enemy, for crying out loud. *I ought to make a eunuch out of him.* She started pacing again, trying to get control of herself. *No good, can't concentrate. When he calls what should I do? I'll just brush the worm off and concentrate even harder on winning the election.*

The phone rang. She answered.

"Hi, Sa—," Steve began.

Sally interrupted, saying, "You bastard! I just saw you on the news." She couldn't continue. Her eyes filled with tears, so she hung up. She willed herself not to cry but couldn't stop.

Steve tried to call again, but Sally didn't answer. He gave up. This had to happen, but he missed her already. He called Max to tell him it was over with Sally.

Max passed it off. "You knew this was coming. What's the big deal?"

"I treated her like shit and I feel awful," Steve replied.

Max gave no quarter. "You ought to feel bad, shows you have a conscience. Just get over it, Ace. Go on to bigger and better things. I guess I won't be double-dating with you and Sally."

It turned out that Steve didn't feel guilty long. He went to the lab. As he entered, Annie Kim, working at a bench, looked up and, with a big smile, said, "Hi."

Steve felt his knees go weak and his heart thump. He said, "Hi to you. How are your cells performing?"

Annie, still smiling, said, "Perfectly. Take a look."

Annie was already in the lab working when Val arrived the next morning. Steve arrived a few minutes later.

"Good morning, Annie," Steve said and went straight into Val's office. "My spy caper is over. Sally saw a news report, I guess, and cut me out.

"On my part in doing the spy thing, everything was for a purpose but became fun. As I got to know Sally we became intimate and I admire her. It's tough knowing that she now thinks I am the pits, and I guess I am."

Val said, "Steve, you were only following through on my request to discover who masterminded the panty incident. Sally gave you important information helpful to our campaign. Look at it as a side issue that you became involved and fond of someone who after all was working for our opponent, and Sally had to learn of your complicity at some point. Well, you've arrived, and both you and Sally will survive and move on. You carried out your assignment. Ron and I appreciate your work."

CHAPTER 57

THE GONSOLIC-BROWN MERGER NEWS CONFERENCE the next day became the lead headline for all the radio and TV stations and the morning paper. Charles called Ron immediately upon hearing the news. He broke into a meeting Ron was holding with Art and one of his assistants on council relations. Ron called the meeting off. Charles told him he and Mike had just been discussing approaching Benson about his support, but obviously, Gonzo had beat them to the starting line.

"Shit, we should have moved faster," Ron said.

At the news conference, a news reporter had asked Benson why his group chose Gonsolic over Steadman. Benson responded, "Gonzo's environmental position is close to our position. We have more in common with him than we do with Steadman."

News people started calling Ron for his comments on the merger.

After consultation with Ron, Charles prepared a news release for Ron that stated, "I just learned that some of Will Brown's supporters have joined the Gonsolic campaign. We will welcome everyone who wants to join our campaign. My position on issues has not changed. My efforts and time will continue as before. I have listed the accomplishments of our administration these past three years and have and will continue to state the programs we will concentrate on during the next four years. I am running a positive campaign, trying with every resource we have to explain to our citizens how important my proposals are to the economic health and posterity of our great city and how these can be accomplished without diminishing our important environmental programs. I welcome the support of all citizens in striving for the accomplishment of our common goals."

The next afternoon, Gonzo called a news conference challenging Ron to a special debate on issues.

When asked for his response, Ron stated, "I would rather hear Gonzo explain why his programs would be better than mine. This might not be accomplished in a debate. At least, not much was accomplished in the two debates already held. He has skirted the issues so far, preferring personal attacks. But I will have my staff contact his staff to arrange a debate. Maybe we can learn more about how he would govern the city."

CHAPTER 58

FRIDAY EVENING, RON AND VAL attended a political event. The congressman for Centerville held a fund-raiser dinner for Ron at the Centerville Country Club. As they drove to the club, Ron mentioned to Val how such fund-raisers were vital to a successful campaign, but their existence was ironic in some ways.

"Tonight, the purpose is to raise money for me. Next spring, during the run-up to the primary, I will be obligated to hold a fund-raiser for the congressman and will be expected to make a nice contribution to his campaign. The contribution must be at least as much as his is to me. This way we both can raise additional funds without the donors feeling we have our hands in their pockets. If I held all my own fund-raisers instead of others holding them, I couldn't raise as much money, and even if I did, there might be resentment or a feeling that they are buying me.

"Politicians explain large contributions as not buying votes, only access to us. Think about it. If one person has access but another does not, who has the audience? Fund-raising is a necessary evil. I wish there were a better way."

"You have a point," Val replied. "I believe our system becomes worse the further the distance from the voters. A governor is more remote than a mayor. A congressman and senator are more remote than a governor. Special interests have the most influence at the national level because of the remoteness and distance. You, as mayor, cannot avoid the spotlight of any voter. You are right here with the voters. They can hear and watch everything you do. You have to listen to and respect their comments."

They arrived at the country club, the valet parked their car, and they entered the well-appointed social room of the club. Golf paintings and photos covered the white walls. One wall held an enlarged photograph of a local professional putting the ball in a national tournament. Chandeliers glowed brightly. Dining tables, set up with four, six, and eight chairs, were placed around the room. The congressman and his wife greeted them effusively and pointed out the head table.

Congressman Handley looked healthy in a well-tailored black suit, white shirt, and natty bow tie. His ruddy, round face looked as if he had received a facial massage. What white hair he had left provided a nice top to his smiling face. His wife, Helga, wore a beautiful white dress, pleated down the front with a bare back. She had beautiful blonde hair framing her demure face. Her smile was most welcoming. Ron kissed her cheek and told her she looked beautiful.

Ron then started working the room by greeting and shaking hands. He came upon Julie Carrico, who apparently was there by herself. He didn't see John Carrico. He thought back to Charles's comment about divorce and concluded that the separation had started. Both Ron and Congressman Handley made speeches after introductions, and contribution pledges were received, even though the cost of the dinner was $100 per person. After several other speeches, Ron made his campaign speech. The dinner broke up, and most people stayed for dancing to a local band hired for the occasion.

Ron told Val about the Carrico situation on the way home as they discussed the evening's events. After they arrived home, Ron told Val how upset he was about Will Brown and reviewed for her the comments he would make the next day at Brown's memorial service. He would give many compliments and deplore the loss of such a fine person. He would say that no one who kills deserves to live in our society.

"The police are working hard on the case, and I have joined the detective team."

Val laughed, "You just can't stay away from a criminal investigation. It's like Old Home Week."

"There may be something to that. I believe, however, I can contribute to solving the case."

Ron moved on to the debate set for Sunday, saying, "I am not too concerned about the debate. The only thing new is the establishment of the stem-cell research lab, and we have thoroughly discussed it. My statement supporting it has been released, so I have to be consistent with my public statement when responding to questions."

CHAPTER 59

THE DEBATE WAS SET AT the convention center, in a room holding about two hundred people. Since the debate time was 6:00 p.m., and the TV competition was college basketball playoffs, Ron did not expect much interest, either from people attending or the TV audience. One of the local TV stations was sponsoring the debate. The station consistently won the annual award for best news casting. A longtime news anchor for the station acted as debate moderator. Charles had tried to stack the audience with Ron's supporters, as Sally had with Gonzo's supporters. Both Ron and Gonzo greeted people attending.

The room was about half full when the moderator started the session by introducing the two debaters. He then laid out the ground rules. Introductory remarks were limited to five minutes and then audience questions and then concluding remarks of five minutes each. Gonzo lost the coin flip and went first with opening remarks. While the moderator was presenting the introductions and other preliminary matters, Ron looked around the audience and saw Steve and Annie sitting with Val.

Gonzo zoned into his candidate role. By this time in the race, of course, both candidates had their speeches fine-tuned; and Gonzo made his case for changing mayors by criticizing Ron's record and his administrative approach as being too controlling.

He said, "He doesn't delegate decision making down to the proper level, yet he pays his management people high salaries, indicating they are competent enough to make decisions on how to operate their departments. He either ought to cut their pay or let them earn the money. According to news reports, even city council members have complained that the mayor encroaches on their decision making." He explained in general terms how he would govern, especially emphasizing a broader and larger program for open space and more emphasis on environmental improvements.

Ron paid polite attention and appeared to be listening closely. Knowing him so well, Val knew he was reworking his remarks to counter the accusations without appearing to be defensive.

Another accusation made was toward Ron's inability to carry out his promise of working with the school board and administrators in education improvement. This was an Achilles' heel for Ron. He had run into clever stonewalling by the school people on every overture he had made. The school system was separate from the city government. The city had no sticks, big or small. The only effective carrot was dedicating city money to the schools, and money was always short.

Gonzo directed his final attack toward the protection of the water supply by better conservation programs and concluded, "I can solve these problems. I will work with the US Forest Service for more open space. I will fund parks adequately. Water conservation will be a top priority. I will replace department heads not doing their jobs. Then the directors will run their departments, not me.

"My fellow citizens, let me repeat, I can solve these problems. About twenty-five years ago, I bought a small electronics business and made it a thriving business. Now we own six stores and are still growing. Being in charge of the city government is not much different from other businesses. What I am trying to do is show you I can do the best job of taking Centerville to the next generation. Thank you."

Ron took the floor. He started out, "Ladies and gentlemen"—he hesitated for a few seconds—"goodness gracious, based on what other people have said, I thought my administration had

195

been doing a great job of running the city government. Yet we now have been informed that I am running the city down the tubes. What a letdown, if true. But could it be the person making the charges is running against me for mayor? Are the charges substantiated by the record? He obviously thinks we have flopped, but I submit he is wrong. Our record over the last three years, although not perfect, shows an entirely different picture from the one just presented.

"First, let's discuss decision making and how it really works in city hall under my leadership. I do make many decisions. Nearly all of them involve policy direction for city activities. I believe I have good working relationships with department heads. They run their departments under the policies set by the city council and me. At times, if there is a question on policy, the department head brings the matter to me for a decision. He also brings to me one or more proposed solutions. He knows I want his input. A decision is made. He carries out the decision. In short, on matters of policy or policy interpretation, I welcome and receive the recommendations of those who should be involved in the decision.

"Many times recommendations may differ between those involved or affected by the decision. To resolve the differences, I make the decision. President Harry Truman had a sign on his desk saying 'The buck stops here.' Well, in city government, the buck stops with the mayor. Since the charter does not spell out what is administrative and what isn't, council members and the mayor sometimes disagree on who should make a policy decision. Naturally, both try to be protective of their territory. Every council and mayor must expect an occasional disagreement on authority questions. Remember though, councilors represent districts, but the mayor represents the whole city. The irony of my opponent's accusation on control is this. If I were not making decisions, he would have been up here clamoring that I am wishy-washy. I submit his comment on control and decision making raises the question of whether or not he understands what is entailed in such matters. I personally would not want a mayor who deferred decisions he or she should be making to those who are under his or her supervision, who are not—and I repeat, *are not*—elected by our citizens to make those decisions."

Ron proceeded to stress that campaigning is different from governing. The former required commitments on what one would do. The latter was the doing or carrying out the commitments.

"No one is perfect. I have listed for you my promises made during the last election and where we stand on the commitments. I estimate we have accomplished 85 to 90 percent of the goals.

"The only commitment not accomplished is education improvement. We are working on addressing how we can assist the school board and its administration. Remember though, they must agree to accept our assistance by contract, because we have no authority over the schools. We have made overtures and will keep working to find mutual grounds for an agreement. Another meeting with school officials for discussion of new proposals has been scheduled. Education includes higher education. Just last week I met with President McKinley at the university. We discussed areas of concern, identified those we feel are most urgent, and have started working on those. You will be hearing about them shortly.

"Regarding open space," Ron continued, "we are all in favor of expanding open space, and the first forty acres were obtained last year. My opponent and I agree we need more, and more will be obtained if I am elected. The same attention will be given to water conservation. Water is the nectar of life. It must be conserved.

"In conclusion, let me repeat, we accomplished about 90 percent of our goals set for the first term. We want to finish the job and accomplish goals I have identified for my next term. I am asking you for another four years to work on your behalf, and I trust my record warrants your supporting vote to do that. Thank you."

Roy Smith, the moderator, said, "Gentlemen, we thank you for your opening remarks. I am sure we have interesting questions. I will ask the first question to get us started. Mayor, you mentioned economic prosperity. What do you have planned for your next four years to enhance our economic conditions as we grow? After you respond, Mr. Gonsolic will comment."

"Growth is a given. We can't stop it if we wanted to. The question is whether or not our city limits expand. If not, it occurs in unincorporated areas or in our neighboring cities. I prefer that our city limits expand but those who control development money make the final decision."

Gonzo replied, "Growth isn't always good. We have to make sure our existing citizens are protected environmentally when approving growth."

A young female stood up, introduced herself as Ann Abeyta, a reporter, and asked, "Mayor, would you comment on the so-called panty incident that occurred in your office recently and the subsequent murder of the woman?"

"I will comment, although I feel this incident has been thoroughly discussed. We performed a detailed investigation into who instigated the incident because I did not know the person except to greet her as a volunteer worker in our campaign office. We found evidence that the incident was a political trick set up by a person who at that time worked on the Gonsolic campaign. You'll have to ask my opponent whether he was a party to planning the incident. Let me state that the murder investigation is proceeding. The police chief has been keeping me informed daily. He expects charges will be filed in the near future."

Gonzo responded that he had nothing to do with the panty incident. When reported to him, he severed connections with the person alleged to be behind it.

Further questions addressed matters and positions discussed in previous debates. The candidates made their final pitch for votes, and the debate ended with each side claiming victory.

CHAPTER 60

T HE PREVIOUS FRIDAY, MAX, THE chief, and the mayor had prepared for the El Paso trip to meet with the task force.

Ron stated that he intended to discuss the investigation informally with Josh Thompson, the task force chair and the lead FBI agent in El Paso, noting that he and Thompson had worked together on a couple of cases while Ron was an agent, and they respected each other.

Max, Ron, and Delaney met at the airport early Monday morning for the short flight to El Paso. Ron planned to attend the meeting and discussions most of the day and then fly back to Centerville. Max and Delaney would spend the night in El Paso in case other matters would be pursued on Tuesday. A rental car took them to the federal building housing the FBI offices and other federal agencies.

They proceeded to the security stop in the building lobby, using their police ID cards for clearance, and then rode an elevator upstairs to a fifth-floor conference room.

Max had telephoned Thompson on Friday asking for a brief conference with him prior to the task force meeting.

The three were ushered into a large room, the director's office, by a nice-looking middle-aged secretary. Max glanced around quickly and saw two windows on the two sides facing east and south, offering views of downtown, the Rio Grande River, and Juarez. A haze of industrial pollutants hung over Juarez city like a light-gray blanket, almost extending into downtown El Paso. Population wise, the over one million population of Juarez dwarfed the three hundred thousand plus of El Paso.

Director Thompson stood up from his desk to greet them, and he seemed pleased to see the mayor. Thompson wore a black suit with a white shirt and a conservative tie. He sat down behind his massive desk after inviting the delegation to have seats. Max glanced around the office. In addition to the desk and chair, a small conference table with four chairs sat on the other side of the room. The credenza behind the desk held photos of a woman and three children, a photo of a young male in a cap and gown, and a telephone.

Max observed several framed citations, awards, and diplomas on the wall behind the desk. One, a diploma from Harvard Law School, impressed Max. On the other wall were three paintings illustrating southwestern landscapes. Max commented on the attractiveness of the paintings. Thompson noted that his wife painted them and said, "She is a commercial artist."

Thompson asked, "Well, gentlemen, what can I do for you today?"

Ron said that Lieutenant Maxwell had a concern.

Max stated his concern was about a potential leak through the Juarez police official on the task force.

Placing his hands together with fingertips touching, Thompson appeared to think about Max's statement for a moment, and then said, "Max, normally your concern would be justified, but I will give you some confidential information. It is important to our operations against the drug cartels that this information remains in the stated that his concern."

Max replied, "I understand, sir."

Thompson continued, "Ramirez, the Juarez assistant chief and task force member, does not have any relatives in the Lopez-Carbona cartel. He does have relatives in the Chavez-Sedillo cartel. Since Olivas is in the Lopez-Carbona cartel, we feel Chief Ramirez will assist us rather than thwart us in apprehending Olivas. I am not accusing Ramirez of colluding with the Chavez-Sedillo people. He might say something to relatives if they become targets. Then again, he might not. Family ties are strong over there though."

Josh continued, "The Juarez Police Department is heavily infiltrated by the cartels, so your concern is justified. We have some names of people we suspect are corrupt, but the task force can never have enough information, if you know what I mean. A well-informed and connected cartel member such as Olivas helping us would be a godsend."

"Sir, I appreciate your confidence. We want this guy badly," Max said.

Josh responded, "Go for it, Max. We'll get the SOB if the opposing cartel doesn't beat us to him. Al Romo is DEA point man on the Carbona cartel. He will be your main contact with DEA, and I will be your FBI contact. I suggest you meet with him after the task force conference ends."

"Thank you, sir." They all proceeded to the conference room for the task force meeting.

Max entered the conference room, noted twenty-four chairs in a circle, leaned over to Delaney, and asked if he would introduce his team to the attendees when the meeting started. Delaney said that he had already asked Thompson about that, and he would have everyone introduce themselves.

He escorted Max over to introduce him to Romo. He called to Al, who was standing to one side talking with two people, to come meet Lieutenant Maxwell. Al, a stocky Hispanic of average height and dark curly hair, greeted Max with a smile. They arranged to meet after the conference.

Thompson called out, "Let's start."

Task force members took their seats in the circle with the two Centerville police sitting beside each other.

Thompson said, "For the benefit of our new arrivals, I will mention the reason we have a circle. Everyone is equal on the task force. Every agency represented here is fighting the criminal drug industry, and all are equally important."

He continued, "First, introductions. We'll go clockwise around the circle, and I'll start."

After introductions were completed, Thompson announced why the Centerville police were present. He noted that Mayor

Ron Steadman was present, an old friend and former FBI agent. He asked Ron to take the floor.

Ron stated the reason Centerville had requested the meeting—Centerville needed help in solving a murder case. Lieutenant Maxwell, the lead investigator, will summarize the case.

Max reviewed the Brown murder case and the reasons why he believed Olivas was the perpetrator.

He then stated, "We have enough on Olivas to go after him but not enough to arrest him or make a case that would hold up in court. Obviously, if we are correct, Olivas contracted with a local Centerville person. That person is believed to be a citizen named Simon Martinez. We forwarded to you and I have reviewed for you the bank withdrawals by Martinez, the money sent to Tomas Martinez, and the association between Tomas and Olivas. We have discussed possible motives and have a favorite. We think it is political, a part of the mayoral election, and it was made to look like a hate crime against homosexuals. We would appreciate any assistance from the task force or its individual members. Are there any comments or suggestions?"

Thompson replied, "Depending on the evidence and border problems, RICO might have been violated. The cartel certainly is a criminal gang, and two gang members are possibly involved. The criminal act occurred on US soil, even though the gang is located in Mexico. I have checked with our legal people about this possibility. I have a preliminary finding that RICO does apply."

"That possibility has been mentioned to us, and we would welcome task force intervention in this case," Max said.

Chief Rameriz, the Juarez representative, stated, "My force is well-informed about Olivas and his activities. Unfortunately, Juarez cannot pursue arrest because no witness will testify against him. If one would come forward, the person likely would be killed before the case could be prosecuted."

"Another thing," the chief said, "these crooks are killing each other. Murder is murder, but the reality is we have fewer criminals when that happens. What Juarez police will do is keep Olivas under surveillance and inform the El Paso police and sheriff when he crosses the border."

Arturo Sanchez, from ICE, stated, "I too will alert the agencies when Olivas crosses the border."

Thompson stated, "The FBI will immediately set up electronic and visual surveillance on US sites Olivas visits. If he violates federal law, we will move in. If it is state or local, we will notify the local authorities and hopefully will have evidence of the violation."

Max stated, "That's good. Monitoring the Tomas Martinez business should prove worthwhile."

"I've put it on my to-do list," Thompson said.

The meeting then turned to other task force business. Max listened while members reported their programs and efforts to contain illegal drugs. After the meeting ended, Romo approached Max with the suggestion that he and the Centerville team pick up coffee and meet in his office.

The mayor stated he would visit with Thompson while they met with Romo, and left.

Romo started the discussion with a status report on the cartel crime in Juarez. "The cartels are fighting over drug dealing, extortion, and prostitution control. They're even moving into legitimate businesses, having purchased stores and hotels, for example. Local law enforcement has been corrupted or compromised along with many others."

Romo continued, "The Mexican government has sent the army to Juarez, where they are patrolling the streets. Our people believe the army has some officers on the cartel payroll but do not have names. In short, it is a real mess. The cartels are like octopuses, with tentacles everywhere. Mexican provincial law enforcement agencies are assisting local law enforcement when possible.

"One murder occurred on a street in broad daylight within sight of an army guard on the corner. The assassin drove away before the guard could respond.

"For now, the far-reaching cartel control is limited to Mexico. That does not mean they keep their drugs in Mexico. To the contrary, the cartels supply most of the drugs coming across the border. DEA feels that it is imperative that the US government assist the Mexican government in regaining control of Juarez, but we are limited by long-standing suspicions of our motives. Mexicans still remember our military invasions."

Max commented, "In Centerville, we are trying to solve three murders, while here you are trying to save entire cities and states—quite a contrast."

Romo said, "Yes, a contrast in effort and resources, but our goals are the same. We want to catch the criminals, and we will be assisting you and the FBI with your mission. You have our reports on Olivas. You will be receiving everything we learn about him as we proceed. Let's talk frequently. We should keep each other informed. Be aware that you are not limited to the task force. If direct contact is needed, we are here."

"Good point," Max said. "We will stay in close communication with you. Thanks, this has been a productive day. We will spend the night and head back to Centerville in the morning."

Ron and Josh sat down with coffee and visited old times for a few minutes, and then Ron said that it sure would be helpful if Josh could catch Olivas for a serious criminal act on US soil, something that might warrant a death penalty. Josh said that might happen, and they would watch for an opportunity.

The Centerville contingent left the building, with Max almost dancing a little jig. "Fellas, everyone makes mistakes," he said. "With the whole world watching him, we will catch the asshole Roberto Olivas when he makes his mistakes."

As they approached the car, they saw a parking ticket stuck under the windshield wiper. Max shook his head as he removed it. He looked at it and then slowly tore it in little pieces. He threw the pieces up in the air and watched the wind scatter them over the street.

Delaney said, "I hope the meter maid didn't see that. She would write a littering ticket."

"No matter," Max said, "I would do the same with it."

While they were having a beer in the hotel bar, Thompson called Max on his cell phone to inform them that RICO definitely applied in the Olivas case.

They had ordered Dos Equis in longnecks and enjoyed the first taste, as anticipated.

Ron excused himself to catch his plane to Centerville as he finished his beer.

"Let's get food out of the way. Where are we going to eat?" Max asked Delaney.

"Are you referring to country or restaurant? Based on what we learned today, I'm not crossing the border to eat. Let me ask the bartender where the closest good steak house is located." He obtained a recommendation and directions.

The next morning they met for breakfast and checked in with Romo, who had nothing new. They caught a plane back to Centerville.

After arriving back at the police station, Max gave Chief Pirwarsky his encouraging progress report and wrote up the report for the task force and murder book. He then called Barb for a dinner date. Stud headed out to Simon's construction yard to say hello and to shoot the dog if it was loose.

Steve headed to the lab to catch up on work and to enjoy seeing Annie. He felt that a relationship was developing personally as well as professionally.

Max sent Davis to follow up a tip on another case.

Meanwhile, the FBI set up surveillance on Tomas Martinez. He owned a small Internet coffee shop where people played Internet games or just surfed the net. Thompson suspected that the shop was being used for laundering cartel money as well. Late that night two wiring specialists visited the shop. They tapped the phone landline and obtained the name of his cell phone company so his cell conversations could be monitored. Listening bugs were placed in strategic spots in the shop. The Centerville FBI office handled the same arrangements for the Martinez Construction Company. While Simon was in his bank, a bug was placed in his pickup.

Juarez police set up a surveillance crew on Olivas and bugged his van.

In El Paso, Olivas was observed entering the Internet shop. During a discussion between Tomas and Olivas in the small office, Olivas asked about news on the Brown murder case. He said he had been busy in Juarez with no opportunity to follow the news out of Centerville.

Tomas informed him that the police apparently were keeping the lid on the case because nothing had been reported by El Paso news. This recorded conversation did not prove murder but did indicate unusual interest toward it. The FBI forwarded a recording of the conversation to Max.

The FBI also heard Olivas tell Tomas he had been assigned the job of picking up some girls at the Los Altos training site for transportation to Juarez and El Paso. They were to be delivered to whorehouses owned by the Carbona cartel in Juarez and El Paso.

Located about three hundred miles southwest of Juarez, Los Altos was known as a site where women, kidnapped or bought, were physically and mentally abused to prepare them for prostitution. Roberto told Tomas that three girls had been bought by the cartel. Another one, a blonde Russian, was a gift to Carbona. Roberto expected to return in two or three days and would check back with Tomas. This conversation was immediately reported to Thompson.

Thompson arranged a meeting with agents of Mexican law enforcement, immigration, DEA, and Juarez and El Paso police where he proposed surveillance that visually recorded Olivas's trip to Los Altos and back into El Paso. He intended to establish a complete record of the prostitutes being brought into the United States by Olivas. Olivas would be arrested after the women had been delivered to the brothel. He pointed out that Olivas, in carrying out the cartel's assignment, would be violating several US laws, including the Mann Act, kidnapping, and sexual abuse of minors. These likely would be enough to sentence him to life imprisonment or, possibly, death. On top of the federal laws, Mexican and Texas laws would be broken, and potential prosecution existed there.

The plan developed for reeling in Olivas included being stopped on the highway to Los Altos by the Mexican highway patrol on a minor violation, such as informing him he had a broken taillight on his van. It was fortunate that he did have a broken taillight, which had mysteriously been broken the night before. The real reason for stopping him was to identify him.

He also would be stopped on his return trip with the women for a good, logical reason, again to visually identify him and the girls. He will be filmed and photographed at customs bringing the girls across the border and then delivering them into the El Paso brothel.

Thompson listened while a lively discussion took place about getting the girls out of the house. Should it be a raid? Should an agent go in and obtain the services of one of the delivered girls? Should there be photos of customers going in the house? Three agents volunteered for obtaining a prostitute's services, if that was selected as the preferred alternative. Josh did not appreciate the humor, giving them a silent, hard look, but he let it play out.

The approved plan included keeping the house under observation after the girls had been left there and then use a subpoena for raiding the brothel. Girls arrested would be used as witnesses against Olivas.

Thompson, by secure phone, reported the plan to Ron. Ron reported the news to the chief. Pirwarsky decided Centerville should have someone on site, so he sent Max back to El Paso.

CHAPTER 61

EARLY THE NEXT MORNING, OLIVAS entered his van and left the cartel compound, giving the gate guard a wave as he passed.

The compound, located about five miles from Juarez in relatively flat country, served as cartel headquarters at times. The ranch house and land still operated as a working cow ranch as well. The flat landscape provided good vision for protecting the fortlike ranch buildings. Over five hundred acres, the ranch was one of Carbona's favorite headquarters.

Carbona moved frequently between five such sites, another ranch and three heavily fortified houses in Juarez, usually at night and usually in a caravan of five armored Mercedes cars. When traveling, he could be in any one of the cars. His purpose was protection. If attacked, the attackers would not know where to concentrate fire. Carbona currently resided at this ranch and planned to spend a few more nights.

When Carbona was present, security, always tight, became tighter. Comprised of four adobe structures, one being the ranch house with a six-foot-tall adobe wall surrounding the complex about one hundred yards from the house, the property was designed for defense against any attack. Along with movement sensors scattered around and cameras covering all areas, guard stations and roving guards provided protection. The cameras provided visual monitoring 24-7.

Over a Mexican breakfast of huevos rancheros with chorizo, Carbona and Olivas discussed the Los Altos trip. Carbona's gift from the Acapulco cartel was one topic and delivery of the girls another.

Later, a small Mexican army plane observed Roberto's van leaving the ranch and turning on the highway leading to Los Altos. The Federales plane used a geographic information system (GIS) device tuned into the bug on the van.

Located in the mountains southwest of Juarez and south of the well-known Copper Canyon National Park, Los Altos sat on a remote mesa. An Acapulco cartel specializing in prostitution controlled the site and facilities.

Olivas anticipated having a party with one or more girls, so he made good time until he entered the mountains where the rural road was poorly maintained, hilly, and with many curves. The last ten miles were severely rough, having rocks about the size of footballs, both loose and stuck in the road. No one but serious sightseers and people on a mission would drive this road.

About twenty miles from Los Altos, before turning on the bad road, he had been stopped by a courteous highway patrol officer, who checked his license and informed him that one of his taillights was broken. The officer reported the stop to headquarters, as previously directed.

Upon arriving, he drove up to a building compound of six small barracklike cabins located on top of a small mountain mesa with spectacular vistas of two valleys and a large slightly sloping mesa toward the east. Serpentine canyons defined the sides, and the end fell off sharply into a river, at least 150 feet below. Olivas was immune to the great view. He had girls on his mind.

The poor or modest structures, mainly built of rough wood and mud, sat facing one another. They appeared old, but one small barrack cabin appeared to be of more recent vintage.

Several men and women, standing in front of the cabin in the yard, smoking and talking, watched him arrive. The women appeared to be young girls, except for one who looked middle-aged. Olivas knew her as Rita, a matron. The older woman acted as a substitute mother and handled the young girls' training.

A taller girl, about five feet ten inches, naturally blonde, and absolutely drop-dead gorgeous, visually overwhelmed the other girls. Her blue eyes were almost magnetic and her body so sensuous, especially in a flimsy white shirt. Roberto wanted to merge with her immediately.

Roberto assumed her to be the Russian who would be the gift to Carbona. He decided to have her tonight, all night. He greeted the group and entered the building.

Inside, two men jumped up, joyfully greeting Roberto. He made one or two trips per year to the site and transported girls back to Juarez or El Paso each time. The men treated Roberto like the longtime favored customer he was.

Carbona's relationship with Los Leones, the Acapulco cartel that ran Los Altos, stayed good because no competition existed. Girls brought to the compound were tortured, raped, and beaten until they became submissive. When ready they were sold into sexual slavery. The camp director, Juan, took Roberto out to meet the three girls Carbona had purchased and presented the Russian as Sasha, from Odessa, Russia.

Roberto asked her if she spoke Mexican. She said, "Un poco."

When he asked about speaking English, she said, "Some, better than Mexican. I learned in school in Odessa."

"Good," Roberto said, "we will speak English. You know I am here to take you back to Juarez where you will be presented to Don Antonio Carbona. He is a great leader, and you should be honored. We will leave tomorrow. You and I will spend the night together. You will show me all the tricks you have learned."

Juan said that Sasha, being a good Russian, liked vodka.

"I hope you have plenty of Oso Negro vodka. Sasha and I will have a big party. We will eat dinner first. Do I have the usual cabin?" Roberto asked.

Juan said, "Yes, you can eat there or in our small dining area."

Roberto requested two plates of food and two bottles of vodka be brought over to his cabin. He placed his arm around Sasha and said, "Let's go party, pretty one."

The next morning Roberto woke with his head feeling like it was being pounded by a sledgehammer. Sasha's head was lying on his arm. Through his bloodshot eyes, he could see a beautiful breast rising and falling gently. He thought about doing it again but rejected the idea. His head hurt too much. As he slid his arm out from under her head, she moaned and rolled over. He gently raised himself to a sitting position on the edge of the bed. After a few moments, he mustered the courage to stand up. He staggered over to the fridge, took out a bottle of water, drank a couple of sips, and hurried over to the toilet to throw up. He was on his knees with the dry heaves when Sasha came over to join him in throwing up.

When Roberto was able, he drank some more water. It stayed down, so he downed a can of Pacifico beer. After that, he admitted that he might live.

He gave Sasha a bottle of water and a beer. She had crawled back into bed and was holding her head. She sipped the water. It stayed down, so she drank the beer and said, "I might live too."

He looked at her naked body and decided to have her again. After his orgasm, they drank more beer. Both sponged off their bodies with cold water, dressed, and reluctantly decided to face the day.

He opened the door facing a bright sun and almost fell from the shock of the light. His eyes hurt, but his head was better. He stepped out, seeing Juan in the yard.

Juan offered breakfast but all Roberto could handle was a glass of orange juice and a bite of tortilla. He took a glass of juice to Sasha. She thanked him, went over to the open vodka bottle, and poured a splash into the juice.

Roberto watched her sip and then said, "Let me have a drink." He took a large swallow.

Now slightly tipsy, he told Sasha to load up a cooler with ice and beer and get her things. She would be leaving here forever.

Juan had the other girls ready and sitting in the van. Sasha placed her things in the back, the beer in the floor behind the front seat, and sat in the front seat. Waving a hand and saying adios, Roberto started back to Juarez with his cargo.

Some twenty or so miles from Juarez, he was stopped by a highway patrolman, who informed him again about his broken taillight.

The patrol officer asked who the lovely young ladies were.

Roberto stated that Sasha was his fiancée, and the girls, his nieces. None of the girls in the backseat looked to be over sixteen to the officer.

Roberto said that they are going to Juarez for his and Sasha's wedding. The patrol officer congratulated him. As they drove off, the patrolman reported the stop by radio as instructed.

Roberto, who had been monitored by the small plane all the way back, headed directly to the cartel compound. As he walked Sasha into the house, he told her she was the best he has ever had, and he would ask Don Carbona if she could be his if the don ever became tired of her.

Sasha, well trained by now, said, "I would like that."

After leaving Sasha at the compound with his happy boss and his instructions confirming which girl would be placed in the Juarez brothel and which would be going to the El Paso brothel, he checked fake identification cards for the El Paso girls. Dropping one girl off at the Juarez brothel, they drove to the border. He told them to reply to the border guards' question on nationality as "I am Mexican." He was ready to present the IDs if asked, but Roberto was surprised at the easy passage through customs. Of course, he was unaware of being photographed and recorded on camera. An unmarked car with two FBI agents followed him to the brothel and snapped photos of them entering the brothel and of him leaving in the van by himself. He headed toward the international border.

Arrangements were in place to arrest Roberto at the border before he crossed back into Mexico. He headed straight to the border and was arrested by representatives of ICE, FBI, DEA, and El Paso police. First, Roberto was taken to jail for booking, but rather than being placed in a jail cell, he was escorted to a safe house and kept there under heavy security, including constant video surveillance. Located in an eastern El Paso suburb, the house, although separated from neighboring homes by several vacant lots on each side, looked similar to other homes in the development. A major structural difference had been built for two of the three bedrooms. Windowless, the walls, ceiling, and floors had been reinforced with steel.

That evening the agencies raided the brothel, arrested the matron and prostitutes, including the two new arrivals, and started an interrogation process.

Thompson expressed his thanks to all involved in the joint operation but also expressed anger and dismay about the young ages of the two girls and some of the other girls. Thompson had a teenage daughter himself. Through questioning the girls, the agents learned that they were kept under close watch and never allowed to leave the brothel except under close guard. Four other underage girls identified Roberto Olivas as the person who previously delivered them to the brothel from the Los Altos training camp. He had intercourse with three of them either at the camp or on the way to Juarez.

CHAPTER 62

CHARGES AGAINST ROBERTO CONTINUED TO mount as the investigation continued.

Max had been monitoring the operation with Thompson. Elated, Max asked Thompson to congratulate everyone for him. He also asked Thompson if he could participate in the interrogation of Roberto, specifically about the Centerville murders. Thompson agreed but informed Max that two actions must be taken that day before detailed questioning.

The first was an arraignment before a judge where prosecutors would have a strong case to prevent bail. The second was to keep Roberto in a place safe from assassination but adequate for interrogation. He welcomed Max's participation in the processes. He would like Max's testimony at the court arraignment that Roberto was a flight risk and a danger to society. Max readily agreed.

Max reported the successful operation to Chief Pirwarsky, who then called the mayor with the update. Ron, elated with the news, asked about a news release. The chief suggested a release first be issued out of El Paso so they would not upstage the FBI. Besides, they might not be ready for a news release. Centerville police could supplement it when it happened. Ron reluctantly agreed but called Charles to update him and Mike so they could readily follow up any El Paso FBI news release with their own release.

Thompson explained the arraignment of Roberto, who would not be present. Instead, his appearance would be by closed-circuit TV. After denial of bail and conclusion of the court proceedings, the interview team would start Roberto's interrogation. Max would sit in on the interview.

Roberto had not requested an attorney yet, according to Thompson. He apparently did not want Carbona to know of his arrest. Roberto knew firsthand what happened to people in his position, having helped dispose of some of them.

Thompson buzzed his secretary to send in Len Alcorn and Viola Mendez, two interrogation specialists who would be in charge of the Roberto Olivas interrogation. He stated that he and Max would be present for the interrogation.

Alcorn appeared to be in his late thirties. Even with wire-framed glasses, his brown eyes seemed to show amusement. Added to that, his brown hair sprouted a cowlick, emphasizing his large ears. Mendez obviously was Hispanic, with black hair, tan skin, dark eyes, obviously large but modestly contained breasts, a sort of chunky build, and a beautiful smile showing even, white teeth. She shook Max's hand.

CHAPTER 63

ALCORN STATED THAT HE WOULD take the lead during the initial stage of the questioning. "It is my understanding," he said, "that the goal is to suck Olivas dry of information on the cartels so that the cartel drug supply routes and people can be neutralized on the USA side of the border. He'll provide adequate information for the Mexican government to battle the cartels in the Juarez area."

Max stated, "I don't intend to preempt Centerville's position, but you should know that we are willing to deal with Olivas regarding the Brown murders if he is willing to give up his contractor and testify against the person." He asked Alcorn his opinion on the minimum he would have to give up to obtain Olivas's cooperation.

Alcorn stated, "Let's play that by ear. Maybe you'll have to offer a New Mexico sentence to run concurrently with federal sentences."

The team walked down the hall and entered the interrogation room, a room that was bare of everything except a table and three chairs in the middle of the floor and two chairs next to one of the walls. One wall held a one-way mirror, and a video recorder sat on the table. Roberto sat in one of the chairs at the table with one hand manacled to the floor.

Alcorn introduced himself and his associates to Roberto and stated that there were a few formalities that must be handled before starting the discussion. He and Mendez sat down at the table.

He then turned on the recorder and camcorder, stated the time and date, identified those present, and stated the purpose of the meeting.

He said, "Roberto, please state your name and where you live." Roberto gave him the information, using a Juarez address, so Alcorn asked his citizenship. Roberto told him he was both American and Mexican.

He then asked Roberto his occupation. Roberto stated, "Bill collector." This brought wry smiles from the agents, who projected in their minds how he collected.

Alcorn said, "Roberto, do you mind if I call you Roberto?"

He responded, "No."

"Roberto, I am going to read you your Miranda rights again, just for the record." He did so and asked if Roberto understood his rights. He received a yes.

"Also, once again for the record, you do not have an attorney present. If you want an attorney before proceeding, please say so now."

Roberto answered, "I don't want an attorney."

Alcorn said, "Let me remind you that you can stop these proceedings with a request for an attorney at any time."

Prior to going into the room, Alcorn had informed Max and Josh that during the initial stages of the interview, he preferred no interruptions. At a certain point, he would call a recess when the team could go out in the hall and discuss how to proceed. Mendez would carefully observe Olivas while Alcorn was handling the initial interview to help her decide on her interview approach.

Alcorn looked at Olivas and said, "Roberto, I have reviewed the charges against you. They are substantial. If I were you, I would be particularly concerned with the RICO charges, which can carry the death penalty. This isn't my case, but the FBI agents tell me they plan to go forward with a death penalty. I am going to show you videos and photos, plus law officers' sworn statements. These are only for the last trip to and from Los Altos. The reason I am showing you this is to illustrate how tight you are tied up in these charges.

"Another thing, we are going to request a change of venue to another city for the trial. A city far enough away where the cartel cannot influence the trial. I suspect Carbona might let you hang out on the line alone, if he can't find a way to put you down. Take a look at the evidence we have against you."

Alcorn then showed Olivas the video taken from the airplane of his trip to and from Los Altos. "So far, seven underage girls have sworn that you had sex with them. When we add up all the charges, you have twenty-eight charges, just on sex with the girls. When all the charges relating to prostitution are added, the number is forty-nine. This does not include the racketeering charges that carry the death penalty," Alcorn said.

"Fuck you and the other motherfuckers over there. This is all bullshit," Olivas said.

"No, Roberto, you're wrong. It's you and you alone taking the rap. Carbona will keep his operations going. You'll have to make do with your fellow prisoners until you are executed. Let's take a break. You keep your seat, Roberto. The rest of us are stepping outside."

"Fuck you," Roberto said. "Where would I go, I'm chained to the fucking floor."

In the hallway, Alcorn looked at Mendez. "What you think, Viola? Have you developed a feeling on how you want to handle Olivas?"

"He's a scumbag and not too smart. I think he has a hang-up with authoritative women. I'm going to be aggressive with him," Viola said.

"Well, let's see how it goes," Alcorn stated. He turned to Thompson and Max and asked if they had any comments or suggestions.

Both responded with, "No, sir."

The team reentered the room. Viola took the chair facing Olivas.

She looked at him directly in the eyes for a few seconds and then said, "Olivas, I am Ms. Mendez. You may call me Ms. Mendez. I refuse to be on a first-name basis with scum like you. You deserve to die. I plan to attend your execution and will applaud your death. Who do you think you are, raping fifteen- and sixteen-year-old children and taking them into a life of prostitution? You kill people. It now is time for you to face the reaper. You will pay your debt to society for all your crimes against humanity in general and your victims specifically. You probably think you are a real stud, but I know you are nothing more than an animal, a scavenger like a hyena. I doubt if any woman, if given the choice, would have sex with you."

Olivas interrupted, "Fuck you, you bitch." He started to stand up but was stopped by his manacles. "I don't have to take this shit."

"Oh, yes, you do. I plan to continue feeding it to you. I suspect your father beat your mother, and maybe you did too. You think it is all right because you think women are beneath you. Well, this one woman knows you for what you are and is telling you—look at you, you're helpless. You can curse, rant, and rave but can't do a thing. I am talking down to a person who deserves what he is going to get, the ultimate penalty—death! Now that we know what I think of you, I want you to think of me as one of your jailors, whom you hate. I want your hate. I ask you, how old were you when you killed your first victim?"

Olivas looked at Mendez, obviously still angry. Finally, he responded, "I was sixteen."

Mendez asked, "What brought it on?"

"I was a member of the Lobos. He was a Coyote. We was enemies. I ran into him in a Juarez alley, taking a shortcut. He pulled a knife. I pulled a gun. A gun is better than a knife. I shot him."

"Were you and he alone?"

"Yes. When I got to our hangout, I told some of the Lobos. We expected a rumble and started preparing for it, but nothing happened. Guess they didn't want to take us on."

Mendez asked, "Did the Coyotes find out you were the killer?"

"I don't know. I didn't tell. Maybe they never knew who did it. They should have figured it was a Lobo," Olivas said.

"Did that make you a hero?"

"It resulted in me being a made man, a Primo Lobo. I became a member of the inner circle only Primo Lobos belong to."

Watching, Max thought, *Olivas is enjoying the conversation.*
"Did the Lobos and Coyotes ever rumble?" she asked.

"There was one big one. We fought with any weapons we could find—bats, knives, guns, rocks, you name it. So did the Coyotes. We had them outnumbered slightly. It became a free-for-all with lots of guys hurt. No one was shot, but several shots were fired. Didn't find out who won. The police arrived and everyone scattered," he said.

"How long were you in the Lobos?"

"Slightly over a year." Olivas said, "I then joined Don Carbona. Been with him ever since, over ten years. Life's funny. Some ex-Coyotes are also with Carbona."

"We hear you are the person Carbona called on to carry out assignments requiring permanent solutions," said Mendez.

"I do many things for Don Carbona," Olivas boasted. "He knows I will finish my jobs."

"How many people have you killed for Carbona?"

"Ha, all of them. I don't think I want to get into that right now. Maybe someday I'll write a book. I know it is tough out on the streets, not safe. That's all I say now."

"What about Carbona? What kind of guy is he to work for?"

"He's okay. Sometimes he is erratic when he is high on coke. He expects success, and he can be tough when people don't get the job done. One time a mule claimed he lost a large shipment to the Federales. The don checked with his sources in the Federales and found that was a lie. Ha, no more mule."

"Did you do the mule?"

"No, he died from torture."

Mendez then said, "It sounds like the Don thinks highly of you. What would he do if we kept you a few days and then released you with no charges?"

"He is always suspicious of anything unusual. He would start checking me out and would cut me out of things until he satisfied himself I'm still loyal."

"What would happen if we released you and dropped rumors in the right places that you had provided good information against the cartel?" Mendez asked.

"He wouldn't take a chance. I would have to run, or I'd be dead."

"It's just a thought, but we could save the taxpayers a lot of money if instead of taking you to trial, we planted rumors you were spilling your guts and then released you without charges."

Olivas, startled, almost panicked and said, "You can't do that. I know you can't. It would be against the law."

"You standing on the law, Olivas? What a laugh. No, no law against it, and we can't control what people say. This is America."

Max noticed a change in Olivas's demeanor. He now appeared uncomfortable, squirming in his chair, as if he now, only now, understood that he was in an impossible situation in relation to Carbona. If he hung tough, took the rap, even got the death penalty, Carbona still would worry about Olivas's loyalty, and as he didn't like to worry, he would take action.

Olivas looked up from the table at Mendez and stated, "You are aware that Carbona likely is planning a move on me and will make it soon."

"Olivas, that is the message we have been trying to get across to you," Mendez said. "You are a danger to him. He will make an attempt on your life. We have to protect you. In that sense, we are your friends. We want to keep you alive," Mendez said. "We want you to talk with us. We want you to completely debrief on cartel activities. We will make commitments to you about your safety in the future. No question your life will change. You can never go back to what you had. You will be somewhere else, under another name, when you are released from prison, but you will be alive and safe. You could have hopes for the future. Frankly, I have been authorized to tell you this, but I hope you turn it down. You deserve to die for what you have done, in my opinion. Mr. Alcorn, I suggest we take a long break, let Olivas go back to his room and think about all this."

Alcorn said, "Okay, we'll take a break. We'll reconvene in an hour."

Three guards were called into the room; they removed the shackle from Olivas and took him back to his secure room.

"Let's take a ten-minute break and reconvene in the conference room," said Alcorn.

When the four convened, Alcorn stated, "I don't want to sound too optimistic, but we are further along than I expected to be at this time. He already is thinking about his position, which he first accepted during Viola's interrogation. He has no good options, and now has realized that fact."

Max said, "I agree. He struck me as a person who has survived a dangerous world for a long time, so he has good survival instincts. If those instincts overcome his loyalty to Carbona he will be dealing with us."

Thompson asked, "Should we take a direct approach on Carbona's vicious solutions to problems like Olivas or just keep reminding him in roundabout ways?"

Viola responded, "I brought it up directly once and believe we should continually talk about it. Maybe an approach where we take it as a given and ask his opinion on how Carbona will try to get to him so we can be prepared."

"I like that," Thompson said. "We ask him to help us save his life. No doubt Carbona is now aware we have him and is trying to figure how to get to him."

"Yes, it would be the first step of cooperation," Alcorn responded. "Viola, if you agree, I'll start the session on the survival matter."

"Fine with me."

The meeting broke up with some time to spare before starting again. Max took the opportunity to call Stud. He asked Stud how things were going up there.

Stud said, "Everything is quiet. I was out to the construction yard, and the damn dog was tied up. I want to shoot that dog bad."

"Stud, I know that dog is important to you, but what's happening on those other important things, like murders?"

"Shit, Max, Simon may as well be spending all his time at Mass. He is doing nothing. We did see him have an out-of-the-way meeting with Gonsolic last night, lasting about fifteen minutes."

"That's interesting. Gonzo said he severed relations with Simon. Doesn't sound as if it's a clean break. I hope you have the meeting noted in the report."

222

"Not to worry, Max, already done. How they hanging down there? Any progress?"

"We're making fast progress." Max said, "I believe Roberto will come over to our side. The FBI has two expert interrogators working him, and they are good. I enjoy watching them work. It is a learning experience."

"Maybe the FBI will loan them to us for our next session with Simon," Stud replies. "'Course, he is lawyered up."

"Okay, they're ready for our next session. See ya." Max cut him off.

Guards brought Olivas back into the interrogation room and shackled him. After everyone sat down and the sound and video turned on, the interview started again.

This time Alcorn sat at the table facing Olivas.

Alcorn said, "Olivas, we both mentioned that an imminent attack by Carbona was likely. Do you have any suggestions on how we should prepare for it?"

Olivas replied, "He'll have scouts out to find where you have me. I am not familiar with this building or even what's around it. I know he recently bought some war weapons—grenades, bazookas, and mortars. His move will depend on what problem this place presents. A few of his people know commando tactics. It could be an assault by them, using bazookas and grenades. He could wait to see if he can get me when you move me, but that is not as likely since he would not want to give me time to talk."

"How would he get commandos over the border?" Alcorn asked.

"Most likely, he will use his tunnel."

"What tunnel?"

"About two years ago, he had a tunnel dug under the river. It starts in a house over there and ends in a house here. The tunnel hasn't been used yet. He said he would save it for an emergency. He uses other tunnels for moving shit."

"Where is the unused tunnel located on this side? Be specific," Alcorn asked.

"I am not sure. I haven't seen it, and he just mentioned it to me one day. I think it is east of downtown—maybe two or three miles."

"Josh, is it worthwhile to pass this info up the chain right away?" Alcorn asked Thompson.

Thompson said, "Excuse me, I will be back in a few minutes. I'll report this." Thompson left.

"Roberto, do you know where the tunnels currently being used for shipping drugs are located?" Alcorn asked.

"Sure, get me an El Paso map from Columbus to Fabens, and I'll show you."

"We will do that later," Alcorn replied. "We'll stop for a few minutes. If Thompson does not return shortly, we'll proceed without him."

After five minutes, Thompson had not returned. Alcorn said to Olivas, "We will continue, Roberto. We picked you up at the border right before 5:00 p.m. We took you to jail. Booked you and arraigned you before the judge. Your appearance was by TV, especially approved by the judge before we picked you up. We brought you here and fed you at about half past seven. It now is 9:20 p.m. What is your guess as to how long it will take Carbona to find this place and arrange an attack?"

"He will find me by putting word out on the street he is looking for me and who has me. The person who reports where I am correctly will be given a cash reward. Others will be given small amounts for their effort. I guess he will know this location before eleven. His attack will occur before 2:00 a.m., probably between one and two," Olivas replied.

"Do you think he has this place under watch now?"

"It is possible but not likely. He hasn't had time."

Thompson came back into the room. Alcorn reviewed Olivas's comments made while Josh was out of the room.

Thompson said, "We will stop the questioning now and commence again later. Olivas, we are moving you. There is a field nearby. An air force Apache helicopter will pick us all up. The guards will escort you to your room, pick up everything you have. We won't be coming back. We'll meet you in the front room."

Guards escorted Roberto out. Thompson noted, "The boss doesn't take chances. We're out of here. The copter will take us to the air base where our FBI Brasilia airplane's waiting to fly us out. Destination Dallas. Meet in the front room in five. Max, we need you too."

Max had a weekender bag with him. Fortunately, he had not checked into a motel. He grabbed his bag from the hall and joined the group in the front room where ten people had congregated—the four law enforcement officers, Olivas, and five guards.

Thompson said, "Four guards and Olivas will go in the lead van. The rest of us plus a guard will follow in the second van. Our arrival at the field will be timed with the copter landing. Move fast when we enter the copter. Our guards will take positions outside and enter last. Olivas will enter first. Let's go."

In the garage, two gray vans were waiting with drivers and motors running. They loaded the vans as directed, the lead van driver hit the button opening the garage door, and they drove rapidly to the field. They heard the helicopter before they saw it, and then its landing lights went on. They drove up just as it sat down. Side doors on the helicopter opened up, and they climbed in. The copter took off. The whole operation didn't take more than eight minutes, Max noted.

Within another ten minutes they were landing next to the Brasilia plane at the air base and climbing into the plane. Max looked around the interior. The plane easily could seat thirty, but the custom seating arrangement held about twenty seats around a conference table.

The plane taxied to the assigned runway, Max heard the captain receive clearance to take off, and then they were airborne. Max asked Thompson, who was sitting close, what would happen to the safe house. He said, "We left it abandoned with some lights. If none of Carbona's people saw our departure, they will attack an empty house and probably destroy it. Our director considered a firefight but didn't like consequences—too close to other houses. More importantly, some of us could be killed, and the incident would have international repercussions.

"The boss decided to let General Flores, Mexican Federales commander, know about the potential attack with the idea he might intercept the assassins when they arrive back on Mexican soil. He has to locate the tunnel area. We will be helping with infrared surveillance of the intruders on their way back. This solution may help close down another tunnel and avoid an international conflict."

The plane touched down at Dallas/Fort Worth International Airport at 12:35 a.m.

Two gray vans were waiting at an auxiliary hangar where they off-loaded. Thompson did not appear as rushed now. He made a cell phone call and, after a short conversation, said, "I'm changing van assignments. Olivas, we have to keep you shackled, but I'm sending Alcorn with you and placing a guard in our van. We are ordered to Oklahoma City. It's about a three-hour drive. Alcorn offers you someone to talk with."

He went over to Alcorn and said quietly, "Make sure you record everything."

Louder, he said, "We'll make a pit stop in the hangar and then be on our way."

The vans were loaded and started through Interstate 35N toward Oklahoma City.

"In case you are wondering, Max, Oklahoma City has the best security of all our cities," Thompson said. "This is because of the federal building disaster a few years back. Law enforcement there leaves nothing to chance anymore. By using vans to go, Carbona will have a harder time tracing where we are taking Olivas. Oklahoma, here we come."

Max dozed a little on the way, shortening the trip for him. They arrived at a building near the federal courthouse that turned out to be a detention center. Several governmental and private office buildings surrounded the federal building. Olivas was herded into a secure cell with the suggestion he get some sleep. By this time, it was close to 4:00 a.m.

Olivas was told there would be a wake-up call at 10:00 a.m. that morning, and a hot breakfast would be waiting. The federal officials and Max rode over to a nearby hotel commonly used by federal employees and were instructed to meet in the lobby at 10:00 a.m.

CHAPTER 64

WHILE THE FBI WAS ABANDONING the safe house, Carbona was awaiting word on the location of Olivas. He had his commando unit organized. Fourteen men, led by a mercenary ex-marine, were waiting for the go command. Their orders were to rescue Olivas and bring him back, if possible. If not, they were ordered to kill him. They were told not to leave him alive in the hands of the FBI.

A telephone caller notified Carbona of the safe house address. He checked it out on a map with Amos, the commando leader. Amos, an American who had become bored with his civilian life before joining Carbona, originally had been hired for boot training some of Carbona's men. Carbona was paying him well to stay on as the commander of the troops. He stood a good six feet three inches and carried about 220 pounds in weight. With his shaved head and his brown eyes supporting his hard chiseled face, his physical presence cowed others. He had already proved himself tougher than any of his men, but as he learned about the raid, he started developing serious reservations about leading an attack on US soil, especially if it could result in injury or death of federal law enforcement people.

Amos listened to Carbona and his second in command, Rojas, as they checked the best route to the safe house. He made some comments but was trying to think of a way out for himself. Amos was not going to become an American traitor, but he was in a tough position. He couldn't back off the assignment if he wanted to live. He couldn't participate if he wanted to remain loyal to the United States.

When his commandos hit Texas, he decided to just disappear, and the plan he developed allowed this. The attackers were split into two teams, each with a leader.

He informed them he would control the attack at a command post from the house. In his briefing to his men, he informed the two group leaders to stay in radio contact with him.

After his men were on the way to the target, he planned to grab a car and leave for the airport but would keep in radio contact. He dressed in light civilian clothes and put his commando fatigues over his civilian clothes, intending to discard his uniform and guns in a sewer or other safe place. At the airport, he would jump on the first plane going anywhere except Mexico. *Sounded like a plan*, he thought.

Amos held his briefing and he presented the attack plan, which was set up exactly as a military operation. Each man was issued a revolver, an Uzi machine gun, a grenade, and a knife. Two men, sniper types, had rifles. One carried a bazooka. They were driven to the border house in two six-wheel military trucks. Tension, almost electrical, hung heavy in the trucks. A few men spoke quietly but most were silent. They arrived at the house above the tunnel, jumped out of the trucks, entered the house, and waited for orders to enter the tunnel. Amos reviewed the attack instructions again. The main one was the assignment of the first four men through the tunnel to assure that the building over the tunnel exit was secured and two vans for carrying the troops to the target were ready. Each van would carry a driver and six men.

Amos informed the teams he would control the operation from the US house command center. He noted that a Mini Cooper was available if he needed to join them in the attack. In the Mexican house, communications equipment received a final check. The invaders ran through the tunnel and out of the building on the other side. Vans were loaded, and they set off for the targeted FBI safe house.

After the vans left, Amos told his man handling the command radio that he would move closer to the action in the Mini, but for him to remain at the house. He reviewed the abort commands with him and said that he would remain in radio contact.

Amos drove off, taking the road leading to I-10 and the airport, to board the first flight as planned. He stopped in a remote place and discarded his commando clothes and equipment. Most of the money Carbona had paid him, a hefty nest egg, was safe in a Denver, Colorado, bank. He had enough to last until he found another gig. Hasta la vista, baby.

The teams arrived at the safe house and reconnoitered with night-vision goggles, although a couple of lights shined from the house. The house, completely quiet, was attacked, exactly as practiced previously at a house on the ranch. The bazooka took out the front door, and they charged in with half the men going upstairs and half securing the downstairs. Closed-door rooms received grenades before entering. The teams quickly determined that they had found an empty house and radioed the information back to Amos, who had just parked his car at the airport. He ordered them to clean up spent ammunition, set fire to the house, and hustle back to the ranch through the tunnel as planned. He knew Carbona would be pissed about failure to take care of Olivas. This fortified his departure decision.

The FBI surveillance plane, using infrared equipment, followed the vans and reported the tunnel location, which was relayed to General Flores. Flores, who had three companies of troops standing by, ready to roll, relayed their destination and ordered their departure. He reminded his colonel in charge how important it was to arrive at the battle site before the invaders so an ambush could be set up. The timing would be close.

Colonel Flores, nephew of the general, called for a left turn at an intersection, rather than the correct right turn. Valuable minutes were lost before the caravan of vehicles could be turned back to the correct road. By the time the army arrived at the ambush site, the invaders were past it and well on their way back to the ranch. Colonel Flores radioed for instructions. He was ordered to secure the tunnel and building with guards. Later, explosives would implode the building and tunnel.

When he learned Olivas had escaped, a furious Carbona ordered another search for him. Much later, he learned that an FBI plane had left El Paso the previous night with a number of people. Olivas likely had been aboard.

Since the failed commando attack would be reported to Olivas, Carbona expected Olivas to tell everything, and he knew a lot. Many operational changes became necessary, including major changes in drug supply routes and distribution points, especially in the United States. He couldn't make changes in prostitution houses or in extortion methods, but he could cut back on extortion until the smoke cleared. The legitimate businesses he controlled would be exposed, and problems would develop when that information became public. One matter that would cause major operational disruption was exposure of those who had been bribed. This included federal, state, and local officials in Mexico and a few American law enforcement people. In addition, the missing Amos was a mystery. After his last radio command, he'd disappeared. Carbona decided to put word on the street that he wanted Amos and the Mini Cooper located. The car was found in the airport parking lot with the keys in it, but Amos was never found.

He and Rojas, his assistant, started making calls, alerting everyone to the Olivas danger.

The next morning, TV news reported a blurb on an El Paso house explosion in the northeast heights. The cause was unknown, but police were investigating. A late edition of the El Paso morning newspaper carried a similar article.

Since he was only a low-level distributer, Tomas Martinez did not learn of the Olivas capture for several hours. When he heard, he recognized his danger. The El Paso police would have evidence of his trafficking and possibly his participation in the Brown murders.

He and Simon had avoided contact, but now he had to alert Simon of the danger. He called Simon on his cell phone, using a coded sentence indicating an emergency. "How are you and Megan making out?" This sentence would let Simon know they had to talk on a secure line. Tomas said he would be at the emergency number in one hour.

When Simon called one hour later, Tomas told of Olivas's capture and said that he was going to run. Tomas didn't know when he would be talking with Simon again.

Tomas went home, packed, and then went to his bank and withdrew $20,000 via cashier's checks, even though he knew the withdrawal would be reported to federal officials. He had previously planned an exit when things became too hot. This was it. He took another $30,000 he kept at his house, loaded his pickup, and headed to Phoenix, where he sold his pickup at a used car lot. He caught a taxi to a bank, cashed his cashier's check, and placed the money in a suitcase. He took another cab to the Phoenix airport and disappeared. Tomas had no ties to El Paso. His wife had divorced him three years back. They had no children.

Simon, on the other hand, had family, his business, and now a shot at becoming public works director. He felt he had to take the chance and stay.

CHAPTER 65

Tomas's message received, Simon started driving around while thinking of his situation.

He was under suspicion for murdering Amy, but no evidence existed. *Be cool on that one,* he thought. To save himself, Olivas would give Simon up on the Brown murders, and he had real problems there, but with Tomas gone, the money connection may not be proven, so there was a chance. If Gonzo was elected, he may work with Simon to mitigate some of the Brown case pressure. The mayor's race is closer, but Steadman still had the lead. He remembered he had thought about killing Steadman instead of Brown originally but still felt his decision was correct. Now it was time to remove the mayor, leaving Gonzo as the sole candidate.

How to do it? he questioned himself. There can be no more large payments that can be traced. A small payment or two could be hidden in a construction job cost without any chance of discovery.

He needed a low-cost hit man. He remembered a migrant he had hired on a recent job with typical MS-13 tattoos. He drove to his office, took his payroll records out, checked the small road project the fellow worked on, and came up with the name.

Luis Orasco. He made a couple of calls and tracked Orasco down. He was living in a south valley house. Simon found him there. Orasco, with a beer in his hand and obviously plastered, agreed to meet with him the next day in a south valley city park.

Simon met a sober Orasco the next morning and successfully negotiated a hit on Mayor Steadman for $2,100. He paid $1,000 up front with the rest to be paid after the successful execution of the mayor. Orasco started to explain his murder plan, but Simon said that he preferred reading about it.

CHAPTER 66

I N OKLAHOMA CITY, THE FBI group and Max met the next morning with Olivas, who opened the meeting with, "After thinking it over, I am going to cooperate fully by answering your questions, but before we start, I want an attorney to negotiate the best deal he can get for me. I need a name of a local criminal defense attorney. Give me five names. I will hire one of them, and after we negotiate a deal, I will talk with you."

Thompson, surprised, had Olivas escorted back to his cell.

"And that is the guy who I said was not too smart," Mendez said.

Alcorn replied, "But we are achieving our goal as soon as he gets his deal."

Max agreed. "If he gives up our killer, I am sure the city will deal, but I want to confirm this with the district attorney and chief of police. Does anyone have a problem if I call them?"

No one said anything so he left the room to call Chief Pirwarsky.

After filling in the chief on pertinent facts and raising the plea-bargaining question, Pirwarsky said he would clear the offer with the district attorney and get back to him.

He alerted the DA. The DA brought in Bracken, the attorney assigned to the city, and they agreed on plea bargaining.

She sent Bracken to Oklahoma City as the city's legal representative. Max was notified.

Thompson called the senior FBI attorney in the Oklahoma City office, Harlan Wilson, to discuss local defense attorneys. Wilson said he would discuss this with a couple of his trial attorneys and have five names shortly. About one hour later, Wilson called Thompson with the five names. He said, "These are the five most active defense attorneys in town. Our office has high professional regard for them."

Thompson took the names to Olivas, who said, "I'd like to discuss these people with a public defender attorney. Could that be arranged?"

Thompson said, "I need to discuss that request with our attorneys. I will be back in a few minutes." A few minutes lasted until early afternoon before Thompson reported to the group and Olivas that a public defender attorney was lined up.

Later that afternoon, an attorney from the public defender's office called Thompson. Introducing himself as Hector Johnson, he said, "Mr. Wilson gave me your name and suggested I talk directly with you because you have a case with unusual circumstances."

Thompson explained Olivas's request and requested that Johnson meet with Olivas as soon as possible. "The guy wants to confess, but he wants a plea bargain. He just wants you to pick an attorney from the five names we gave him. How do you feel about coming over tonight?"

"Listen," said Johnson, "I'm completely bushed. I had three cases in court today and three more tomorrow, none of which I have prepared for. This workload is crazy."

Thompson, becoming frustrated from talking with attorneys all day, came up with, "Why don't you hang onto the phone, and we will connect you with Olivas. Let him give you the names. You suggest one or give him another name. We don't give a damn which one represents him. We want to move on with this case."

Thompson quickly connected Olivas with Johnson. After Johnson listened to the names, he suggested Otis James, saying that he thought James was the best for plea bargaining.

Olivas told Thompson he selected James. "How do you want to proceed?"

Thompson said, "You get one phone call under the rules. You can call James in the morning, first thing. Make your deal, and our attorneys can start discussions. We will be pushing for action. Get James to give you first priority on his cases. After you hire him, you know the rules. We don't talk except through the attorneys. Good night."

Max again phoned the chief. He said, "Chief, is this is a secure line? I have confidential information."

Pirwarsky said, "Let me set up the scrambler and we are secure."

Max gave his updated report and asked, "What is the limit we can offer Olivas on a plea bargain? The feds suggested we could give him a sentence running concurrently with the federal sentence. They then will take responsibility for jailing him in a safe federal prison. He will testify that he was hired for the killing and identify the contractor. I support the recommendation. It solves our case and will convict our criminal."

"I'll check this out with the district attorney for our answer," the chief replied. "I don't see a problem. Let's talk when I have answers."

Later in the day, Pirwarsky called Max with the information. "The DA supported the plea bargain you suggested—concurrent sentences with the condition that he give us the contractor and testifies fully against him. She has sent Bracken to Oklahoma to assume the attorney negotiations for us. She also plans to brief the mayor on a strictly confidential basis. I will bring Stud and Davis up-to-date but will emphasize the top-secret aspect of this case. Keep me informed."

Max reported receiving approval for the plea bargaining and the city sending an attorney for participating in negotiations. Thompson said, "We are out of the picture until plea bargaining is over. Then we start again. Anybody for lunch?"

The team left for lunch at a nearby restaurant. Max warmed to Viola while there. She was witty, quick with banter, and took nothing from the men. Making a point to walk back to the federal building with her, he asked if she got hit on much by other agents.

"Only once from each of them," she responded. "I do not mix pleasure and business in the office."

Max asked, "Does that apply to me? I'm alone in Oklahoma City and need a dinner companion. I will even buy dinner."

She responded, "Now that is a real concession. Tell you what. We'll eat together but go dutch. None of us should have to eat alone in Oklahoma City."

"Let's meet for a drink in the hotel bar and discuss where to eat," Max suggested.

"Fine, I'll meet you at six thirty."

Max felt good. He had a date that wasn't a real date but was close enough.

Arriving back at the federal building, Thompson suggested they spend the afternoon working on questions for Olivas after his plea bargaining. Max, of course, was most interested in obtaining the name of the murder contractor and in any possible activity of the cartel in Centerville. Raising one question seemed to lead to several other questions. They had not finished by the five-o'clock closing time and agreed to continue the next morning.

Max entered the bar at six thirty, cleaned and refreshed, but was wearing his last clean set of underwear and shirt. Tomorrow, he'd have to go shopping for additional clothes. He ordered a Dos Equis beer, but the waiter said they had none. So he ordered a draft. Viola entered, he waved, and she came over and slid into the booth opposite him. "I'm having a draft. What would you like?"

"A glass of the house white wine."

Max ordered for her.

She asked, "How long have you been with Centerville?"

"Seems like since I was a baby boy, but it's only been eleven years. I joined the force after being discharged from the marines."

"You made lieutenant that quick and you are in charge of homicide?"

"Yes to both, and if this case is resolved favorably, I'm likely to become captain. We have a good chief, and he rewards good work. Police work is hell on a personal life though."

"We have the same problem in the FBI. Len and I travel a lot. I feel my divorce happened because of continual separation. We became strangers. Have you been married?"

"No, never had the time to really develop a relationship. Are you in a relationship now?" He sipped on his beer.

"One does not waste any time, does one? We had better slow down a little. No, I'm not. Where are we going to eat? Do you have any clues?"

"One of the local freebees recommended Joe's Steak House as the best for beef. Is that agreeable?"

"Sure, shall we go? We can continue exploring each other's psyche over food," she said as she finished her wine.

As they were rising, Max said, "You go right to the jugular in a conversation. Your approach with Olivas was a masterpiece. You had him talking in about two minutes."

"Len, with his soft approach, helped set him up. We work well together."

At dinner, they exchanged funny work incidents and found they were comfortable with each other. Back at the hotel, they had an after-dinner drink, and Max walked her to her room. They did not kiss good night, but Max felt that a closer relationship was possible.

The team worked on the question list the next morning. Late morning, Bracken arrived. He and Max separated from the others, and Max brought Bracken up-to-date and then took Bracken to Wilson's office for introductions.

Leaving Bracken with the attorneys, he said that he would see him again later.

Also, that morning Olivas contacted James by phone, and he accepted Olivas as a client. He demanded an up-front fee of $10,000. Olivas stated that he would make a wire transfer from his bank account to James's account, which was accomplished later that day with the cooperation of Thompson. James contacted Wilson, and they agreed to start plea-bargaining negotiations at 4:00 p.m. that day.

Wilson decided to take the government's lead in the negotiations with a senior attorney, Joseph Hines, who had participated in several negotiations, as his backup. They met with Bracken and determined the base offer acceptable to the government—a thirty-year term, twenty-year minimum served, eligible for good time reduction and parole after twenty years. All other charges not included in the indictment would be dropped.

James met with Olivas and immediately started intimidating him with his brunt countenance, dark hair, low forehead, bushy eyebrows, flaccid face, way overweight body, and gruff voice. He tried to browbeat everyone, client or opponent. In just a few minutes with him, Olivas definitely was cowed.

James told Olivas the feds had a strong case against him with plenty of evidence. He asked Roberto, "Just what do you think you can accept as a plea bargain?"

Roberto said he wanted less than a life sentence and a commutation of his sister's life sentence in Mexico to time served. He could offer most everything the cartel was handling—names at all levels of Mexican government, operations, information, everything. He could also name the contractor for the Brown murders in Centerville and a murder in El Paso. James asked him why his sister's jail term was important. Roberto said, "My mother was upset over it."

James said, "That'll require Mexican governmental action. You have a lot to offer. I feel good about our chances for successful negotiations, if something doesn't blow up."

CHAPTER 67

RON DROVE TO HIS CAMPAIGN office early Monday afternoon, eight days before the election. He talked with Charles and Mike about the get-out-the-vote campaign and asked how the absentee ballot contact was working. Early in the campaign, Mike had started sending a worker by the City Clerk's office daily to obtain names and addresses of absentee voter applications. Letters were then sent to the voters asking that Ron be supported.

Mike told Ron the program was ongoing, and several vote commitments had been obtained. Some people would not state their intentions, usually just saying that their vote was a private matter. Mike laughed and said, "One person contacted said he is a relative of Gonzo, knows him well, and would never vote for him."

"Too bad we can't make that public. Gonzo tried to get nasty in the last debate. Maybe we ought to get nasty. Just kidding. You know I don't campaign that way and won't start now. Have we finalized our assignments for the get-the-vote-out election-day campaign?" asked Ron.

Charles said, "Almost. We have sixty-four people who will work their precincts on election day calling likely supporters, or visiting them, to encourage their voting. We have a few who will stand by for contacts who say they need a ride to the polls. With the widespread absentee voting efforts in place now, we don't get many of those. Another twenty precinct workers would be nice, and we will likely pick up some this week."

"What did Alice say when you saw her?" Ron asked, referring to the executive director of the Chamber of Commerce.

Charles replied, "She said she had been working in the background and expects you to carry 65 percent of the business votes. Workers will be calling members on election day, encouraging them to vote. After last night's debate and your stand on the lab issue, the figure might go to 70 percent. Most businessmen vote their pocketbooks."

"Any word on election-day surprises Gonzo may be planning?" Ron asked.

"We haven't picked up any rumors," Charles replied. "If he comes out on Sunday or even Monday with a surprise, we are prepared. We are saving some money for a last-minute response and need you to be available to record a last-minute telephone message, if necessary. Mike has your latest telephone message going out today. We'll alert the TV stations if Gonzo brings up last-minute charges and will have a taped response for airing."

"I'm surprised nothing has been said about abortion," Ron said. "We know city government, the mayor, or council has no authority on abortion, but emotions run high on the issue. Right-to-lifers appear more militant than right-to-choose people, or is my opinion off base?"

Charles raised the point of numbers of people taking one side or the other.

"Maybe there are more militant-type people who are anti-abortion than militant-type abortion people."

"Maybe they are just louder. It's a tough issue. I think that Gonzo, being Catholic, would take the anti-abortion position. At least, he should've brought up the issue in the Catholic precincts. These are mainly heavily populated Hispanic areas. Charles, have you heard anything on the issue from our Hispanic friends?"

"Not a word."

Ron said, "I talked with Councilor Cisco yesterday. He and I will be walking together in his council district Saturday morning. I hope no one brings up the issue. The only response I have is that the abortion issue has never been raised in city government. We've no authority and don't need any. The state and feds are the proper place to argue abortion. "What about trying to obtain free TV coverage of our walk?" Ron asked. "The media love Cisco. If they decline to cover, let's do our own ad. Check with some of the other councilors. Maybe one or two may want to walk with me. I know they'll want paybacks, but enough issues will come up where I can do that. Obviously, I only want those who have safe council seats."

Charles said, "We'll follow up."

Ron continued, "I finished telephoning my legislative friends we've helped. A few notified their supporters about our assistance on city issues they've called about. We should be in good shape there. Have we covered everything?"

"I think so," Charles said. "I want to mull over why Gonzo has been quiet on abortion. We'll call you if we missed something."

"I saved the best news for last." Ron smiled. "Chief Pirwarsky informed me the Brown murders were contract killings. The assassin has been captured. He is talking, and we will have the name of the local contactor soon, before the election."

"Wow," Mike said. "That is great news. Should I distribute a news release?"

As he stood up, Ron said, "The chief nixed that right now. I'll let you know when we receive clearance for a release."

Ron walked through the work area, waved at the people, and told Charles he would be in his office.

When he arrived at city hall, Lupe handed him a note that said he should call the chief immediately, and he did.

CHAPTER 68

T HE CHIEF SAID, "STAY IN your office. I'm coming over."
When the chief came hurrying in, he closed the door and said, "I have startling news, not good. There's going to be an attempt on your life. One of our undercover narks, who acts the role of a wino, was sitting next to a wall at a street corner, all balled up with his cap pulled down. Two Hispanics were discussing taking the mayor out. They had the markings of MS-13 thugs. One said he would be in the parking garage when the mayor came out of city hall at 5:00 p.m. to get in his car, and he would blast him. He asked the other thug to back him so he could get away. The other guy agreed to back him for $400. We have to protect you, but we have to handle this so the shooter and his backup are caught or killed or they'll try again."

"My God, Chief," Ron said. "I am at a loss for words. What is going on? Has this Martinez guy put out another contract?"

"We don't know who arranged this yet. Our first job is to stop it. Our first priority is protection of you and people leaving city hall through the garage.

"We can't let you go out. It's too dangerous. We either have to dress up one of our officers to replace you or stop the guy after he gets in place before you go out. My people are discussing the options right now. We likely will brace the guy before you or your replacement goes out because that is the less dangerous option.

But these guys usually are high on drugs, so we have to be ready for a shoot-out. I have our officers scouting out the garage right now so we can position our people where they won't be seen but will be able to take the guy."

"Okay," said Ron. "It's in your hands. What do you want me to do?"

"Stay right here until we give you clearance to leave. I have a couple of officers headed up here for protection and one officer sent to your house to check it out. I was told Val was at work. I called university police and requested they place a couple of men at Val's lab. They said they would provide protection immediately."

The chief left. Ron, of course, could not concentrate on anything. He sat there in a daze for a few minutes and then called Val. He related the information and said he had no idea when he would be home. He advised her to refrain from discussing the matter with anyone until more information became available and assured her that he personally will be kept safe. Already the chief had assigned two more officers to his detail, and his other bodyguard was still on duty.

Pirwarsky joined the meeting with Stud, Davis, and two officers known to be accurate with guns, Suarez and Prince. Stud, who had been assigned the job of evaluating ambush sites, reported his selected positions for the four team members—one in the hall leading to the garage, one in a booth at the garage entrance, one in a van located next to the driver's side of the mayor's car, and one in a van parked a couple of spaces away on the other side of the mayor's car. The logical place for the gunman to position himself was behind the van located on the driver's side of the mayor's car. If he tried to break into the van, the cop in the van would arrest him as he radioed the others. In the meantime, two cops in civilian clothes would come out the door from city hall, yelling back, "See you tomorrow, Mayor."

The next person out would be a cop impersonating the mayor, wearing full-body armor. Employees would be stopped from entering the garage by diverting them into the auditorium next to the hallway.

Pirwarsky had taken charge of the operation and made assignments. He authorized gunfire in any questionable situation after the standard warning. "This guy is MS-13. He may ignore warnings and start firing, so be ready."

Stud took the van assignment next to the driver's side of the mayor's car. The two civilian-dressed cops were to walk by the car, turn, and be ready for action.

As the workday was coming to an end, two Hispanic men dressed in worn jeans, dark shirts, and ball caps entered the pedestrian entrance to the garage.

The police officer in the booth radioed the information to the team.

One gunman took position by a concrete structure that housed garage equipment about thirty yards from the door leading into city hall with clear vision of the door. A cop was on the other side of the structure in a car.

The lead gunman took a position at the side of the van holding Stud, as was anticipated.

The cop on the other side of the structure and another one converged with the man by the structure at the same time. The two cops came out the door and yelled, "See you, Mayor." The gunman appeared to be readying himself to fire.

Then Stud exited the van by the side door and, using the door as a shield, said, "You are under arrest. Drop the gun, get on the floor." The man swung his gun arm up to fire at Stud, but Stud fired first, as did one of the cops who had just left the door. Both bullets were lethal shots, as determined by a later autopsy. The other assassin was disarmed, read his rights, and taken to jail.

The chief called the mayor, told him the results of the operation, and said, "You and your bodyguard are free to go."

As Ron entered the garage, he was ushered to a police car with the explanation that his car was part of the crime scene.

Media converged into the garage as the police car carrying the mayor left. Another police car followed.

After he was in his house, both remained on guard duty outside. The chief told Ron, "We don't want to save you at one place and lose you at another."

Val was waiting for Ron. He walked in, kissed her on the cheek, and bee-lined for the liquor cabinet. Pouring a substantial measure of scotch into a glass and then taking a gulp, he said, "Amazing. This whole campaign is amazing—in fact, unreal."

Val walked over and hugged him, saying, "It's almost over. Everything is going to be all right."

Once again reporters and film people converged on the mayor's house and he was under siege. Although Chief Pirwarsky gave a press conference on the murder attempt, and Ron made a statement from his front porch thanking and praising the police actions, the media still stayed camped out at the mayor's house until late evening.

Later, the chief called to inform Ron that the second gunman refused to talk, except to ask for his one phone call. He apparently called a fellow gang member to arrange for an attorney.

Although Al, the captured gunman, was held in jail overnight and spent most of the night being questioned, he stayed mute. Finally, late at night he was placed in a cell with a cellmate who had been wired with a recorder.

The next morning the gunman was charged with assisting in attempted murder. A high cash bail of $800,000 was set. The prosecution argued for no bail, stating he was a flight risk and the charge was serious. His attorney argued that his client was an innocent bystander and deserved bail. But his gang could not raise such a large amount of bail money anyway.

Al and his cellmate talked about various matters, but soon the discussion turned to why they were in jail. Luis, the cellmate, said he had been charged with robbing a store at gunpoint. Al reported the garage shoot-out and how he was disarmed before he could shoot. Luis asked, "Who authorized the attempt on the mayor?"

Al said, "Ah, Juan didn't tell me. I think it was a Spanish brother."

Luis reported this comment while he supposedly was meeting with his attorney. The comment was passed on to homicide. Since Stud had been placed on paid leave—a common practice for a policeman after shooting someone—and Max was in Oklahoma, Davis informed the chief about the conversation.

Val, the mayor, and Gonzo all received 24-7 guard protection. The chief joked about the mayor supporting a police department budget increase, but he knew one would be needed. It helped his budget that Val's lab was protected by university police.

CHAPTER 69

SOME OF THE EQUIPMENT FOR the lab expansion had arrived and been placed into service. After the new lab procedures developed by joint staff work were in place, stem-cell testing commenced with in-house fanfare. At Val's request, Dean Lorensten presided and broke a bottle of sparkling grape juice over a centrifuge. Alcohol was not allowed by the federal government.

Initial results presented interesting data, including the observation that the stem-cell failure rate of those tested varied greatly between laboratories. All labs had some failures, but some labs consistently had lower failure rates than others, varying from 15 percent to 44 percent. This information was reported to NIH contacts, who requested a Washington meeting on the subject. Val invited Annie and Steve to attend the meeting. As the election was down to the last few days, she needed to stay home.

Steve was ecstatic but kept his feelings from showing. Val, knowing him so well, could see his jubilation and was amused. Actually, she had decided she was in favor of Annie and Steve matching up, being fond of and admiring both. They were compatible. Love was blossoming. Any second thoughts about turning down Steve's move on her in Washington were long gone.

An afternoon conference on the Washington agenda prepared the two for the meeting, and they left the next morning.

Once again, the NIH meeting went well. Annie and Steve received guidance from NIH scientists, and NIH committed to fund the university, sending investigators to other labs with the intention of transferring successful procedures used by low-failure labs to the higher-failure labs.

Annie and Steve enjoyed a bottle of champagne and their late-afternoon and evening hotel activities.

CHAPTER 70

SITTING IN HIS CAMPAIGN OFFICE, Charles looked over at Julie working at a phone and decided he couldn't take it anymore. He had honored her request for separation during divorce proceedings, but had had difficulty. He asked for a private word with her in his office and closed the office door as they entered.

"Julie," Charles began, "I assume your divorce is proceeding, but we haven't even talked. Can't we even be friends who just talk? I would love to have a cup of coffee or tea and be a resource for you through these difficult times."

Julie looked at Charles while she thought of her response. "I think you know why I demanded complete separation. Our physical attachment to each other is too strong. I can't handle those complications while I go through this divorce. If you think we can have friendly chats, I am willing to try."

She smiled. "Thinking back on it, we didn't talk much, did we?"

Charles laughed and said, "That's an understatement. I'll get the coffee. Yours was black with Sweet & Low, as I remember. How's the divorce moving?"

"I told him I knew about his affair. I'm filing for divorce and asked him to move out of the house. He apparently moved in with his mistress. We are at the point where attorneys are trying to allocate assets. I'd like to enter court with everything settled, but we may not. He suggested we try to work out our problem, but I turned him down."

"At the proper time, do you see me in the picture?" Charles asked.

"Charles, have you considered the fact I am several years older than you?"

"Age is not an issue with me."

"Are you thinking of continuing the affair or of engagement?"

"I haven't thought that far. I just know my feelings toward you are different than with other women, and I am assuming it is love."

"Well, at this particular moment you are busy winning an election, and I am busy with the divorce. We can pursue this when we have time to explore it more fully," she said.

"That sounds testy. Did I say something wrong?"

"Not really. I'm surprised a man your age is not sure he recognizes love. While we are pursuing the other things, you might ask yourself what's love got to do with it?"

"Oh!" was all Charles could say. He'd done it again. He was getting a feeling that song would be haunting him forever. With gloomy thoughts, he went back to work.

CHAPTER 71

I N THE OKLAHOMA CITY FBI director's conference room, James started plea-bargaining discussions with Wilson, Hines, and Bracken.

James opened the discussion with the comment, "Here I am again, outnumbered and in enemy territory. Should I surrender or should I gird my loins and take you on?"

"Otis, don't gird your loins. By the time you finish, the day will be over," said Wilson.

"Ow, that hurt," said James. "I will not banter at that low level. Keep the fight above the waist. Let's resolve this and go get a drink. Give Olivas five years' probation, and you will learn things guaranteeing the demise of the Juarez cartel."

"We were thinking along the lines of removing the death penalty in exchange for his cooperation. He was the cartel's main hit man, you know. We have his confession of one murder, evidence he murdered Mr. Brown and his partner in Centerville, and a lead on a murder in El Paso. He is not a person we want on the street," Wilson replied with force.

"Hell, one more like him on the street would be like throwing a pebble in the ocean. Give him ten years' probation, a new name, a safe place to live, help him with a legal job, and check on him occasionally. In a new life, he might be an asset to society."

"More likely he'd be running a prostitution ring of teenagers or distributing drugs. People don't change. Why would he try to learn something new that pays much less than the illegal stuff? No, we want him off the street. He has to be punished for his crimes. Let's talk about appropriate punishment, not free rides," Wilson countered.

"Harlan, this guy may help you bring down a complete organization of criminals who are terrorizing Juarez. The action could spill over into El Paso at any time, and the drug distribution network probably covers the whole United States. I would bet this could be the biggest scalp you ever take. He is a valuable resource and deserves appropriate compensation. For my interests and my fellow Americans' interests, you must destroy the cartel. I feel strongly about this. But I also feel strongly this witness should receive fair compensation for risking his life, giving up his existing life, and heading out into an unknown future."

"I agree Olivas deserves tit for tat. But we are discussing what is tit and what is tat. We disagree on the details. You do not have to remind me how important this guy is. Olivas and the government need each other. We will give up tit for tat. He will give up tat for tit."

James smiled. "I like that—tit for tat, tat for tit. Let's get down to tit. What is your best offer? I'll take it to my client."

Wilson contemplated for a moment. He said, "This is our best and final offer—thirty years' sentence, minimum of twenty years served before parole consideration. We will not oppose parole. The sentence will be served in a secure federal prison. For security, Olivas will be separated from the general prison population. Some people call certain prisons country clubs. After his usefulness as a witness is completed, he will be placed in one. He will be kept safe from harm while in the witness stage. You should consider mentioning to your client how our witnesses fared when we took down the New York mafia. They all ended up safe and sound. We know how to do this."

"I understand the offer but have a question," James said. "What about the Mexican officials? Are they in on the plea bargain? Answer yes to that, and I will take it to my client and will report his answer to you."

"We haven't done anything in that arena," Hines said. "I see a problem. We know the Juarez police chief will support us, but we don't know if we can trust his legal people. Is the legal department in Carbona's pocket?"

Wilson turned back to James. "How about asking your client to give us the names of those in the Juarez and Chihuahua justice departments on Carbona's payroll. Or better, Joe, get the names of the heads of the legal departments and maybe Otis will ask his client if these people are dirty or clean."

James replied, "I don't see a problem there." Joe left the room. James and Wilson chatted for a while, until Hines returned with the names of the Chihuahua attorney general and the Juarez city attorney.

James left to check the names with Olivas. Shortly thereafter, he returned with the information that the city attorney was on Carbona's payroll, but the state attorney general was not.

Wilson told Otis he would work on bringing Mexico into the joint agreement and get back with him. He had his secretary arrange a conference call with the Mexican attorney general.

After a two-hour discussion of the activities and results of the joint operation, with a clear explanation that Olivas was arrested on US soil for US crimes, the attorney general said he would send a representative of his office with the authority to negotiate a plea bargain. He also let Wilson know that he was upset that his office had not been kept informed on the status of the case. Wilson apologized profusely.

Obviously, nothing could be done until the Mexican attorney arrived and had accepted the agreement. Wilson reviewed the proposed agreement with James again and asked James if he would be recommending acceptance. James said the offer seemed reasonable, but he wanted the reaction of his client before commenting.

The meeting broke up. James went to his client, and Wilson asked his people to stay and critique the session. The Mexican attorney would arrive the next day.

Hines said, "We arrived at our offer quickly, and James is taking it to his client. I am surprised negotiations moved so fast. James has been known to walk out when negotiations become stalemated. We have to hope he stays agreeable while we wait."

"Thing about Otis James, he attempts to keep his opponent off balance. Did you notice I made no reference about Olivas's sister and her sentence commutation?" Wilson said. "Just in case James had in mind telling Olivas to reject our final offer in an effort to better it, we can offer the sister's commutation—contingent on the Mexican government granting it, of course. Does anyone have a problem with the commutation?" No one indicated any problem.

Bracken pointed out, "We also didn't mention any deal on New Mexico murder charges. Do you feel you have that included in the offer?"

"Good question. Does James believe I was speaking for the state? If it comes up later, he will argue that I was. We might offer that as another concession when he comes back. We are prepared if he comes back asking for more," Wilson replied.

After requesting the guard to bring Olivas to the witness room, James presented the offer. Olivas said that was a good start and asked about his sister's release.

James said, "I am sure we have it included, and we will add language in the final agreement." He did not mention that he had forgotten to raise the item in negotiations. He then said, "The feds said it was their final offer. It's a pretty good one. With them not opposing parole after twenty years, you likely can get out shortly thereafter, assuming you qualify for good time served. You will still be young. Any danger of revenge from Carbona or friends will have been forgotten by then. A new generation will be running things. We can include a provision in the plea bargain for federal assistance in setting up a new life under parole."

Olivas especially took to the idea that after twenty years, no one would be coming after him, so he said, "Okay, I accept. All charges will be dropped, except the one I plead guilty to. My sister will be released before I start testifying, and the sentence will be thirty years, with parole available after twenty years. I will be kept under personal safety arrangements in a federal prison. After I sign the agreement, I will start talking and give up everything I know about criminal activity in Juarez and El Paso."

James informed Olivas that the case was taking more time then he had planned, and he needed another $5,000. Olivas said that he would arrange another wire transfer.

James went back to report that he had agreement from Olivas, with everything subject to acceptance by the Mexicans. The wording Olivas gave for the agreement seemed to include New Mexico charges, but Wilson decided he would not raise the matter.

Wilson said, "We will have a draft agreement over to your office within four hours. Time is essential. We need to move on Carbona before he can hide or change everything. Call me if you have changes for the draft. We can handle them on the phone and save some time."

After James left, Mark Bracken told Wilson, "Centerville would be helped if the murder contractor for Brown and his partner were identified as one of the first items on the agenda. If Olivas identified our suspect as the contractor, we could move fast on the indictment. Max and I can head back home while the FBI pursues other information you want."

"We will take your stuff first, Mark," Wilson promised.

The next day the Mexican state attorney arrived and was briefed. He said that the Mexican government would support the plea agreement presented, and everyone signed off on it. Since it was late, about 6:00 p.m., interrogation was set for 8:00 a.m. the next morning, with the Centerville murders being first on the agenda.

CHAPTER 72

URING THE DAY WHILE THE attorneys were negotiating, Max made a point of locating Vi. Finding her having coffee and reviewing reports in the operations center, he said, "Hi Vi, I enjoyed your company last night. Let's do it again tonight, and I will buy dinner. That way we will have a real date."

"Sure," she said. "Last night was fun. I have a hard time turning down dinner two times and haven't had a date in at least a month. You pick the restaurant again. Same time in the bar?"

"Yes, six thirty."

By six thirty, the news about the plea agreement had spread throughout the building. Feeling good, Max and Vi decided that the evening would be more than a date—they would celebrate. Max ordered his usual beer and white wine for Vi and said, "We'll enjoy a bottle of champagne with dinner."

Vi's eyes were sparkling. Max told her that she was especially pretty tonight.

She said, "Do you like my dress? I always carry one on trips, just in case. I feel more feminine than in the usual power pantsuit."

"Yes, I like it. My first thought when you walked in was (using cop talk now) 'There's a real feminine woman,'" Max said.

Vi laughed, patted his hand, and said, "Centerville cops are traditional, I take it."

The celebration continued through dinner and late into the night in Vi's room.

As Vi had invited Max into her room, she said that she was counting the previous night as a date also because she never made love on the first date. The next morning, as she slid on top of Max for more lovemaking, Vi commented, "Wearing a dress once a month is not often enough. I need to do it more."

Max replied, "The dress is beautiful. Wear it again tonight when we have dinner. I will be better at helping you take it off now that I'm experienced."

"Well, I'll send it out for cleaning and pressing. Someday, maybe I can show you my other dress." Vi smiled.

Max laughed. Changing the subject, Max said that he was happy the Centerville murders were first on the agenda. "It is one of those situations where we know the answer, but we must wait for confirmation." They dressed and went to the hotel coffee shop.

Alcorn entered; they saw him and waved him over. As he sat down, he said that he had been organizing his questions for Olivas by subject matter. He asked Viola if she would take a look at his notes before the session starts. She agreed and asked if he had them with him.

"Yes, most of them. Centerville is first, Max. My questions are 'Did you do the murders?

Who contracted the job? How much did he pay? How did he pass the money to you? Explain how you did the job. Had you met the contractor before the job? Describe how he looks.'"

"Max, do you have any others?" Alcorn asked.

"Just two. How did the contractor obtain Olivas's name? And where is the gun?"

"Oh, yes, the gun," said Alcorn, making a note.

Viola said, "I'll start looking over the others you have worked up." She picked up the papers, noticed how many there were, and exclaimed, "My God, it might take weeks to cover all these!"

Alcorn said, "At least a few days for sure. Remember though, we will have him available for a long time."

Bracken entered the shop. Max said, "I'm going over to his table for an update. You guys have a lot of work to do."

Bracken brought Max up-to-date. James had demanded a document from the New Mexican district attorney granting Bracken the authority to sign off on the Olivas agreement. The assignment had been faxed, with the original being sent by FedEx. It should arrive by one o'clock today. James had agreed that the fax was adequate for starting the questioning.

Arrangements included a telephone call to the mayor and Chief Pirwarsky with the name as soon as it was given so that an arrest warrant could be issued and served. Davis would make the arrest.

Max noted, "What started out as a local murder case is now a part of an international investigation, with several law enforcement agencies involved. This slows down our work, but it can't be helped. We have to go with the trickle and wait for the flow."

They killed time by making phone calls back to Centerville.

The meeting with Olivas started in the same room as before with the same people, and now included James and Wilson. Olivas testified. He answered questions with, "Yes, I murdered Brown and his partner. The contractor was Simon Martinez. I was paid $14,000 using Tomas Martinez as the conduit. I threw the gun in the river off the bridge and will show you where." Through the questioning, he related his complete Centerville itinerary. Max excused himself and left to call the chief to proceed with the Martinez arrest. He returned to the interrogation.

During a break, Max alerted Vi that he probably would return to Centerville the next day, assuming he and Bracken would finish with Olivas today. He asked Vi if she and Alcorn conducted interrogation training sessions for other agencies.

"Yes, we hold one about every six months for other agents and other agencies."

"Do you think I could obtain approval for you to conduct a training session for the Centerville Police Department and other local law enforcement agencies who may be interested in Centerville?"

Vi smiled. "What an interesting thought. When I next talk with my boss, I will bring it up and let you know. I really don't see a problem. If I come out there, I hope it won't be a boring trip. Is there anything interesting in Centerville?"

"You mean other than me? Not to worry, darling. If we ever get tired of bed, I'll show you around the hotel lobby, but bring both dresses," Max replied.

CHAPTER 73

I N CENTERVILLE, CHIEF PIRWARSKY CALLED the mayor while he was at breakfast and said, "Mayor, we got him. Olivas testified on everything. He targeted Simon Martinez as the contractor for the Brown hits. My guys are on the way to pick him up and will call dispatch when they have him. We'll put out a press release immediately thereafter, and I suspect there'll be a big media reception for Martinez when he arrives at the jail."

"Here it is six days before the election and we have our man. At one time, he was a key person on the Gonzo team. We have no choice but to discuss with Gonzo and some of his people whether they are involved in the murder. What this means for me is I am toast if Gonzo is elected, so, Mayor, you continue to work hard."

Ron informed Val. She said, "Gonzo is the one who is toast. I don't see how he can overcome this. Even if he didn't know about Simon, he must have held suspicions. You had better check with Charles and Mike to make sure this is handled the best way."

"I'll call Charles right now and have them over. Can you stick around?" he asked. "I want your input."

"Sure, I'll call in to say I will be late." She reached in her purse for her cell. With her enhanced status as lab director, she didn't need permission; she just notified someone.

Later, Charles and Mike entered the house, elated with the news.

"It couldn't happen to a nicer guy," Charles said in a sarcastic tone, talking about Gonzo.

"It's a death blow—right to the heart," Mike said.

Val said, "Not quite. Our response, if good, will be the death blow."

"You're right, Val," Charles said. "If we commiserate with Gonzo, people will know it was tongue-in-cheek. We can't offer our assurances he is in the clear. He may not be."

"About all we can do is make a statement that allows people to make their own determination," Charles continued. "Our statement should be along the lines of wait-and-see-what-develops. The issue is in the hands of our police force."

Ron reflected on the discussion. "I would like to make a distinction between a bland statement and a wait-and-see statement. A wait-and-see statement is a logical stance for me since we don't know everything. We must wait for some answers to the questions, and the answers aren't there yet. Now we know why Gonzo has not been physically attacked. One of his key people has been identified as the instigator of the murder of one mayoral candidate.

"We don't know for sure about the attempt on my life. Yes, that's our position. We have to wait and see."

"I will write a press release for your review," Mike said.

Martinez's arrest, along with the announcement that a cartel criminal had confessed to the shooting and allegedly was paid $14,000 by Martinez left Gonzo's supporters in a frenzy.

Gonzo released statements and gave interviews stating that he had separated Martinez from his campaign well before the murders because of other problems and had no knowledge of Martinez's actions.

Sally had assisted him in preparing his statement. His statement had little impact on public opinion. Polls taken before the arrest showed 52 percent for Steadman, 44 percent for Gonsolic, and 4 percent undecided. Two days after the arrest and five days before the election, a poll showed 76 percent for Steadman, 22 percent for Gonsolic, and 2 percent undecided.

Wes Benson, former Brown campaign manager, publicly rescinded his Gonsolic endorsement. Sally knew Gonzo was a sinking ship. With the murder question hanging over his head, Sally began thinking about her association with Gonzo detrimentally affecting her career. She told Gonzo that she wouldn't desert him publically, but she was leaving his campaign to look for another job.

When Steve heard the Martinez news, he was in the lab. He called homicide and Davis answered.

First, Steve asked if the information was correct. When Davis confirmed Martinez's arrest, Steve said, "When Max returns, ask if my temporary assignment is finished. If so, I'll turn in my badge."

On the Sunday before the election, Catholics leaving church after Mass found flyers on their windshields calling Steadman a baby killer who supports women having the right to choose abortion. His wife works on baby stem cells. Gonsolic supports the right to life and opposes abortion. Vote for Gonsolic.

The Steadman campaign responded, using the only abortion counter available. "Why is this issue being brought up in a mayoral election? The City of Centerville has no authority on the abortion issue. It is a Supreme Court issue. Gonsolic should try to be elected on matters relating to city government operations and policy. The abortion issue is a smoke screen from Gonsolic because he has no standing on issues facing the city."

Gonsolic claimed he didn't authorize the fliers, saying he had no control over supporters not part of his campaign.

On the Sunday paper editorial page, the local paper endorsed Steadman, using much of the Steadman campaign platform to justify the endorsement.

CHAPTER 74

STUD RETURNED TO DUTY AT homicide after serving his three-day mandatory leave and was assigned to lead the team until Max returned from Oklahoma City. He led the interrogation of Simon Martinez.

Jason Knott continued being effective in preventing any meaningful discussion with Simon about Amy's murder during initial sessions.

Stud obtained Simon's hand imprints on a large ball of silly putty. Steve had suggested silly putty as a perfect material for hand imprints. The only problem with the putty was in handling it after obtaining the imprints. A board was placed under the putty to aid in handling.

A laboratory analyst compared the handprints taken from Amy's neck bruises to those on the putty and stated he could testify that the handprints match, but he could not exclude other matching hands of the same size.

Simon pled not guilty to the Brown murders during his arraignment. Stud still wanted him for the Johnson murder, but Bracken would not support that action until more evidence could be found. Martinez also refused to comment on the attempted murder of the mayor. The prosecution requested no bail for Simon, citing he was a flight risk. His brother, Tomas, had fled and had not been located.

The judge turned down bail.

Stud placed a cellmate in with Simon who would relay Simon's conversations back to homicide.

Of course, prosecutors believed that Knott warned Simon not to discuss anything with his cellmate, but some inmates still make the mistake of doing so. Some need to brag. Others accidentally make damaging comments. Some heed the warning and say nothing.

The next afternoon Max and Bracken arrived back at the police department from Oklahoma. The team met for a complete review of the case and reviewed everything to assure it had been handled properly. They reviewed the Johnson case also.

After the review, Max raised the question of proceeding against Martinez by filing first-degree murder charges in the Johnson case against Martinez. He argued that such charges would add to the pressure on Martinez. This might lead to mistakes by Martinez and something might break. Bracken finally agreed.

The new charges were filed.

Although the police had no political motives in filing the charges, the action offered more fodder for the news media to use against the Gonsolic campaign. The media speculated whether or not Gonzo was involved with or had knowledge of the panty incident.

Gonzo's denials carried little public weight. Politicians always deny all charges at first. When charges are true, many times confirmation results in confession.

CHAPTER 75

WITH COURT CHARGES FILED FOR the Brown murder case, Max was still unsatisfied. The Amy Johnson murder was still unsolved. Being aware the Brown murders were connected to the election, he knew justice was being served in that case.

He and Viola talked daily.

She called to inform him that Centerville had been mentioned at least two times by Olivas while being interrogated—once in responding to a question about cartel and gang association and another about drug distribution.

Olivas was testifying about corruption and conspiracy in Mexico big time. He had fingered two New Mexico government officials. It was true corruption was spilling over into the United States, on a small scale right now, apparently all along the border between California and Texas. Several cartels or cartel wannabes were fighting over territory. The Carbona cartel had tentacles and connections even in Centerville.

Max discussed Viola Mendez's report with Bracken, and they took the matter to the chief with the request for travel approval back to Oklahoma. Max felt that the city police needed to know the extent of cartel operations in Centerville crime, especially drugs and prostitution. The attempted attack on the mayor had become an eye-opener.

Their stay in Oklahoma City was approved, and they were told to drain Olivas of all he knew about Centerville. They left for Oklahoma City on Monday, eight days before the election.

Before they left the office, the chief informed them that the mayor was arranging a public commendation ceremony for those who had worked on the two murder cases.

Upon arrival back to the Oklahoma City federal building, they met with Viola and Alcorn for an update on Olivas's interrogations.

Alcorn stated, "Based on what Roberto has said so far, cartels are becoming more and more dangerous to the United States. According to Roberto, cartel competition for drug and prostitution is spread along the border. Profits are almost unlimited. Drugs are being shipped all over the USA. A key area for entry points lay in southern New Mexico and West Texas. The heaviest-used route lay south of San Diego, California. The high value of shipments calls for any effective distribution method, regardless of cost. The cartels can afford expensive delivery operations, such as tunnels and small airplanes, because that way they can deliver larger loads with less chance of interception by the border patrol. Would you believe that the mayor and police chief in Columbus, New Mexico, have been arrested on weapon-smuggling charges?"

"I believe the border patrol is way understaffed relative to area of land requiring patrol," Alcorn continued. He had discussed the matter with border patrol agents. The border patrol and other organizations, public and private, also were concerned that the leaky border also offered opportunity for terrorist infiltration. Although ICE received an extremely large budget increase and had been hiring new agents and the National Guard had a large presence on the Mexican border, Alcorn pointed out that to place one agent on patrol on a twenty-four-hour, seven-day coverage required five agents if they worked eight-hour, five-day weeks."

Olivas had stated that Carbona's cartel acted as a gatekeeper for an area between Columbus, New Mexico, and West Texas. Anyone using the area for smuggling of any kind had to pay a toll fee to the cartel. The violence along the border was increasing as other cartels tried to encroach on Carbona territory. The border patrol was experiencing more violence against agents. Steps had been taken for better agent protection, but border agents recently reported that agent assassination contracts have been placed with the MS-13 gang.

Max knew of five or six suspected members of this gang living in Centerville. His concern about organized crime expanding into Centerville grew.

Another concern, Alcorn said, was corruption; he emphasized that corruption in Mexico had become rampant. Most every Mexican law enforcement organization had officials being suborned with drug money, including the military. Cartels offered officials a choice—take our money and leave us alone or face assassination.

A police chief in Nuevo Laredo had been elected in the morning and killed that afternoon. USA officials were concerned about some of their law enforcement officials accepting drug money. Local sheriff employees or even border patrol agents were being paid to look the other way during contraband shipments.

"In the past, agents operated individually while patrolling, even at night. With increased violence, changes have been made, but the problem had become so huge, knowledgeable people are questioning whether or not they will be effective," Alcorn said.

The border patrol union had stated concerns about misguided efforts being funded in Washington and had suggested a different policy direction for increased funding.

Alcorn offered Max and Bracken a copy of Olivas's printed testimony to date and informed them that the interrogation would continue in one hour. Max looked at the large folder and said, "There's no way we can review all this in an hour, but we'll jump-start it. See you and thanks."

The FBI interrogation had started on the subject of drugs. Prostitution and money laundering through cartel-owned legal businesses would follow.

Max learned that the cartel dealt primarily in coke, heroin, and marijuana, although other drugs were handled. Supply primarily came from Columbia and Mexico. Contraband supply problems were minimal for cartels in Mexico due to bribery and simple lack of enforcement. Suppliers, kept informed of roadblock locations, avoided them. Trucks shipped most drugs, although trains also were used on most main rail routes.

Drugs going out of Mexico into the USA were a different matter. It was a game of cat and mouse. When border patrol interdicted an existing route, new routes were established. Delivery methods changed based on expediency as enforcement concentration changed. Tunnels and small aircraft were best but required frequent replacement. The cartels forced innocent immigrants to act as smugglers if they were to be allowed to enter the United States. If the immigrant refused, he might be assassinated. Good highway transportation existed in New Mexico, and the state held huge unpopulated areas. The drugs left the border area to Centerville and Dallas or Houston, where they were distributed locally or sent to further urban areas, such as Denver and Chicago.

Now that he had a grasp of Olivas's testimony so far, Max was ready to participate in, or assist with, the questioning. He commented to Bracken, "We need MS-13 names from Olivas and we need organizational information. Who was the head, and who were key associates? Can he estimate the size of MS-13 in Centerville?" They listed the questions for Viola and Alcorn to use during the Olivas interrogation.

During the next interrogation session, Olivas supplied most of the information needed by the Centerville police, such as the names of drug supplier wholesalers, the extent of the MS-13 community infiltration, and drug routes.

After obtaining the information, Max and Bracken returned to Centerville on Wednesday.

CHAPTER 76

Back in Centerville, Simon had been in jail since his arrest. He hadn't made any mistakes during interrogations, and questioning sessions had slowed down.

He had too much time to think and his thoughts flew everywhere. Much of his waking time was spent cursing Olivas, "the dirtbag son-of-a-bitch traitor." *If only he were standing before me with my .45 pointed at him, I would blast him into mincemeat. If only I had left Brown alone. They did not have enough evidence on me regarding Amy, and still don't, according to Knott. I could beat that charge. They haven't found Tomas yet. He did a good job of covering his tracks and could be anywhere. I don't think he would turn on me, but to them he offered another piece of the puzzle. Maybe I should have run, but I didn't have the cash resources he had, so I probably would have been caught anyway.*

He ran through these thoughts two or three times each day, and he couldn't help but wonder about facing the death penalty for the death of Brown and his partner. He had been keeping his thoughts off that subject—it was too scary. He recognized that he stood a good chance of being convicted. They had the Olivas testimony, plus the $14,000 he had paid him, directly connected to him. Olivas would get a deal out of fingering him. He wondered what they offered him. Maybe he could deal with them. Gonzo will lose the election. Maybe he could give them Gonzo. He didn't have anything to do with it, but no one knows that for sure. Gonzo sure was quick to throw him to the wolves when he was arrested. Gonzo claimed that he fired him when he really hadn't and hadn't even contacted him since the arrest. He owed Gonzo nothing.

Maybe this should be discussed with Knott, he thought. He might have an idea what the district attorney would give for a bigger fish to catch.

Later on Wednesday Simon met with Knott. Simon asked, "I haven't mentioned this for several reasons, but I had a person behind me on the Brown thing. I wasn't going to give him up, but I may change my mind if the DA will work with us on a plea bargain. Would you discuss this possibility with them? Find out what they'll offer me?"

Knott was surprised. "What! Why are you telling me this now? Why didn't you tell me before? Are you holding back anything else? I can't defend you properly if you are operating this way. In fact, I will withdraw as your counsel if you continue to hold information back."

"I'm sorry, Jason. I'm not holding anything else back. On this, I didn't want to involve the person unless our position looked bad. I think the DA has a stronger case than I previously thought and I now have no choice but to deal."

"This information probably would have had more weight earlier," Knott said, "but they will still have to consider it. I'll take it to them."

Knott went back to his office and called Leon Messina, the lead prosecutor on the Brown case, and requested a meeting to discuss a plea bargain for Martinez. Messina's secretary said that she would check on his availability.

Messina came on the line and said, "Plea bargain? You must be kidding. We are going for the death penalty."

"I have some new information and believe you will want to hear it," Knott responded.

They scheduled a meeting later in the day at 4:00 p.m.

Knott checked through the guard station at the courthouse, moving in the line with everyone else and headed for the elevator.

The courthouse, finished only six months before, still had the fresh smell of a new building. In keeping with tradition, most of the building lobby and public areas presented beautiful marble walls and floors. The mural in the lobby highlighted the tricultural nature of the city—Native American, Hispanic, and Caucasian. The Native American panel showed three Indians on ponies overlooking a river; the Hispanic, two soldiers in full armor holding muskets; and the Caucasian, a man making a point in a court scene.

The district attorney's offices were located on the third floor. Jason entered the reception area, gave the receptionist his name, and stated that he had a meeting with Mr. Messina.

The secretary escorted him into a medium-sized conference room, with walnut-paneled walls and hardwood floors. Completely impersonal, there was nothing on the walls except a couple of windows with views of other large office buildings across the street. A large conference table reflected ceiling lighting. Twelve chairs surrounded the table.

Messina entered the room with his assistant attorney, Liz Booth. Knott knew both well, having litigated cases with them before. The Centerville legal community was closely knit with most attorneys well acquainted with each other.

"I hope you have something worthwhile to discuss. This place is a madhouse, and we don't have time to sit around and pass time away. Notice I said 'pass,' not 'piss'." Messina said.

Jason said, "Leon, I hope you like surprises because I have a dilly of one for you. Notice I said 'dilly' as in 'dilly.'"

Leon smiled. "A dilly, you say?"

"Yes, a dilly. And you will agree. Martinez informed me that he has a person behind him who was the instigator of the murder. He is willing to give him up if a deal can be made.

"Now before you comment about why he is presenting this now and not earlier, he claimed he thought he could win the case and didn't want to give up the person, but he now realizes he could be convicted, and he's scared of the death-penalty possibility."

Messina asked, "How do we know whether this is bullshit or not? And notice I said 'bullshit.' What will he be giving us? Just a name? Does he have something to back it up?"

"He will testify against the person, providing details of discussions between them," Knott replied.

"I wonder if it's Gonsolic. At least, he comes to mind as the first candidate," Messina speculated.

"He hasn't given me the name yet," said Knott.

"Liz, have you noticed we never are assigned a case that is just a straightforward, run-of-the-mill murder? Okay, Jason, we'll discuss the offer and get back to you." After Jason left, Messina said to Liz, "Let's run this by the boss," referring to Mandy Citron, the district attorney.

Citron's secretary buzzed them through. Not known for her small talk, she upheld her reputation by saying, "What's up, Leon?"

"Martinez is claiming he collaborated with and fronted another person in the murder of Brown and his partner and is willing to give the person up for a plea bargain. Knott said Martinez didn't offer this before because he thought he could win the case but now has second thoughts and will deal."

"What do you think?" asked the DA.

"This came out of the blue," said Messina. "My first reaction was he is blowing smoke. My second reaction was we have to consider dealing because of the public flak we would get if we don't deal, even if it is smoke. He apparently can't produce hard evidence, just his word against the other person's."

Citron thought for a few seconds, twiddling a pen in her right hand. She said, "I really want the death penalty for this jerk, but they obviously will want that off the table. If he pleads guilty and takes a life sentence, no parole, we can deal. Is that acceptable to you, or do you have another thought?"

"No, that's agreeable to me. Wait, maybe we should add the Johnson murder and the attack on the mayor to his guilty plea. These pleas would not add anything to his life without parole. Olivas managed a better deal with the feds in that he will be eligible for parole in twenty years. Knott will want the same deal, but we had other evidence in that situation and Olivas had more to trade. We ought to hold firm, nothing more than removal of the death penalty. His word against another person's word is an iffy case."

"Take this to our litigation committee," instructed Citron. "Get approval from the committee. I want a united front out of the office, no backstabbing or leaks that we aren't doing the right thing," she said.

"We'll get on it," Messina said. Nodding to Liz, they headed out.

He directed his secretary to set an emergency meeting with the lit committee, as it was called in the office, at eight the next morning.

Normally, the lit committee acted as a mock court, whose purpose was to listen to the prosecution's arguments to be presented in court and critique them. The committee met on important cases. Early on Thursday morning, Messina presented the plea-bargain proposal, stated the justification for it, and asked for comments.

After questions and a discussion, the committee blessed the plea bargain.

Leon called Knott after arriving back at his office. He reported that the prosecution would discuss a plea bargain where Martinez would be sentenced to life with no parole in return for fully reporting his participation in the murders and answering all questions regarding his association with the other person in carrying out the murder, a guilty plea for the Johnson murder, and a guilty plea for conspiracy to commit murder for the mayor incident.

Through the attorney negotiations, Knott committed Martinez to name and fully testify in court against the person who contributed money for the Olivas payoff and provide any documents, fully describe details of the times and places the murders were discussed and arranged, and provide any written records of the meetings. He also must testify in court against the person.

Initially, Simon argued against the guilty pleas for Johnson and the mayor cases, but then Knott pointed out that the pleas did nothing to him because they did not increase his jail terms. Knott reported back that Martinez had agreed to the terms of the plea bargain.

As anticipated, Knott had wanted the same deal as Olivas. Knott said that the DA had clearly stated that the death penalty would be all they would offer and that is final. Take it or leave it.

Martinez reluctantly agreed. The parties wrote up and signed the agreement.

Messina, Liz Booth, and Bracken met with Martinez at the jail. Martinez said, "My partner was Wilber Gonsolic. In a meeting in my car early evening on a Friday before the Tuesday murders, we held a discussion about getting rid of Brown, and Gonzo agreed to reimburse me the cost of Olivas's services. I have nothing in writing on the agreement and haven't been reimbursed yet."

On the walk back to the courthouse, Messina said, "We knew we had an 'I said, he said' case, unless Gonzo confessed. But the agreement is good. Martinez is pleading guilty without a trial and will spend the rest of his life in jail."

The DA called a press conference that Thursday afternoon to announce the terms of the agreement and the arrest of Gonsolic for murder. Five days before the election, this became the final nail in Gonzo's election coffin.

A happy Chief Pirwarsky called Ron to give him the news and then called Max to congratulate him and the team for wrapping up the cases.

Gonsolic screamed that he was being framed. He was innocent, and his innocence would be proven in court. When a media person asked if he was withdrawing as a candidate for mayor, Gonzo replied, "In America, everyone is innocent until proven guilty, and I am innocent anyway. I am in the race to the end."

Max called Bracken to ask who would be conducting the interrogation of Gonzo.

Bracken said that he would have to check with the DA.

Max suggested contacting the FBI to see if the state could borrow Viola Mendez as the lead interrogator.

Bracken thought the suggestion a good one and said that he would present it to the DA.

After Bracken had strongly endorsed Viola's interrogation expertise, Citron made an official request to the FBI for assignment of Vi to the DA as lead interrogator on the basis that the feds and the state were working the same case.

Upon learning about her assignment, Vi immediately called Max with the news. She said, "Max, I know you initiated this, but I didn't know you could move mountains."

He said, "Don't forget your dresses, Vi. Why don't you move in with me while you are here? We will save some driving and state expense money."

"Sounds like a winner. I'll bring a couple of teddies also. We might just go straight from power suits to teddies. But promise me we will go out for Mexican food at least twice if I bring both dresses."

Max surprised himself when he said, "Vi, I love you, and I'll take you wherever you want to go."

When she arrived at the Centerville airport, Max greeted her, and they proceeded to his apartment.

While she was settling in, he reviewed the status of the case and told her about Gonsolic. "The case will be an 'I said, he said' unless you can obtain a statement from Gonzo condemning himself."

"I'll take you over, introduce you to Messina and Booth and then the DA," Max said. "I want you to observe that we are hardworking public servants trying to protect the public during work hours, and then I want you to find out we go forth with that attitude during play hours. Just like we did in Oklahoma."

Vi said, "I remember Oklahoma well. God, it's good to see you." She moved into his arms and to a long, passionate kiss. "What time do we start the work part? Is there time to play?"

"Well, I want you refreshed and ready to go. I told the DA we would be there after lunch. We have time."

They went into the bedroom. Vi noticed that the bed had been freshly made. They helped each other undress, embraced, and fell on the bed. Later, they jointly made bologna sandwiches to go with potato chips and Cokes. While downing her sandwich in dainty bites, Vi asked about Gonsolic.

"You'll be impressed. He's a big man and can be charming. At the moment he essentially has clammed up, not answering questions," Max said.

"Messina hopes you can get him talking. I have a hard copy of Gonzo's limited discussions with our people. You can look at it on the way to the DA's office. He kept repeating that that bastard Martinez was trying to frame him. He knows nothing about the murder, other than what he read in the paper."

"During one discussion, he admitted meeting with Martinez the day Martinez mentioned but said they did not discuss murders, only a discussion of Martinez raising campaign funds and his going to work for the city when Gonzo won."

"When we arrive at the DA's office, I would like to listen to the previous Gonsolic interrogation tapes," Vi said.

Max rounded up Messina and told him what Vi wanted. Messina ushered them into a small office like room with a table and several chairs and left to get the tapes.

He returned with Liz, his assistant, with a tape player and two tapes.

Messina set up the player, inserted a tape, and all listened.

On the tape, Stud handled the questioning. After stating the preliminary tape information, Stud asked, "Mr. Gonsolic, do you understand the charges against you?"

In a strong manner, Gonzo said, "I did not have anything to do with the Brown killings. Martinez lied to obtain his plea bargain."

No matter what question was asked or comment made, Gonsolic gave the same answer. After a couple of answers from Gonsolic, Messina told Vi that she could listen to the rest if she wanted, but his answer never varied, no matter what the question was or how it was phrased. All he had given them differently was his side of the discussion with Martinez in the parking lot.

Vi said, "Maybe he believes if he keeps saying it everyone will start believing it. If he is taking that approach, I don't know if I can swing him off it. Tell me what you know about this man."

Turning to Liz, Messina asked, "Liz, would you bring the file on Gonzo, the one with his bio and all his campaign information, as well as our interviews with Sally Larson and Johnny Bustos."

Turning to Vi, he said, "We interviewed all the people who worked in Gonsolic's office, volunteers and all. Everyone, including Sally Larson and Johnny Bustos, two of his main campaign people, denied ever hearing any incriminating discussion between him and Martinez. Martinez claimed they only had two discussions, and both were in isolated parking areas in cars. Larson said that in her opinion Martinez was lying. Bustos said he found it hard to believe Gonzo's guilt."

"Let me review all this material," Vi said. "It looks about three hours' worth. By that time, your working day will be over. I would like to let the information work in my mind awhile, so why don't we start with Gonsolic in the morning?"

At 5:00 p.m. most of the people started leaving the offices. Max came in and asked Vi if she wanted to call it a day.

She said, "I have been through it all once and have gone back over a couple of documents. I read this Mr. Gonsolic as a strong opinioned individual. Do you see him that way?"

"Yes, you have described him well," Max replied. "He can be charming, but he likes to be in control. He also has a reputation for being, well, if not smart, at least clever."

"Yes, I can call it at this point. Are we going back to your place?" Vi asked.

"We can go home, freshen up, and maybe let things develop, shower, and have some dinner. I bought an interesting-looking chicken dish at the deli and a nice bottle of champagne to celebrate your visit. I'll tell Messina we're leaving."

As they headed for the parking garage, Max asked, "How many dresses did you bring?"

"Would you believe two? But guess what? I brought several teddies."

"That's good thinking,"

Early on Friday morning Vi and Max were sitting at the kitchen table, she in a teddy, he in shorts, having juice and coffee. Vi said, "I don't look forward to this interview. I keep asking myself how I can get Gonzo to open up. Then I think about it and don't like the answer. Well, if I can't get him to open up, I'll go back to Washington with my tail between my legs, and I probably would have to leave soon. If I can't get motivated by such consequences, I can't get motivated."

Max said, "Yes, do get motivated. We need at least three days together. One or two won't be enough. It would be good if we don't have to work the whole weekend."

"If I don't get anywhere today," she said," I'll request a couple of days leave, but I had been hoping for a couple of days work to add to the leave."

"I know one thing. If you can't get him talking, no one can. Do you want the first shower?" he asked.

CHAPTER 77

VI, MAX, AND MESSINA HELD a short discussion while Gonzo was being brought from his jail cell to the interrogation room. To Vi, the room appeared to mimic every interrogation room she had ever been in—centered table with chairs, nothing on the painted-gray walls, and a one-way mirror. A tape recorder sat on the table. When asked how she planned to proceed, Vi responded that much of her approach with a defendant depended on her reaction to the individual.

"In other words, I wing most of it, with an exception of establishing an overall goal. In this case the first chore is to get him responding."

Gonzo was ushered into the room and sat with one leg chained to the floor. Messina introduced Vi to Gonzo as a person brought in to discuss his situation with him since he hadn't discussed anything with others.

Gonzo's attorney, Wayne Zimmerman, also was introduced to Vi. She had been informed that Zimmerman was recognized as one of the top three criminal lawyers in the state. After the introduction, Zimmerman said he wanted to note that Mr. Gonsolic faces an adversarial proceeding, and he will advise his client on some answers, if Mr. Gonsolic decides to respond.

"I understand," Vi said. "We would like to hear Mr. Gonsolic's side of the story, if he deems to inform us."

"Mr. Gonsolic," Vi said, addressing him directly, "I have no idea where any discussion between us might lead, but to me, it could be in your interest to answer some of the questions. For example, I have reviewed your personal information from DA files, but I haven't had the opportunity to learn anything about Simon Martinez, except for his participation in the murder of Brown and his partner and his accusation against you. I would like to learn how you became involved with Martinez originally."

"I'll be happy to talk about that bastard son of a snake," Gonzo replied. "The son of a bitch not only has falsely accused me of setting up a murder, he is solely responsible for sabotaging my mayoral election. Although I'm not dropping out of the race, I am dead meat. Even after I am cleared of this ridiculous murder charge, I am still ruined in this state forever, just because I was charged."

"When did you become acquainted with the 'son of a bitch'?" Vi asked with a serious expression on her face.

Gonzo smiled, knowing full well Vi was trying to manipulate him with her remark, but he provided the information she asked for and proceeded to discuss Simon.

"I decided to run for mayor after checking with some of my friends and started making the rounds. One friend introduced me to Simon. He asked me some questions, must have liked the answers because he said he would support me and help me raise money. He was good, raised more money for me than anyone. I offered him a seat on the committee. He was very active."

"His main problem," he continued, "was that he tended to come up with an idea then run with it without consulting me. A good example is the panty incident with Amy Johnson. He set it up with her, and she did it before I even knew about it. When it backfired, I had to tell Simon he was out of the campaign. That was the purpose of one parking lot discussion. He didn't like being cut out but didn't argue. No other subject was discussed in that meeting.

"At a later time the bastard called for another meeting. We met in a parking lot again. He wanted to know if he would be the public works director when I was elected. I had promised him the job previously, and I confirmed it would be his job. Again, no other matter was discussed in the meeting. He seemed to be relieved about the job. That was my last discussion with the son of bitch."

"Why the clandestine meeting?" Vi asked.

"When Steadman found out Martinez had set up the panty incident, I told Steadman I would remove Martinez from my campaign. I didn't want Steadman finding out I still communicated with him."

"And that was the last discussion you had with Simon?"

"Yes, and if he says otherwise, the son of bitch is lying," Gonzo repeated.

"Regarding the Martinez-Johnson relationship, were you aware of it, and would you inform us if you know anything about Martinez possibly killing her?"

"After what that son of a bitch has done to me I ought to tie him up with that murder, but I have to say he never indicated in any way that he knew Johnson or was involved with her until the panty thing."

"I think this is a good time to take a break, about twenty minutes," Vi said.

After pit stops, Vi held a conference in the hall with those listening in through the mirror and those who had been in the room, minus Gonzo and his attorney. She asked for any questions or comments.

Messina said, "He just gave us his basic defense for the trial. As we expected, it is an 'I said, he said' defense." They all concurred and he continued, "And Gonzo's attorneys have all the tapes of Martinez on both cases, Johnson and Brown. I mention this because Martinez lied in his first two interviews regarding Johnson. If they use the information, our only witness will have been shown as a liar in previous situations. I think we have a big hump to overcome. I had better take this to the DA. Vi and Max, why don't you come with Liz and me. We will stop the interview for now."

As they walked into the reception room, Mandy's secretary looked up and said, "Why the gloomy looks? You haven't lost a case today."

"True, but the day is young. We need to speak with Mandy," Messina said.

The secretary punched a button and said, "Mrs. Citron, you have a delegation of lawyers who wish to speak with you."

"Send them in."

Messina started out. "Mandy, we need direction on the Gonsolic case. The basics are this, part of which you know. We have the Martinez plea bargain for life sentence without parole for giving up Gonsolic. Viola was able to entice Gonzo into telling his side of the story instead of just claiming innocence. He admitted meeting with Martinez on two occasions in parking lots but claims nothing was discussed except political matters—first, removing Martinez from his committee because of the Johnson panty incident and then, at the second meeting, confirming Martinez would be appointed public works director. This commitment gives Martinez the motive to take Brown out.

"It also sets up the 'I said, he said' confrontation for the court case, but we face a real disadvantage on that. Martinez is a proven liar evidenced by two interviews he gave detectives investigating the Johnson murder. Gonzo's lawyers have copies of those interviews, and we believe they will be used to attack the veracity of our witness. Unfortunately, it appears to be an effective tactic. Without other evidence we don't stand much of a chance of winning."

"Vi, do you think you can wrangle some more information out of Gonzo?" Mandy asked.

Vi said, "I never know, but I can try. The basic question in my mind is whether Gonzo was involved in the murders. I haven't interviewed Martinez, but reviewing his testimony, he is more likely to be lying than is Gonsolic. I think Gonsolic told the truth.

"Also, we have to seriously consider the point in the second meeting that Martinez sought verification he would have the public works job. He asked for that before he proceeded to set up the murders. There is his motive. I suggest we go back to Martinez and ask if he verified his public works job when he met Gonzo the second time."

"Leon, let's get an answer on the job offer from Martinez before we talk again with Gonzo," the DA directed.

Messina said, "I'll call Knott, and we'll run over to jail and take care of that."

"Then we can decide on how we proceed," the DA said.

The group sat in an adjoining room, making small talk and having a coffee break while waiting for Messina to return from seeing Martinez.

When Messina returned and the team had reconvened, he said that Knott advised Martinez to take the Fifth on the question, but he pointed out they have a plea bargain in place for a life sentence. To stay with that agreement, Martinez agreed to cooperate in the Gonsolic prosecution. They need the information for prosecuting. Knott withdrew his objection, so Martinez confirmed he raised the question. "Let's decide on whether or not we proceed on the Gonsolic case."

Max said, "I believe the decision is strictly for you attorneys. I'll support your recommendation."

"Liz, what do you say?" asked Leon.

"I believe we should dismiss the charges. Our case is weak. We can work on it and file again at any time. We have a murderer who has pled guilty and will be given a life sentence with no parole," Liz replied.

Messina said, "I agree. Mandy, you have our recommendation."

"Okay, I concur." She called in her public relations officer, told her what had been decided, and instructed that a news release be prepared.

Max and Vi walked out to the parking lot, and Max said, "I think you and I need to go back to my place, take care of some immediate needs, and maybe start exploring a life sentence for us. Afterward, we'll go to Padilla's for chile rellenos. They have good ones."

"Vi, that scumbag Olivas is getting off too easy. That grates on me. In twenty years, I'll be retired, and I won't be required to sign his plea agreement. I will attend his parole hearing and oppose parole strongly.

"Also, I intend to participate more in the fight against cartel activities in New Mexico. If the chief will assign me as liaison for the city to the DEA and immigration service, we would establish direct contact with them without always going through the task force. I want to be on top of MS-13 before they become a major crime force in Centerville.

"Excuse me while I report the news," Max continued.

He called Chief Pirwarsky and reported the decision to drop charges against Gonsolic. The chief took the information in stride and took the opportunity to inform Max that he, Stud, and Davis were to appear that afternoon at 3:00 p.m. in the mayor's office. The chief had proposed, and the mayor had approved, a major change in the police department organization. A Homicide and Major Crimes Division was being formed. Max would head the division with the rank of commander. Studdard would be promoted to Detective Lieutenant, and Davis to Detective Senior Grade.

Max called Stud. "Stud, if you were a detective lieutenant, do you think you could still put up with Davis's bullshit? The reason I ask is that we all will be receiving promotions this afternoon. I'll be commander, you a lieutenant, and Davis a sergeant. Also the DA is dropping charges against Gonzo. Relay all this to Davis, and you two be in the mayor's office at three today."

Stud said that he was almost acclimated to Davis and would give him a chance, and they would see him in the mayor's office.

Stud then said, "By the way, you know that damn dog out at the Martinez Construction yard? It occurred to me that no one was taking care of it. Sure enough, no one was, so I took it home with me." Laughing, Max told Viola the tale of the dog.

CHAPTER 78

GONZOLIC WAS RELEASED FROM JAIL on Saturday morning. An immediate press conference was called on tthe courthouse steps. Gonsolic's main points with the press were that he was innocent of any participation with Martinez regarding his crimes, and was not aware of them until he heard Martinez had been arrested. He is still a candidate, and would make the best mayor.

On Sunday, the newspapers endorsed Mayor Steadman for a second term. A poll taken on Saturday showed Steadman with 72 percent and Gonsolic with 26 percent, 2 percent undecided, and this was reported in the Sunday papers.

On Tuesday, Mayor Steadman was elected with 72 percent of the vote, Gonsolic received 28 percent.

A large crowd happily celebrated the election win at the victory party held in the ballroom of the Hyatt Hotel. Campaign workers, friends, other politicians, and other supporters all celebrated. Gonzo had called Ron early in the evening to concede victory.

Upon receiving Gonzo's concession, Ron and Val left the suite where they had been watching returns. They entered the ballroom amid a frenzied victory party. People swarmed toward Ron, trying to shake his hands, pat him on the back, or kiss him. All were happy the campaign was over and victory was theirs.

Ron made his victory speech, noting Gonsolic's concession, thanking everyone, and reviewing the major issues he intended to resolve in the next four years.

After the speech, he and Val made the rounds, trying to make personal contact with everyone. Impossible, of course, because of time constraints and the desire of many to hold short discussions, but he made the effort. At the appropriate time, they retired back to the suite. Charles, Mike, Steve, Annie, Max, Stud, Davis, and the chief, and Julie Carrico were invited to share the champagne victory toast.

Earlier in the evening, Charles had searched the ballroom for Julie and finally located her with some friends.

After greetings, he asked her to move into the lobby for a private conversation.

They found a quiet corner and Charles began, "I thought about our last conversation and want you to know it was not my intention to equivocate on my love for you. I love you, and there is no doubt about it. The election is over. Where do you stand on the divorce?"

"Just today we resolved all the asset and property issues," Julie said. "We hold no differences about sharing our teenagers and our relationships with them. In fact, the house is mine. Would you like to see it?"

"I would love to. How many bedrooms does it have?"

"Well, why don't you wait until I can show you? Would you like a tour tonight after the party?" she asked.

"Absolutely," he replied as they hugged.

She leaned back and said, "I'll mention it has two walk-in showers."

"How interesting. I look forward to using them."

"I have some information for you," Julie said. "The mayor offered me a job as a mayoral assistant. We will be discussing it tomorrow."

Charles said, "That's wonderful. Although my job with him has concluded, the strongest candidate for governor, Walt Carson, wants me in his campaign. The election is a year away. I will operate primarily out of Centerville, so we will have a chance at a long-term relationship. I can tell you right now my interest is long term."

"To answer a previous question, love has a lot to do with it," Julie said and smiled.

They went back to join the ballroom party.

Not everything can be a worst-case scenario.

PROLOGUE FROM NEXT BOOK

COMMANDER JOE MAXWELL, HEAD OF the City of Centerville Police Homicide and Major Crimes Division, sat in his office going over activity reports of the previous evening. His mood today couldn't be much worse. His wife, Viola Mendez, had been called for an assignment in Chicago. Viola and a partner, Len Alcorn, formed the premier interrogation team for the FBI. In fact, her job resulted in Maxwell meeting her. The interrogation team helped break open a major Centerville murder case through their questioning expertise. Joe and Viola fell in love and married. She routinely was called out of town on work, but this time the call interrupted a scheduled Pacific cruise. Between the two, they had yet to plan a vacation that they took, and he was getting tired of cancellations.

Stud, Lieutenant Studdard to others, stuck his head in the door, looked at him, and asked, "Bad night, Chief?"

"No. Just the usual shitty morning. The only good thing is no major crimes or murders last night. You heard about Detective Thomas wrecking his police car in a high-speed chase? He's in the hospital with a broken leg and minor injuries, none life threatening. He'll be on medical leave for weeks. The perp escaped, but he'll be picked up soon. We have the license number. Viola was called to Chicago on a case, and I had to cancel our vacation, so you once again miss the opportunity to be acting commander."

"Our people will be upset. They thought you would be gone twelve days, and we would all party while I was acting chief. I was sort of looking forward to it myself."

"Well, they'll just have to live with me. If they were planning to roast you, I'll authorize the go-ahead for that." The intercom buzzed and Max answered.

His secretary informed him that Josh Thompson, from the FBI, was on line two.

Max picked up the phone and said, "Hello, Josh, are you calling to inform me that Carbona has been arrested?" Carbona, head of a large Juarez, Mexico, cartel, had managed to stay in control of his cartel, even though the FBI and DEA had seriously damaged his operations by arresting and turning one of his inner-circle members, Roberto Olivas.

Josh said, "No, he slipped our net, reorganized, changed his distribution network, and is back in operation. The Zeta cartel tried to take over some of his stuff without success but with loss of several Zeta members in a shootout. But that is one reason I am calling. I'd like you to come down to El Paso to discuss going to work for us. We are planning new expanded operations in our cartel fight. We believe we have a job you would find interesting, and we like you for it."

"What kind of job?"

"We think Mexico could better perform against the cartel if the army had a trained commando outfit along the lines of our Navy SEALs. We need a strong leader to set up the training, select the people, and handle specialized attacks on cartel terrain."

"That does sound interesting. When do you want to meet?" Max responded.